PRIVATE
FORCE

PRIVATE FORCE

RICHARD MALMED

Kravitz & Sons

INNOVATORS IN PUBLISHING, MARKETING AND ADVERTISING

Kravitz and Sons LLC
1301 Farmville Blvd, Suite 104
Greenville, NC 27834

Published by Kravitz and Sons LLC.
ISBN: 979-8-89639-142-5 (sc)
ISBN: 979-8-89639-141-8 (e)

Library of Congress Control Number: 2025905634

Because of the dynamic nature of the Internet, any web addresses or links contained in this book may have changed since publication and may no longer be valid. The views expressed in this work are solely those of the author and do not necessarily reflect the views of the publisher, and the publisher hereby disclaims any responsibility for them.

CONTENTS

CHAPTER 1

I led my group of clients out of the New York subway and up to the monolithic Madison Avenue tower of steel and glass which housed the enormous law firm where we had an appointment. Tom Katinek, the founder of K Form Apps was selling his software company to Nano-Bridge today. Some of his key software nerds had been given stock and would soon become millionaires. I too had helped Tom out early and been given a nice percentage for my money and efforts. So, today was a big day.

As we had walked off the elevator on the 49th floor, there was a wooden floor of inlaid teak forming star patterns. Over this was an immense ivory and blue Persian rug. The entire room was dominated by a large red, white and blue cloisonné figure of a Chinese warrior brandishing a curved sword. The walls were also covered with red and blue Chinese paintings of angry Han warriors. In front of us, at a gigantic glass desk was a trim and attractive blond woman with exquisite gastrocnemius muscles. In the interest of being politically correct, I cannot comment on the gluteus maximus. Her English accent was full BBC.

"May I help you?"

"I am Peter Stern, an attorney from Philadelphia. We are the K Form group for the Nano-Bridge Merger."

"Quite right. Follow me."

I would have followed that exquisite little tushy to the ends of the earth, but alas, it ended at the door to a conference room that extended half of a New York City block.

I invested a small sum, did some legal work – contracts, incorporation and general day to day advice. Tom had been an old friend. I put in the money, but had not expected much. I had a 20% share in the company and taken a personal interest in the day to day operations. Tom had not disappointed me, he had worked his butt off creating script and numerous incompressible lines of data along with the handpicked bunch of techies he had recruited.

I had arranged for them to work in an abandoned office area of one of my firm's clients. He had located used and cannibalized computers and peripherals, desks and equipment.

As yet, for tax purposes, K Form Apps had not made a dime, but it had sold a number of its apps in future royalty deals which could be hocked to the bank to pay off debts and cover the payroll. It was only in the last two years that Tom could take a salary from K Form and let his wife start the family she had lobbied for over the past few years.

Tom sat at the table next to me along with three of his code writers who had been given small shares in the company. I guess the best way to describe them collectively was stunned. The size and opulence of the New York law office was staggering. My little troop of clients were dressed casually – not even office casual. Tom wore his black T-shirt from some long forgotten rock tour and sandals (Oh no! with socks). His jeans still had a carpenter strap for a hammer. The others were not much better except Helen Chu. She was a petite, delicate woman with a neat, trim figure. As always, her hair was cut into a shiny black helmet with strict bangs. Someone had styled the back to hang neatly to the contour of her scalp. Helen was not only a code writer par excellence, but she played a delicate and precise violin without an expression on her face, but a weeping in her tune. Somehow, the math propensity had been wed to the music propensity. She murmured her thanks to me for her sudden prosperity.

Meanwhile, the lawyers fussed imperiously around us. Law firms are divided into four types – the finders, the minders, the binders and the grinders. The finders are the rain makers – often ex-politicians, or fund raisers, all with big egos or some financial or family connection that gave them access to moneyed clients, whom they could attract to the firm. Once clients were securely tied to the firm, the minders met often with them, got to know their business and pounced on ways to stir up legal business from them. They also apologized when the bills were too high. The binders are people who specialized in the area the clients needed most often and, by a long term of maintaining regular contact with the client, make themselves indispensable. Lastly, the grinders are junior associates who do most of the work – whether research, drafting mammoth documents, or by doing whatever is necessary to deal with the client's current problem – anything from delivering documents, walking the client's dog, listening to his airhead second wife or bailing his son out of jail at 2:00 AM.

And they dress in the appropriate costumes. The grinders have polyester suits from J.C. Penney and the always acceptable blue oxford button-down shirt in 50% cotton 50% polyester. The finders wear print shirts of English striped spread collars with tailored pin stripe suits. The minders affect a bow tie and suspenders, and French cuffs and try to look either English or country club WASP. The grinders and minders walk around with a look of permanent annoyance on their faces and make extraordinary efforts to look busy and important.

K Form Apps was a rather simple company which owned the property rights to a number of interesting and useful applications for specialized engineering usage. At present, it had some specially adapted versions for about 300 companies, and was actually profitable. None of the shareholders, including me, were rich or had gotten a dime in dividends. But Nano-Bridge had access to over 100 million users and saw this instant opportunity to dominate a business sector's software by acquiring these apps and making them the flagship of its sales effort to this business niche. Viewed that way, $85 million was a steal. Tom could hardly get the words out when he called me, however. He would come out with $65 million and a long-term contract to service Nano's customers. The other techies got a million each, and long-term contracts as well. All were agog as I explained the deal in more detail.

The deal was mostly a simple tax-free stock swap. I knew that the lawyers on both sides knew that, and we also knew that 80 - 90% of the language for the deal was in their computers from the last deal and could be spit out in half an hour needing few modifications. Yet the

Finders-Minders-Grinders and Binders had to parade around in their office finery with annoyed looks on their faces as if they were doing some heavy lifting.

Actually, Tom, the techies and I had elected to take our end of the deal in Nano-Bridge stock and a little cash so they could drown their spouses in some temporary luxury and shut up their in-laws for all eternity. We paid some small tax on the cash and got the Nano stock tax free of capital gains for the time being. We would get Nano dividends and could sell small bits and pieces of the Nano stock as we needed the money, which, given the employees' life styles, would be never.

In short, everyone from K Form Apps had more than enough to retire and were still mystified that anything like this could happen. Tom, of course, was very tightly wound today.

Every once in a while, some of Nano's lawyers would come up to us and ask some inane question – "in the exercise of due diligence." Nano's accountants had been sniffing K Form's butt for about six weeks looking for something to kill the deal, and now their lawyers were trying to do the same and thus proving they had not read the accountant's very expensive report. In answer to each question, I would cite them to the accountant's report page and ask if they had read it.

One snotty young binder (or maybe a high-level grinder), suggested that "my sarcastic tone was unavailing. He would serve his client as he saw fit."

I muttered "at $450 per hour." I didn't add "for unnecessary work." I could have used the word redundant, but thought that would be unavailing as well.

While we sat there at our end of the conference table, minions came from some hidden kitchen area bearing coffee, Danish, fruit platters, tea, and water. We had made the early train up from Philadelphia and had only gotten on the subway at Grand Central Station. The food was welcome.

Of course, as the morning wore on, we were handed menus from what was obviously an expensive delicatessen. Again the food was welcome. Because I was in New York, I ordered a warm corned beef special and a chocolate egg cream. I was almost at the point where I would not hate New York, the Yankees or the Rangers, when another minder walked up to us with the Nano VP of Human Resources and began to explain the rules of Human Resources at length at Nano-Bridge. Since I would not be working there, I was not bothered, but Tom and his techies blanched. No head scarfs, side burns shaved to tragus, no alcohol on the premises. When we got to the point about sexual harassment, I could see the VP eyeing Helen Chu with her black helmet of shiny hair, her delicate little fingers and her form-fitting silk blouse. Here was a man who had lust in his heart. Helen looked at me with a beseeching look. I would explain the rules of sexual harassment to her later.

Fortunately, our techies would be exempt from most rules. They could work when or where they wanted as long as they were logged into their computers for 40 hours a week. They had no dress code outside the tech room which was amply supplied with caffeinated drinks and candy bars. Every month their production would be reviewed.

The VP of Finance for Nano then put everyone to sleep with a talk on the 401(k) plan, the ESOP (employee stock option plan), the health insurance options, etc.

Eventually, a stack of papers was put at one end of the table each with colored tabs where they should be signed. The process of paper shuffling, sealing, and notarizing took about an hour. In anticipation of the length of the closing, Nano had made reservations for rooms at the Omni across the street. We trundled out into the twilight with numbed looks on our faces. Unfortunately, the trim blond receptionist with the BBC accent was not there to show us the way out.

Tom looked over at me and said, "I could use a drink."

There were no counter votes or abstentions. We descended on the Omni bar with our new company's credit cards in hand.

As I pushed back from the huge Omni bar table, I was just starting to feel $17,000,000 richer. My old tensions, my old disciplines, my cases were beginning, only beginning, to slip away as I contemplated a life where I would not have to practice law in the firm of Hartley, Hendler and Howard. I shuddered as I remembered the conference room which we had just left where huge numbers of paralegals, accountants, lawyers and executives were bustling about trying to look very serious, very learned, and very professional as they finalized the paperwork and investigations necessary to finalize the sale of my good friend Thomas Katinek's company, K Form Apps, Inc. to the multinational software company, Nano-Bridge, Inc. for $85 million. Just 24 hours earlier, that could have been me.

I was now 42, but ten years ago, I had helped Tom Katinek start up his software company which wrote a series of applications in the engineering field. Although I had known or understood little of Tom's work, I had invested some cash, consulted on business matters almost daily and helped him solve all the problems of a startup. For my efforts, I had been given little more than an expectation that he would repay me if he was successful in what he did – whatever that was. Well, he had been successful and the repayment was more than I ever imagined.

CHAPTER 2

As I got into his car in an immense parking garage and wound down to the internal concrete coils to the exit, I fingered the receipt for the wire into my brokerage account, and my mind began to drift over to my past. It had started inauspiciously when I was accepted as a CIA trainee after my last year in college. For some reason, I had been recruited by the CIA through a contact with my wrestling coach. Although a so-so wrestler, I had been somewhat successful, after the team had been thoroughly demolished by the major wrestling teams in the East in the first matches of the season. But then we encountered the Ivy League schedule. There, at least, I was meeting opponents without scholarships, without 30-page papers due on Monday after the meet, with no training tables, and without actual audiences at their matches. For our meets, it was lucky if a roommate or two, the coach's wife, and the janitor who was waiting to clean up afterward attended. I had trained on my own invented meals of peanut butter, sardines, and hard boiled eggs. I would weigh in on Saturday before the meet at 147 and by Sunday, after the training meal and lots of rehydration, I would weigh 155 again. I would then lose the same eight pounds each week in mostly water weight. Why had I done this? Who knew? Because it was there. It also helped that I had some of my best concentration on my studies then and got my best grades. I certainly wasn't a masochist. Yet, I could not help but feel jealous when my college buddies partied and drank, chased their dates down the corridors while I sat in sweat pants leaning against the radiator on a Friday night in winter. Some strange impulse drove me and somehow I knew I was learning a mindset that would stay with me my entire life. Even today, I weigh myself every day and go to the gym to lift weights three times a week.

The wrestling coach had been a Sea Bee in the Navy during the Korean War and had gone to the CIA for a few years afterward before he went to coach at Lehigh – then and for many years the powerhouse in Eastern wrestling. The CIA still retained him to "spot" candidates for the CIA training-intern program. At Lehigh, he had been able to spot (what else at Lehigh?) engineers vital to the many technical needs of the CIA in communications, electronic intelligence, computers and lots of secret things no one ever knows about. Coach had then been hired to come to my school. But the CIA wanted "generalists" – people with a knowledge of history and foreign culture, who spoke languages. That was me. He had me go to an interview where the recruitment guy offered full GI Bill and civilian pay. It sounded like an adventure with my graduate school paid for after thee years. So three years it was and what a dumb move!

I went through the CIA training program where we learned many things – how foreign militaries worked, who were good targets for us to "turn," all sorts of weapons, lots of spy craft – surveillance, secret communications, security precautions. Lots of fun – just like John LeCarre, except for real.

Then the real world. Admittedly, life in the CIA is difficult for people with any kind of ego. When you are posted overseas, you are given a cover which is several notches below the level you are in the CIA, although you are, of course, secretly paid at the level you deserve in a separate account. If you have State Department cover, the middle level state bureaucrats and their wives can lord it over you and your wife in the living arrangements, social life, schools, and meetings. Your education resume is faked and so are all your credentials. To maintain your cover, you are given meaningless low level work so these lifer State numbskulls feel they can boss you around. Even if you are lucky enough to have a cover with a newspaper or a private company, you cannot have a job commensurate with your education or ability. This stipulation weighs heavily on you, but more heavily on the wives and children. You can't even spend the extra money you make in a conspicuous fashion.

Inside the CIA, the atmosphere is not much better. Over the

years, the CIA has hired many "contract" employees for their covert paramilitary operations or for training foreign soldiers or intelligence operatives. "Contract" means that they are not civil service and can be released anytime, in theory. In practice, most of these men will have had a career after 20 years in some specialized branch of the military and been hired on by the CIA to live on a new salary while collecting their military pension and health benefits. By the time they have served a few years in the field, they are in their mid-forties and early fifties – and virtually unemployable in civilian life. They have no civilian skills. They will be accepted, h owever, into the old boy network of the agency and given mid-level jobs, by the other old boy former contract employees. They were now civil service and secure in their positions.

What happens is that these men have formal relationships with CIA executives who are grateful for their former paramilitary work. They form a band of middle management, between their senior executives and the college-educated trainees. For the most part these men have been in the military, acquiring military skills and catching college level courses on the run. They bring with them military procedures, military jargon and military attitudes. There is a severe confrontation when they become the bosses of the educated, recent college graduates who are "generalists," speak a few languages, understand foreign cultures' religions and history. It was no different for me. Free thinking, creative thinking, liberal attitudes toward foreigners, going "native" this was all frowned upon. I felt trapped almost from the beginning.

When I was assigned to the Middle East and put on the Iraq desk, I read up on all the past history and even ancient history. Since its founding in the 600's, Islam had been broken up into many sects which often did not get along. The Christians scattered throughout the area were a small minority and were often the target of some religious pogrom by a local warlord seeking to steal their goods and property. I was never able to understand why the U.S., who was so hot on nabbing Osama bin Laden in the rugged hills of northeast Afghanistan, had instead gone after Saddam Hussein. While Saddam was a brutal aggressive dictator who had attacked Kuwait, his country was not a problem in the international theater at the time. We did not need to solve Iraq's internal problems while we had a number of other problems including Al Qaeda, but the Bushes and the right-wing neocons lusted after it.

At the time, the history of the CIA in the Middle East was clouded. In the '80s, the Soviet Union, for little apparent reason, decided to attack and occupy one of the most ungovernable and least economically viable regions in the world – Afghanistan. As a kneejerk reaction, the CIA armed the local mujahedeen in opposition with dangerous and valuable weapons; the most tactically valuable of all was the Stinger missile – a handheld surface to air missile capable of locking into an airplane's heat exhaust and bringing it down. The missile weighs 22 pounds, the launcher 34. Once released, the missile speeds up to Mach 2.54. This weapon was probably the single most devastating device to the USSR. As a result, the Russians eventually left Afghanistan with their tails between their legs and the cost of this effort was a major factor in bringing about Perestroika – the demise of the Soviet system.

To find and kill or capture bin Laden, the U.S. needed to fight the same people we had armed years before in the same areas and against the same tribes that had defeated the USSR years earlier. For some reason, those tribes and part of the Pakistan military structure felt they had to protect bin Laden.

As a "generalist" and a college-educated guy, I was trained to ask questions, not follow in lock step to a military command. I couldn't help but ask all the annoying questions.

Why hadn't the CIA used air cover against Castro and the Cubans at the Bay of Pigs?

Why did we support right-wing dictators against those seeking a democratic government?

Why didn't we engage in talks with Ho Chi Min, Castro and other "socialist" revolutionary leaders before going to expensive, deadly drawn out war with them?

Who was the military industrial complex Eisenhower warned us against?

What had Ollie North done? How was he able to do it?

And now, why were we fighting Saddam Hussein? Were we siding with the Shiites or the Sunnis? Why were we against Saddam Hussein – a Sunni, when Iran – a Shiite theocracy – was our enemy and the enemy of Hussein?

Was Pakistan for us or against us?

And most of all, why were we using the flimsiest piece of intelligence to invade Iraq? The intelligence used violated all the terms of spy craft we had been taught, and, by the way, was obvious to anyone with an inquiring mind.

1. You never use a single source for any decision, but insist on multiple bases for corroboration.

2. If scientific means can be used to verify atomic weapons, you use it.

3. You use electronic intelligence and snooping over human sources.

4. You use the least and safest amount of military action to achieve a goal, but diplomacy is preferable.

Instead, we relied on a doubtful and unproven individual to reach a conclusion that nuclear weapons of mass destruction existed in Iraq which could have been detected by satellite or human handheld Geiger counter. The target was an industrial building which could have been targeted and destroyed from a distance of ten miles by a computer generated bomb run from an F16 which was capable of flying at twice the speed of sound.

Instead "W" and his minions became involved in a massive war against the Sunnis in Iraq for no apparent reason. My questions went unanswered. My attitude eventually left me shunned as the good old boys felt I was not a team player in my performance reviews. After three years, I left to become a lawyer.

Now with the receipt of Nano stock, I was rich and all this was behind me. After saying goodbye at the firm and arranging for my oldest files to find a new home, I began to feel retired. I got up late, made my own breakfast, played on the computer and read the bridge column in the newspaper. Most of my friends were working. It wasn't long before I began to get bored. I had always gone to the gym regularly and, at least, now I could go regularly at lunch time and hang out with the guys there. They came from all walks of life – janitors, med students, retail clerks, waiters. No one knew I had been blessed with the good fortunes because I wore my old sneakers and tee shirts. I did go to the extravagance of buying new socks and shorts.

Two guys who hung out at the gym I knew to be ex-cops. They never discussed it much and I frankly didn't even know their first names. They were just two guys at the gym.

After a month or so, they came up to me as I was leaving the locker room and said they'd like to buy me lunch. Well, I had nothing special to do and a cheese steak place was right next door. So we had cheese steaks and sat in a back booth facing the windows. For some reason, a guy who introduced himself as Hank walked around sweeping a black hand ball device around the room and then joined the other guy named Joe and me.

After a few pleasantries about the gym, Hank began to fidget and then, looking uncomfortable, said "Look, we know you are a lawyer and we'd like to treat this as a conversation with an attorney. Is that alright?

"You know that I am pretty much retired now. I don't take on new cases." "No. It's not like a new case. We wanted to have attorney client privilege and keep what we say confidential."

"I guess I can live with that." Who knew what he had in mind. Was it something dangerous? Illegal? What had they done? I was used to listening to all kinds of stories over the years, and I was curious. What was going on?

"We know you sold all your interest in a computer software company and are pretty well fixed." Oh no, was he asking for money? "We aren't looking for your money." Whew! "You have a good reputation as a straight shooter and a guy who can be trusted." So far, so good. "We have a very unusual proposition for you to act as our lawyer and our conscience in a venture. You have a decent background in criminal law and we want to stay out of trouble. We need you to tell us how. There's no money, but a lot of excitement and maybe some travel. We won't ask you to do anything criminal."

"Okay, I am interested so far. What's going on?"

"We'd like you to come meet with us and our friends tonight at 7:00 in East Falls."

"Okay. I'm available then."

"We'll pick you up at Midvale and Henry and take you there. You'll be blindfolded."

Hank looked at Joe. Joe nodded.

Joe was a guy in his early forties, about 5'10", in great physical condition with a salt and pepper flat top. Hank was a large beefy guy – over 6'3" and 250 pounds – big and strong and imposing – but quiet. The two usually worked on the weights together and kept journals of what they did. They knew I was a serious power lifter and we usually discussed technique, training regimens, and lifting records. I wouldn't say they were secretive, they just didn't mix much with the other guys.

"Before I go, I'd like to have your names. You seem to know who I am, but I need to know who you are."

"I'm Joe Doyle and this is Henry Stanziani. We're ex-cops. You might say retired."

"Okay. Good. See you then."

CHAPTER 3

I couldn't wait to get home and check out the web for anything I could find. I called my old secretary, Angelina, the wandering witch of the web. She, in her spare time, would search anything I was involved in and come up with amazing stuff on the internet. Pictures of houses, criminal records, divorce pleadings, bankruptcies, domestic dispute, clubs, credit checks – somehow, somewhere she came up with this stuff about my clients, my opponents, my opponents' lawyers, my judges, ex-husbands, corporate malfeasance prosecutions, newspaper stuff. I already had a phone message to her, but I decided to start my own search, when blom! There it was! Doyle and Stanziani from the #5 squad prosecution of the narcotics squad in West Philadelphia about five years ago. These two were front page news because they were supposed to be bad cops who shook down drug dealers. They were fired, but somehow, they never were prosecuted. They got 20 year pensions and were mustered out of the police force.

Doyle had been a captain and Stanziani a sergeant. Two very high-ranking officers – never prosecuted, but fired. Very interesting. The newspaper article said that drugs, drug covered money and a number of guns with filed off serial numbers were found in a room in Doyle's house and drugs and a big stash of money were found in Stanziani's car. Before that they had been superior officers with commendation after commendation. Suddenly, their careers were in the dumper. At the grand jury, a number of drug dealers had come forward with testimony that told how these two had raided their homes, stolen their drugs and money and guns. This information which was supposed to be protected by strict grand jury rules regarding secrecy of testimony somehow was leaked to the press. Unfortunately, it was a state grand jury, not a federal one. The FBI would have been on a grand jury leak like white on rice and a federal judge would have been hopping mad, but at the state level, the tired old judge took no action and the criminal case died a peaceful death. Doyle and Stanziani resigned and their case left the front pages. The whole prosecution had a particularly bad smell. Were they set up? Was the prosecution righteous? Who could tell?

CHAPTER 4

Inside the storefront, Arnie Castagnolo sat at a scored and chipped desk. He was talking on the phone getting referrals from his drivers for long or short haul trucking assignments; his phone was planted on his shoulder as he chatted into the receiver, while he scribbled notes on a pile of sheets in front of him.

"Yo, Joe! New Orleans at 6:00 p.m. tonight from 6531. Got it. Any return trip. No. Okay. Truck only." Arnie was in his fifties and had started out as a truck driver himself, but, like many drivers, he developed a bad back, sciatica from sitting on long hauls and had come inside to broker. He got paid by the customers for the delivery, and he took a percentage from the drivers. He had gotten plump over the years, but the constant action on the job was fun. He knew everybody and chatted with them from Philadelphia to California. His office was beat up and tired except for a band new executive desk chair his wife, Francine, had gotten from Office Max to help support his back. Also, Francine insisted on coming into the office to clean up. The men ate a variety of takeout – Chinese, Mexican, soul, KFC and the floor and waste basket was full of detritus. Francine wanted the office to look like the home of any decent Italian wife. She also wiped Arnie's phone down with disinfectant and scolded the men to put their trash in the oil drum outside.

Several men sat on plastic fold up chairs outside Arnie's office and waited for Arnie to shout out their names. More men hunched outside at two battered picnic tables on the sidewalk. The men played cards, or sat staring off into space listening to their iPods. A few of the younger men played on Gameboys. A large garbage can also collected at least some of their takeout. Sometimes, the cart lady would come by and sell them hot dogs and sodas.

At each shout from Arnie, one of the men would jump up and grab the slip from his desk telling them where to go to pick up their load. Some of the men were part-timers, some full. They got paid by the mile and, in good times, work was plentiful. You could make about $200 a day for a decent load. All the men had gotten CDLs, commercial driver's licenses, through a school they had seen advertised. Some of the men were filling in gaps in their employment and worked seasonally elsewhere. Others were fulltime. But they were the lowest level. A decent trucker had his own rig which he was paying off and would pick up trailers around the country, relying on the brokers to hook him up. Ones without their own truck had to lease one. Ones who had no credit, had the company lease one for them. The lower down the scale you were, the less work you got. Times now were okay so there was a decent amount of work. Arnie was happy, the men were happy.

CHAPTER 5

Yo! Morning! How smart are you?" A rough-looking Mexican guy and an equally rough companion had sidled up to two middle-aged black men outside Arnie's storefront. The Mexican dude was wearing jeans, cowboy boots and a plain denim shirt. He certainly looked out of place in this storefront office in North Philadelphia, but his English wasn't bad. The two black men looked over at him and didn't know what to make of the two Mexicans. They were there in hopes of getting some long-distance hauls; both had their CDLs (commercial driving licenses), and had taken the truck driving course from a local outfit. They had used these trucking assignments to fill the gaps in their employment.

"Smart enough. What you want?" Horace spoke up. Horace was a big beefy guy, Elmo was this little squatty guy sitting next to him. They had lived in North Philly for most of their lives and were no strangers to hustlers, scams, and street guys. Something was fishy about two Mexicans showing up at a trucking broker's office in North Philly and asking them questions.

"We want a driver or two. You wanna talk?"

"Sure. What you got?"

"Two long hauls. Let's talk." The Mexican motioned to a spot on the sidewalk away from the picnic tables.

Horace and Elmo slowly got up from the rough wooden folding chairs and ambled down the street. Both black men were in their 40s and had been around. Horace, instinctively protecting his buddy Elmo, walked in front. "What you want?"

"Like I said, man, long hauls. From Arkansas to Philly. Two day trip."

"What kind of rig?"

"No rig. Rental truck. You pick up in Arkansas, drop it off to be loaded. Then pick it up and drive to Coatesville."

Coatesville was an old mill town about 50 miles outside Philadelphia. It had seen better days when it had a big steel plant. Now, it was a backwater.

"Arkansas to Philadelphia, huh? How we get to Arkansas?"

"Trailways. You bus down, drive back."

"That's four days. For two people."

"Yeah, so we pay good."

"How much?"

"A yard a day each."

"Whoa, a yard."

"Yeah, a yard and under the table, no taxes."

Now that was a good deal. On a good day, they could make $200. State and federal rules prevented them from driving "straight through" and required them to sleep so many hours. Horace and Elmo could make $4,000 a piece for four days work – two down on Trailways, two back on the road. Driving all the way through with each one sleeping while the other drove, they could make it in three days and wouldn't have to spend for a flea bag motel on the way. Good. "Under the table." That meant no federal, state or local taxes taken and, no insurance payments, no Social Security. Pure dollars. That was another $300 at least.

"What are we taking?"

"Don't ask, don't tell."

"No haz mat, no explosives." Hazardous materials and explosives were serious criminal problems for truckers, as well as dangerous to themselves. But this would be a rental truck – so it would be almost new and come from a reputable company.

"No way! Man, no way"

"You got more like this?"

"You do this, we got more for you. Maybe, next week."

Horace and Elmo walked off to huddle a bit. Their parents didn't raise no dummies, and now they knew what they were looking at. Mexicans, long-haul trucking, rental trucks, unnamed cargo and big bucks. This load was worth at least $5,000 to get to Coatesville. It said one word. Drugs. But wait, this wasn't no wetback operation. They wouldn't be carrying illegals in from Mexico.

Horace turned back. "No wetbacks are there?"

"No, man. Clean cargo."

"Okay. When we get paid?"

"Two bus tickets to Arkansas, $400 up front for each for way money. The rest in Coatesville. And, we give you cell phones. You call in every two hours on the trip after you pick up. Got that?"

"Can we use the cell phones to call home?"

"Use them as much as you like, just call in every two hours." "What if we got stopped?"

"Don't do nothing. Just call in."

"Is this dangerous?"

"No. Just call in and keep it simple."

Another huddle, Horace gesturing to Elmo. They both nodded.

"Okay. We in. Where we go?"

"Trailways at 12th and Filbert. Here are the bus tickets and a cell phone. We'll give you the cash when you get on the bus. Someone will meet you in Little Rock and take you to the truck rental – Enterprise. There you get GPS on the phone and a map. You got it."

This was standard practice for the two men. GPS was a necessity now. The men already had two small overnight bags with them in case of a long haul. The men called home on the new phone and said where they'd be. Of course, the money they'd make was not mentioned. Their women did not need to know that. And they were off in the Mexican's SUV to 12th and Filbert. Just like that.

CHAPTER 6

A dark green van followed the Mexicans' SUV to the Trailways bus terminal. Inside, a man sat at the computer screen and was speaking into his call phone to the Germantown headquarters of the Blue Eagles.

"Got it. He got two truck drivers at the Delaware Avenue location of the truck broker. We got the make on them and they were offered $4,000 each to pick up a rental truck near Little Rock and bring it back to Coatesville, all in four days. Looks like we have the connection."

Inside the van, a parabolic receiver had been aimed at the Mexicans and the two truck drivers from about 100 yards away and picked up the whole conversation.

Previously, information had been wrung out of a drug dealer in Germantown that he made pick-ups of his cocaine in Coatesville. He had been tracked to what appeared to be a closed fuel oil yard where he made his contact. The fuel oil yard looked abandoned, but had been rented to a corporation. Surveillance showed a small number of vehicles entering and leaving the premises after short stays. The drivers of the vehicles would come into the old office building and leave with a cardboard box. Two Mexicans would come in carrying several cardboard boxes and stay for about four hours while the buyers would show up and leave with the same cardboard boxes. The Mexicans would leave later with a large metal tool box. The Mexicans had been identified as illegals who had entered the U.S. and been deported twice each. These Mexicans and the activity at the fuel oil office had been recorded on closed circuit camera. The images were transmitted to the Blue Eagles' office in Germantown for the past three weeks. Active surveillance of the Mexicans' movements had been going on for the past week. Once a week, a rental truck came to the office and the cardboard boxes were off loaded.

An entry had been made into the fuel office in the absence of the Mexicans. Aside from collecting fingerprints, there was little of interest inside. There was no trace of either cocaine or meth in the air or on any surface.

Most of the buys seemed to occur on Wednesdays, Thursdays or Fridays in the afternoon. At those times, it was observed that several other Mexicans armed with hunting rifles and scopes were parked around the perimeter of the fuel office yard. Usually three vehicles made up the guard activity.

All this had been reported at the meeting in the Venango Street office.

Hank and Joe sat in the darkened room and reviewed the CD's and photos. Joe had already sent two men by plane to Little Rock with photos of Horace and Elmo to the Enterprise rental office in Little Rock to follow the truck to the pick-up point.

Joe said, when the presentation had ended, "It looks like a good time to hit Coatesville. We want the men unharmed and in custody and we want the money, not the drugs. We now have pictures of the buyers and will go after them soon."

Everyone agreed. A team was assembled to surround the fuel yard on Friday afternoon for a total takedown. Most of the men would have Tasers or tranquilizer darts – a few had silenced AK-47s in case things got rough. Vans were stationed nearby to haul away the inert bodies. Each of the men had a personal body camera on his cap or on his chest. The vans were in place from 12:00 noon and had the parabolic receivers angled at the office as the Mexicans appeared at 1:00 p.m. From 2:00 p.m. until 5:30, six different buyers had appeared and left with cardboard boxes. It was time.

Several of the Blue Eagle men came up on the guards and tased each one quietly and efficiently, and drove their van with the Mexicans securely cuffed off to the Venango warehouse. The rest of the men encircled the office. On a signal from the leader, a flash bang grenade was thrown through a glass window and several men entered blasting away with Tasers at the two Mexicans, who never knew what had happened.

A large metal tool box and a plastic file folder were picked up with dollar bills of all denominations tightly wrapped in rubber bands. A currency counter was unplugged from the wall and wrapped in its cords. A few remaining cardboard cartons were also carried out. The entire operation had taken 12 minutes. It was still daylight as the vans all headed for Route 30 and the Nicetown warehouse.

After the money, drugs and prisoners had been safely and quietly off loaded, Joe and Hank began to count the money. Once $10,000 had been accumulated in a pile, each of the men were called in and given his share, after signing the sheet. Soon the seven men had all received their allotment and left. They all knew that these bills might have drug dust on them or that some of the bills might be marked from a bank robbery. It was their responsibility to cleanse the bills check for consecutive numbers, and launder their payments appropriately.

Now, the interrogation could proceed. Each of the prisoners had been taken to a separate holding cell and chained to the wall, naked. Without clothes, the men would feel more vulnerable. As they came to, a table and chair would be brought in for the interrogation. Next, a surgical table rolled in by a woman in a nurse uniform. She had a large surgical scissors on the table and an electrical apparatus and switch. As the prisoner came to, she strapped electric wires to his genitals and sprayed a solution over his lower region. The interrogator cleared his throat and spoke through a voice altering device.

"What's your name?" No response.

"Where are you from?" No response.

"Who do you work for?" No response.

The first to be interrogated was one of the two Mexicans from the office. His picture had already been vetted through the various government databanks. He was Oscar Avena of Sinaloa Province, Mexico. He was wanted by the Mexican police for several daylight robberies. He had entered the U.S. and been deported previously on several occasions. His information would be useless, except to corroborate what was already known, but he may not have knowledge of more buyers than had been photographed and filmed buying. He also might know more drop off points in the U.S. He might even know some of the higher ups in the Sinaloa cartel or their whereabouts. But unlikely. The cartels were known to be vicious and treated disloyalty or cooperation with the police with heavy brutality, not only to their disloyal members, but their families as well.

"Okay. You want to play games, Oscar?"

"I want a lawyer." The interrogator chuckled.

"We aren't the police. You have no rights here. We are the Blue Eagles. You can't have a lawyer. You can't have bail. You can't call the boss in Sinaloa. You have three choices: One, we can start cutting off body parts. Two, we can electrify your balls, or three, we can leave you with the drugs, guns and money in a motel in northern New York where you will be arrested by the police on a tip from a confidential source. Your boss will think you ripped him off and he'll take care of you in prison. So take your pick: fingers first, balls first or New York motel."

"You can't do this. This is torture. It's illegal."

"Only if someone finds out and believes you. There may not be much left of you to find. So: fingers, balls or motel?"

"I don't know anything."

"Yeah, we know Oscar. Try us. And if you lie, we'll know. So, fingers, balls or motel. We don't have much time." The nurse walked up and sprayed his privates again.

"Okay, that spray aids the electricity. So, Oscar Avena, Sinaloa, Mexico, Sinaloa cartel, twice deported, three times entered illegally. Wanted in Mexico for three robberies in Mazatlan and Guadalajara. Wife: Carmelita, sons: Jose and Martin. Uncle Jose runs a gas station and holds title to the house where your wife and children live. Can we talk now?"

"No, no, that's not me."

"Oh! More games. Okay – fingers, balls or motel. Which?" Silence.

"Okay. Lights and I'll be back. Think this out." The interrogator left. The heat in the room was also turned off. The prisoner stayed spread eagle on the wall and shivered in the dark as the room got colder.

Eventually, all the men caved and gave up what they knew which was very little. Their regular customers they knew by nickname or faces or cell phone number. The customers had already been vetted by the cartel as legit so all the men in the fuel oil office had was a nickname or password and a cell phone picture. The men only knew the contacts in Arkansas and Texas. There were three drop off sites. They did know the drop off site outside Little Rock and word was sent out to the men trailing the truckers. As for the money, the cartel had a messenger pick it up with an accounting sheet showing the deliveries and receipts less the Mexicans' take for the week. The delivery of drugs was to have been left at a storage box in Exton, Pennsylvania for the messenger to pick up Saturday. Obviously, it would not be there, so the cartel would find out then of the ripoff, and would send out some people to find out what happened. Since none of the eight men had texted back since 5:30 Friday, the cartel already knew. Joe and Hank had the fuel oil office cameras on and staked out by Saturday. They would pick up the cartel's investigators and squeeze them as well. The Sinaloa gang had put its hand into a tar baby and every tentacle in the one area that could be lopped off only to be replaced to recreate an endless supply of drugs, but part of Philadelphia would be quiet for a while.

Eventually, all the prisoners were given the best choice. Each was delivered unharmed, but heavily tranquilized to a motel room where a confidential informant told the local cops of a massive stash of drugs, a few guns and a fictitious buy at the motel. The men were caught red handed. They all had prior illegal entries, many were wanted in the U.S. and Mexico on other charges. And the Sinaloa cartel did not look kindly on those who were supposed to be loyal Coatesville agents with a stash of the cartel's drugs on the run. Some of the men actually tried to tell their lawyers or the cops how they had been captured and interrogated by a rival gang or just plain set up. There were no takers for that story, but somewhere in the DA files notes on the Blue Eagles were beginning to accumulate.

CHAPTER 7

The trip to Little Rock was peaceful for Horace and Elmo. As the bus neared the depot, the cell phone rang and they were directed to the Enterprise rental office in downtown Little Rock. The truck was already paid for, a GPS was put on the truck by Enterprise and a map to the barn outside Little Rock was in an envelope. No reason to linger, Horace and Elmo got in and drove to the location. They were met by a Mexican who took the truck keys and drove them to a Jason' s Deli restaurant off I-40 in North Little Rock to wait for the truck to be returned to them in an hour. Simple so far. Horace and Elmo ordered big breakfasts - and a special treat - grits, and biscuits with red eye gravy and coffee with chicory. This was not available in Philly, even North Philly, and they savored every bit, sat back in their booth, held their stomachs and groaned. They went outside and stretched out on a berm in the parking lot for a nap.

The cell phone rang and woke them up. The two Mexicans got out of the truck and handed them the keys.

"Take I-40 through Memphis, Nashville, Knoxville, then 181 North. Don't speed and don't stop except to piss, shit or eat. One of you stays with the truck the whole time. The back is locked. Don't open it. Drive safe. No tickets. Check in on the cell phone every two hours. Got it."

"Yeah, we got it. Straight through to Coatesville." They turned on the GPS and drove off.

The Mexicans followed behind in a red SUV.

A gray rental Chrysler followed behind that. From inside the Chrysler the guy riding shotgun called Germantown. "Okay. The truck is on its way. It's a GMC, Tennessee license plate SLP-1248 with an Enterprise sticker. The two men got in, were handed the keys and drove off. They are followed by a red Jeep SUV, Texas license 149CHP6 with two Mexicans."

"Got it." Several minutes later a return call. "The red SUV is stolen from Dallas. No sweat picking these guys up."

Why would the Mexicans risk driving a stolen car? If they were caught, they got arrested. If they just bought a car for cash and registered in a fictitious name, they'd be home free. Maybe, the cartel felt the Mexicans were expendable or maybe it took too much identification to buy a car. The Mexican had made a mistake.

The truck drove through Tennessee into the rural area of Kentucky, and onto I-81, to the Pennsylvania Turnpike, off onto Route 30 into Coatesville, where the men were told to pull over into an empty lot. The two Mexicans paid off the men and one took them in the red SUV to the bus station in Coatesville. The other Mexican got into the truck.

But he didn't go back to Coatesville. Some place new, he pulled into a suburban driveway off Route 100 and got out of the truck and went inside a pleasant small single family house and handed the keys over to someone inside. He was picked up by the red SUV and both men returned to Little Rock for further work.

The cops were alerted to pick up the stolen red SUV in Little Rock. The driver already had a record, was illegal and was wanted in Mexico. He was bewildered as to why he had been stopped. The passenger also was illegal and wanted. Immigration cops came and picked both up.

After a few hours, the Enterprise truck was driven to a storage locker where it was unlocked and the driver started to unload cardboard cartons. He was hit by a tranquilizer dart and carried off to be interrogated. There were a large number of cardboard cartons in the rear of the Enterprise truck. These were off loaded and taken to a warehouse in Nicetown.

After lengthy interrogation, it turned out that the Mexican knew little of value. He too was tranquilized and placed in a motel with a large stash of coke and little excuse for being there. An anonymous tip got him arrested.

At Nicetown, the truckloads revealed about $1,000,000 worth of coke, meth and, surprise! some heroin. Heroin must be coming back. Yes, Philadelphia would have a drug shortage for a few weeks. This load would be turned over to the cops; it was too big to handle.

When the shipment didn't show up and the Mexicans tracking the truck didn't check in, the cartel went into action and sent out two of its men to investigate. The Coatesville office was vacant and showed no signs of activity. The Enterprise truck had been returned and the credit card had been charged, but no one at the Enterprise office remembered who returned it; it may have been a Latino woman. No one answered their cell phones. Over the next few days, reports began to filter in about the men being arrested for drug possession in different jurisdictions. Had the men divided up the shipment and split? But how had they all been caught so quickly? Where were they going to? Especially with that much product? Did they have an outlet? The cartel got lawyers for them all and wanted answers. The lawyers got nowhere at first; it was obvious the cartel had hired them. If the cartel either thought they had stolen the product or had botched the mission, it might take some serious action. The lawyers could not be trusted; they might sell them out to the cartel. It was becoming obvious that someone had learned about the Coatesville office and taken it down, probably to rob the cash on a Friday. But how would they know about the delivery from Little Rock. The only contact there would be the two Mexicans who hired the truck drivers. Okay, good place to start.

CHAPTER 8

Horace and Elmo were easy to find. They were back sitting in front of the broker's storefront. It was easy to lure them away from the company of the other drivers with a kind of a new long haul. But they knew nothing. They did the job, got paid and went home. They didn't see anything. They never got to the Coatesville office, they delivered the keys at an empty lot, got paid and were driven to the bus station. That was it. Yes, they saw two guys in the parking lot. They were the same two who gave them the truck. They never opened the rear of the truck. It was locked. Yes, they could possibly identify the two men who hired them if they saw them again. No value in that interview. They had nothing to lie about because they knew nothing.

CHAPTER 9

My first meeting at the Venango Street warehouse was a little weird. I entered through what looked like a shabby, but serviceable office, and, went through a large storage room packed with boxes on pallets. A small door concealed in the wall of the bathroom had been opened and Hank stood beckoning me into a shabbier room with an old wooden office table and steel chairs around it. Joe and Hank sat down, and pointed me to a chair. There were two other men and a woman in the room.

"I'm glad you came. I hope we interested you in something that we are very concerned about. I want to introduce you to two other men. This is Al (no last name given). He is a CPA with an undergraduate degree in economics. This is former Army General Lawrence, a graduate of West Point and a specialist in counter terror operations and this is Johnson." She was a very petite black woman. She was apparently only referred to as Johnson. I later learned her first name was Nora.

"I don't want you to say anything except to ask some questions to clarify what you hear. The room has been designed to be resistant to any type of surveillance, or recording device. Anything said here, stays here and is never recorded. We will be saying some things that will be possibly incriminating. You have agreed to be bound by attorney client privilege. We have obtained from your old firm your standard client letter, made a few alterations, and offer to retain you as our lawyer for this meeting. Please review this letter. A check for $10 binds the deal."

I skimmed the letter. It had been appropriately doctored up and suited our arrangement for this meeting. I didn't want it to get out that $10 was an appropriate fee, but then you get what you pay for, and I wasn't asked to do anything but listen.

"Now, first, we have done a considerable background check on you. Aside from your public resume, we know you were in the CIA for three years, had the full training, and served on the Middle East desk. We also know that you have achieved proficiency in a number of weapons including the M-16, Uzi, AK-47, and the Thompson machine gun, the bazooka, the mortar and the use of C-4. You were at marksman level, but not a sharpshooter in several types of sniper rifles. You were superior in hand-to-hand combat. We also know why you left. We like what we hear.

"You speak French, and Spanish, and can read Latin. You spend a lot of your free time on current events and history. You can read 650 words a minute with a 95% comprehension. You learned to speak and read basic Urdu in six weeks in your spare time with tapes and a few hours with a native speaker.

"'You are a bit of a rebel and like to question everything. You apparently can't help yourself.

"You are divorced, have one daughter age seven and have an amicable relation with your ex-wife and dote on your daughter.

"You are 5'10", weigh 185 pounds, and bench 315 pounds. You have wrestled in college with, to be kind, moderate success and played softball and tennis for years now. You can do 20 chins. You are fit and trim.

"You currently have no romantic interest, but had a brief affair with a Chinese-American computer software specialist.

"Whoa. That was just a rumor"

"Please, Mr. Stern, we don't deal in speculation, we only deal in verified facts."

"But..."

"Verified facts and not by your short term paramour."

"Anything else?"

"It's all here in this report which you may read, but only in this room. No printed matter leaves this room."

"Okay. What do you want?"

"Our belief is that the government does a lousy job, and is, on occasion, corrupt. We think we can do better. For free! We intend to demonstrate the ability to privatize a number of law enforcement functions. We will begin with the introduction of drug trafficking in an urban environment as our first project. During any of our work, we will maintain tight security and compartmentalize every participant on a strict need to know basis."

"So you intend to go about arresting drug dealers and cutting off the supply of drugs on your own, without government help, and possibly with their interference. In the process, you may run into corrupt police officials. Do you intend to deal with them?

"On all counts, yes."

"What do you want from me?"

"Legal advice and a moral anchor."

"Whoa! That's a lot. Some of your activities may be criminal and some may expose you to civil liability."

"We want to know which, of what we will be doing, is wrong and assess the risks. We also want to know if our superior operating ability goes to our heads, if, we are engaging in immoral conduct, or if our power has gone to our heads.

"You will know the details of our operations both prior and subsequent to our carrying them out."

"I'd have to know what you intend to do, first, before I can say I'd become your lawyer."

"Okay, we will describe in detail our most recent operation. Tell us what you think. The time, date, names and places have been redacted."

"Within the past month, we paid $100 apiece to four habitual addicts to name each verified drug dealer in a particular neighborhood of Philadelphia. We surveilled seven different dealers to verify their status, and purchased small quantities from each. We took sound and photographic evidence of each purchase. We then made a second purchase, and kidnapped each dealer. They were stripped naked and brought to a safe location where they were questioned extensively mostly about their source of supply. They were advised that if they came clean, they would be returned to the street without further ado. If they did not give us the information, they would be tortured, and it would be let out on the street that they were cooperating with police. CD's of our drug transactions would be sent to the local police. After sitting naked, in handcuffs and leg irons in a cold room, each gave up his supplier along with the times and manner of delivery. The interrogation time was never more than two hours. They and their drugs were returned to their neighborhoods, the proceeds of their drug sales were kept. We calculate the operation cost about $10,000. We retained $5,700.

"So what do you think so far?"

"I think you are fucking nuts. First you've committed so many crimes I can't add them up. Kidnapping, theft, intentional infliction of emotion distress, conspiring to violate civil rights, and probably jay-walking and corner lounging. What were you thinking? If you got caught, you'd be in jail forever."

"Okay. It's risk. But who's gonna rat us out? The drug dealer- not likely! We got him on a CD dealing. And who's gonna convict us? What jury is gonna go after us when we put dangerous dudes off the street, and got their sources?"

"Somehow, evidence manages to show up. What happens when one of these guys get arrested later on and decides to give you up as some sort of plea deal? The DA will cut them a break for getting the goods on you."

"But they won't have squat on us. We surveilled in secret. We grabbed them with masks on and took them to our secret pad in blindfold. We questioned them through a voice altering device."

"Hmm. Okay so far so good. But if you get caught, no judge is gonna allow a nullification verdict. That's where the jury ignores the evidence and delivers a not guilty on their own principles. Like euthanasia cases. Or, righteous civil rights cases. But open, intentional violation of civil rights by some vigilante group no one knows or can trust? I don't think so."

"Part of that is wrong. First, people will hear of us, because we're gonna let them find out. We're gonna be the Blue Eagles, we're gonna leave our signature and we're gonna intimidate drug dealers and clean up whole sections of the city, one neighborhood at a time. We're gonna have a website. We're gonna post some of the CDs, we're gonna name names, and alert the cops to make arrests. We have a few more tricks up our sleeves to get rid of drugs. But we're gonna have extremely high security, complete with cutouts."

"You know as a lawyer, I can't hear in advance about any operation. I could be held as a co-conspirator and I would be forced to invalidate this attorney-client privilege."

"We know. We get that. You will not be told anything about any operation in advance. In fact, you may never know anything about any operation after the fact except what you get from the news or on our public website."

"What am I doing then?"

"You are the public face of the Blue Eagles. You handle all of our external negotiations, and issue statements about us in media interviews. You will be safe to say you do not know anything about future operations and little about past operations."

"Hmm, where are you going with this?"

"After we get a decent rep, and arrest a few high level suppliers, we may go out of the country to intercept a few loads of coke or heroin. We may accept calls from some cities to be deputized to clean their drug neighborhoods up. We intend to privatize some of the more encumbered areas of law enforcement."

"How will you get the funds to operate?"

"Obviously, from the dealers' stock, but we have a few ideas for offshore payments which you will arrange."

"You're going to get some rightwing group to finance you?"

"I wouldn't put it like that. Someone who wants to combat criminal elements without the restrictions our police face against an international, domestic criminal operation. As we progress, the Blue Eagles will be functioning outside the country.

"While the United States may have diplomatic problems operating on foreign soil, we will be able to interdict drug traffic without involving the U.S. or embarrassing the other countries with a U.S. military presence.

"You have to understand that the U.S., while the greatest country ever, has put restrictions on itself. First, we enforce the laws with underpaid policeman. Imagine a cop making about $40K plus overtime sees a drug dealer stash of $50,000 plus $50,000 in drugs. How long do you think the average Joe can resist that temptation before he wants a new car, college for his kids, a summer home, you name it. Once they get a bit organized, they are working for the city, but also for themselves. The end result is they get co-opted by the big guys eventually and all we get are small fry arrests and the drug sales go on business as usual. Plus, these cops are not rocket scientists. Every five or ten years, they get investigated, arrested and all their cases get thrown out because they are tainted by corruption. Some go to jail. For the drug trade, business as usual.

"Next, the exclusionary rule. Back in the '60s, the Supreme Court got a heavy dose of 'let's fix it, Civil Rights.' So any violations of the Constitution by the cops in getting evidence - searches without warrants, coerced confessions, etc. - caused the evidence to be excluded from trial and the bad guys who obviously had committed a major crime walked. They walked! That meant that society was punished because it had the same bad guys back on the streets, the bad guys got rewarded by iffy police work, and the cops who were at fault never got punished. Only the prosecutor looked bad, because he lost a case of an obvious bad guy.

"Then the diplomats sold us out. Just like in Vietnam, we couldn't engage the Vietcong coming down the Ho Chi Minh trail. They enjoyed complete sanctuary and could attack from any convenient place along the long border of Vietnam. We lost many soldiers, the war, and face, because we obeyed our own self-imposed rules. Heroin comes from Vietnam and Afghanistan. We currently need Afghanistan to support its economy with poppies so somehow opium gets out.

"Same in Columbia and Bolivia, we can't use infrared reconnaissance to detect and target cocaine factories, we can't launch bombing raids or paramilitary operations because we might embarrass the native governments. Same in Mexico. We can't kick the shit out of their drug cartels. Against our diplomatic policy."

"Well, bullshit, I say. If we operate in the U.S., we are not making arrests to be tried in court. We are not the cops that are bound by Fourth and Fifth Amendment. Our evidence will never be suppressed. Our men will never be tempted to cheat on us. They are not civil service. They are well paid and will be extremely well supervised. We will conduct our own domestic war which will have the effect of discouraging drug trafficking by intimidation and by making it expensive to operate. We will gain access to the suppliers, and we will operate outside the country unfettered."

"Whoa! That's a lot to digest. I have to be honest. I'm worth a lot right now. I'm not going to take on any risk of criminal prosecution. I can't say I mind being the mouthpiece for a criminal group. Good lawyers are supposed to do that. Let me think about this."

As I went to my car, I noticed that it had been completely detailed, even the tires, but the quarters in my console had not been disturbed. I was a bit upset by this. I would have to check for bugs or tracking devices.

When I got back to my condo at Alden Park in Mount Airy, someone had completely cleaned the place. The fridge has been cleaned out. I am a bachelor now and live like one. My laundry had been done and was revolving cheerfully in the dryer. As I slipped off my sneaks and sat in front of the TV, a discomfitting thought crossed my mind. They didn't send me any female company, did they? I hoped not. That would be really cheesy - but I got up and went into the bedroom. Of course, the bed had been made with fresh sheets; but there was a chocolate mint on the pillow and a note.

"You didn't think we'd send a girl, did you? We are a classy organization, get your own!" I liked it. Very cool.

CHAPTER 10

I had been thinking over the ins and outs of the Blue Eagles offer. It was certainly innovative and appeared to be well funded already. Once I was associated with them, I would be subject to scrutiny of all kinds - the FBI, the press. Every inch of my past life would be an open book. Certainly, my divorce - it had been amicable, no bad blood, no financial issues - just a husband who spent too much time at work and not enough at home. My wife was a very nice woman who deserved better. She had a nice job and had no skeletons in her closet. My daughter was just a kid. Could they be targets of some demented drug lord?

My past might come out. Although I had been CIA, my cover was military. That usually held up. My involvement with K-Form Group would be picked over, but I was clean there. Besides they had been taken over by Nano. I just owned stock now. Anyone looking me up would know I didn't need the money.

My wife and daughter were the only risk I could think of. The Blue Eagles would have to assure me on that.

I was lounging over my breakfast reading the paper when I got to the local news. A big headline read "Germantown man naked on fence." This was too good to pass up. Apparently, a large black man had been handcuffed spread-eagled on a chain link fence near the police station on Germantown Avenue in full view of all morning traffic. He was a large, heavyset man, totally naked, but his genital area had been spray painted light blue and the symbol of a Blue Eagle was also spray painted through a stencil on his chest. He was also apparently a middle class guy who owned a restaurant in the neighborhood. Police were investigating and had a few leads. A large envelope had been delivered to the police station with several CDs. The police had no comment. I knew I was in for it now. The telephone rang about 15 minutes later.

"Mr. Stern, this is Captain Cosworth of the 22nd District Police. We need to speak."

My coffee was still warm, but I invited him over to my apartment which was about two minutes from the police station. He arrived about ten minutes later with four men in tow. I had brewed a fresh pot of coffee. This might take some time – a good sign. They meant to be friendly.

The men came in and settled around my dining room table which was part of an eat-in kitchen. They all took a cup of coffee. Captain Cosworth spoke first.

"Mr. Stern, you have been designated as the lawyer for the Blue Eagles. They are the ones who put George Haynesworth naked on a chain link fence near my police station. We also received a number of CDs and a very long letter detailing who they are and what they did. We want to know what's going on?"

"Well, Captain, first, I need to know who "we" is. I'm not sure I want to do business with all of you. I need a tight and secure group to deal with. I don't want a lot of leaks."

The men began to introduce themselves. One was from DEA, a plump older man, one was from the Narcotics Squad of the Philadelphia Police Department, one was from the Attorney General's Office and one was from the FBI.

"I can see we have a problem right from the beginning. There are too many people and agencies involved. I need to work with no more than two people who will only disseminate information on a need to know basis. There are too many leaks and I can't have too many people dealing with this."

"Who do you want?"

"I want you, Captain, and a senior DEA man. That's it. If I get a sniff of some of the information leaking to the press or other drug dealers, this whole process is off.

The AG man and the Narcotics Squad guy started to bluster and complain, so I said, "I will give you some basic background and explain my status. Then I want you both to leave. If not, I'm out. Is that clear?"

The men looked at each other. They were each interested in receiving maximum credit for any collar, and wanted to be in on what sounded like a high profile case. But I knew this would be a gigantic cluster fuck and I knew I would be caught in the middle.

The narcotics squads over the years had just gotten too dirty. To catch a few dealers, they had to track informants to get information. Informants were usually active drug dealers or unreliable addicts. What usually happened was that major dealers would either sell out their competitors or some of their own dealers. In this way they could protect their own operations and get protection from the cops. Major dealers rarely got arrested.

The DEA was usually above that sort of thing, and maintained a much higher level of internal security. They also had two other benefits - first, they got federal sentences for dealers. Congress decided to approve a series of "Sentencing Guidelines" to make sure all similar crimes were given the same sentences nationwide. In the East, where judges were busy, often were liberals, and a bit soft on crime, sentences were much lower than in the Midwest or South where the judges from the red states were much more conservative. If someone in the East got convicted as a drug dealer, they could easily get at least five years in jail with no parole and often over ten or fifteen years for multiple convictions. A judge in Philadelphia might not give more than two years. Second, the DEA could operate outside the US. I knew this meant they could take the information from a drug dealer and parlay it into the foreign sources in Latin America or the Far East. I needed them.

The AG's office was like teats on a bull. Somehow, they had grown from a statewide prosecutor's office whose main job was to help out towns that were too small to investigate major crimes – murders, drug deals, organized crime, etc. Since the 1980's it had morphed into a massive bureaucracy which the local politicians had easy access to.

Several of the elected Attorney Generals had gone to jail for their illegal connections. Enough said. The last AG was a pretty woman with almost no experience as a prosecutor or running an office. She also went to jail. I couldn't have the inmates running the asylum.

The FBI was somewhat acceptable. They are well trained but do not cooperate well with local police and are very publicity hungry. They love being in the picture with drugs and guns seized.

No. I knew we would be focused on cleaning up Germantown so we needed the Captain and I knew we had to work with the DEA which had the bigger picture.

"So gentlemen, I will explain what I can do, and what I know so far and then insist on only working with the Captain and the DEA. Then I must ask you to leave."

After some brief grumbling, everyone agreed, so I started.

"Gentlemen, I am acting as a lawyer and only as a lawyer. I will have no advance knowledge of any operation that the Blue Eagles may be involved in and I had no advance knowledge, or in fact any knowledge, of this latest caper. I am bound by attorney-client privileges as of now, so I cannot reveal much. I have not officially agreed to be retained, and now am considering a possible long term relationship. With that understanding, I am ready to proceed, if that is acceptable." Hearing no objections, I asked the Captain, "Have you already shared this stuff with the FBI, DEA, etc.?"

"Yes."

"I haven't seen it yet but I have to ask those leaving to erase it from their memories, and to consider this meeting confidential. I don't want my name anywhere, including in the press. That will jeopardize this investigation and my safety. Is that understood?"

Understood from all. The three men got up to leave. The DEA man gave me his card. "Alfred Harbor." He explained that he had been a city cop in Chicago and transferred to the DEA over 20 years ago. He was older, a bit paunchy but otherwise had a somewhat military bearing – a bit on the stuffy side. The Captain was a rather small compact black man, dressed impeccably in a white uniform shirt. He was quite dark, with shining white teeth and clear bright eyes. Even though he was about in his early 40's, he looked taut, as if he spent ample time in the gym. He was alert and quick in his movements, and seemed anxious to get started.

"Mr. Stern, as you know, I also run this station, so I will need an assistant on this matter. I will have to read him in. That will be the limit on anyone's need to know. Is that acceptable?"

"As long as you feel you can supervise him closely, I see no problem."

"No problem then."

"Okay. What do we have?"

"In the package we received, there were CDs – extremely well made and clear, showing a number of drug transactions and interrogations. I just wish ours came out this well. First, we have drug buys with some local street dealers – about seven dealers in all, with multiple buys each. Then we have interrogation of these dealers in a dark location with the interrogator's voice altered by some device. The dealers are then persuaded to reveal their supplier and details about the supply and delivery dates. I have only seen one set so far, but they are very clear and they explain that there are more of the same. Then we have surveillance footage of the deliveries and payments complete with voices - all very clean, all to Mr. Haynesworth.

"Of course, we'd already released Mr. Haynesworth when we found the package. I mean, after all, all we knew was that he had been spray painted, and handcuffed to a fence at that point. We now know he is a dealer.

"Basically, these CDs can't be used as evidence in court. We don't know who took them or when. The court would never admit them without authentication. Of course, we believe they are real.

"The accompanying letter explains a few things. First, it says the Blue Eagles are an independent crime fighting organization that wants to rid Germantown of drugs. The leaders all had military and police training. They do not kill or torture, they target only drug dealers. They also say that they "confiscated" the drug proceeds and are going to use the drugs in future transactions.

"Apparently, Mr. Haynesworth was identified as a supplier by four different street sellers. The tapes confirm his delivery to them. So the

Blue Eagles kidnapped him, but he refused to disclose his sources. (Apparently, other suppliers have disclosed their sources and they are working on that.) When Mr. Haynesworth did not respond to their limited interrogation techniques, it was determined that he would be dealt with "alternatively."

"Part of that "alternatively" is to release him, but chained and naked on the fence and send us evidence of his involvement in the drug trade. We apparently are supposed to use addict street dealers to purchase from him, while we surveil the transaction. We are then to arrest him. If we do not move promptly, the CDs will be sent to the press to embarrass us.

"The spray painting is to discredit him in the eyes of fellow drug dealers who, it is suspected, will learn of the Blue Eagles and steer clear of Germantown."

I had been listening patiently as the Captain ran through his briefing. What had my new clients done! They had certainly been busy. But what a risk. I could feel both men looking at me to judge my reaction. I tried to remain calm, but they had gone too far.

"Well, Captain, I have to say I am totally surprised. I never expected this. I will of course be contacted in time to see what we discussed here. I don't know yet what to say."

"I hope you tell them to stop being vigilantes. This is too much. I can't have every well-meaning person in Germantown becoming unbridled pseudo-cops. This is dangerous business and people are going to get hurt. Besides, we have rules, the Constitution, we live in an ordered society."

"True, true. But who have you caught lately. I'll have to play devil's advocate for them. They know how the game works. Your cops are given a few small fry to pad their stats, and meanwhile whole neighborhoods suffer from drugs, drug-murders, drug-burglaries, drug-prostitutes, yada yada. I wonder how many of your informants are playing the cops while they continue to sell."

"That may well be. But we can't have a private police force."

"They would say, 'Who says?' When was the last high-up supplier you arrested? But I'm a little concerned about something else. When you disturb the existing world order, anything can happen and usually does. Taking an established dealer off his turf and making him look weak can't be good. There are wolves out there ready to pounce. I think Mr. Haynesworth is in a shitload of trouble. He's got a wing down."

"I have already set my men out on the streets to several of his dealers and we'll find out if they're still in business. We will also try to set up some buys."

"All well and good. But I think someone will try to take over his territory, and sooner rather than later. I think he may get killed. I'd put some men on him to anticipate the hit."

"Please, Mr. Stern, let me do my work. I've been here for a few years and I didn't just fall off the turnip truck."

"Have it your way. Just a suggestion." OK, meeting over. Enough said.

It took no more than 15 minutes before Joe and Hank called. "Can we come up?" I was/ busting to have a chat with them after their latest caper. Of course they could come up!

I opened the door to my apartment and they looked a bit sheepish as they came in. They sat at the dining room table and did not refuse some coffee.

"Okay. How did I get involved?" Joe and Hank looked at each other. "I hadn't agreed to be your attorney yet, and now I'm in."

Joe spoke first as usual. "Sorry about that."

"Sorry? That's what you got?"

"Yeah. Sorry. We were stuck in a couple of things and needed to get some distance fast."

"Well, what did you do?"

"So far we have gotten to four suppliers through their street sellers. Three have caved and given up their suppliers. We need to move on them fast before word gets back to their sources. But Haynesworth was a different matter. He wouldn't budge. No one seems to know he's a dealer except for a few very private people and he doesn't get his stuff from the usual sources. So we had to let him go, but then we wanted to discredit him somehow. We were hoping to intimidate others in the

Germantown area as an example.

"So what are the usual sources?"

"Coke comes from Colombians and Mexicans and gets to Philadelphia by mules who are cut outs. They don't know who they work for, they pick up the stuff in Arkansas or Texas and drive it to the North. They meet some local contacts and get paid on delivery at the scene. Then they go back down for another trip."

"We have already intercepted several shipments and taken the coke. The mules get into big trouble, but nothing serious. They're now out of business. Some of the mules we are surveilling and hope to grab their contacts in Arkansas and Texas. Meanwhile we have a ton of coke to make deals with."

"The heroin comes from Afghanistan by boat. Mules pick it up in several port cities on the West coast. We haven't looked into that yet.

"Meth is manufactured in Mexico and also comes across the border where mules truck it north. We haven't gotten into the meth chain yet either."

"So far we are looking into the guys that load up the mules. We hope to pick up their bosses at some point."

"Alright. Now Haynesworth. What about him? He's a fairly prominent guy in Germantown. Runs a nice restaurant. No one knows he's a dealer."

"Exactly."

"But he didn't crack."

"Apparently, he's more afraid of his suppliers than he is of us.

"So he became candidate number one for public exposure."

"Only the cops know he was a dealer now. The public thinks he's a victim of some kind of prank, getting found naked with his genitals spray painted. The cops know different now.

"We have tapes of a number of buys from him in his restaurant. Anytime we want we can release them to the media or just post it on the Internet and it explains the whole thing. If the cops don't act quickly against him, we also release the info we gave the cops and show they were dragging their feet. We suspect Haynesworth has some good cop connections. We want you to tell your contacts who his police contacts are. They may be dirty. If the cops stage a raid, and he gets tipped we'll have his phone and computer tapped to see who gets to him and we'll release that too."

"But I don't think you understand. I think Haynesworth is in deep trouble with his source and may get killed and sooner rather than later. I told Capt. Coswell that, but he didn't seem too interested."

"We anticipated that. We have it covered. He will be under our protection. When the hit is scheduled, we'll grab his hit men and question them if we can."

"I don't even want to ask how."

"Don't. We know more than you can handle right now."

"I've got to say this whole thing bothers me. These guys are very serious about their territories. If Haynesworth gets hit, it starts a drug war. Murders especially, drug assassinations, are messy. They make the news. This is not just business as usual in the drug trade. This gets kicked upstairs to homicide and the feds. If there are a number of shootings that you start, then there are more shootings. Okay. Maybe you are instigating the deaths outside the justice system of a lot of bad guys, but then you screw up the justice system. The U.S. is built on our faith that the justice system works -- the cops get a high percentage of bad guys, the courts give them a fair trial and the vast majority go to jail for a long time; but the whole system works. If we have a bunch of drug warlords claiming territory in open urban warfare, we get a system of lawless warlords outside the system, defending their territories. We descend into a lawless society. Now, if you try to combat that by being vigilantes and you knock off the bad guys, you avoid the justice system. The problem with vigilantes is that they take the law into their own hands and there is no oversight. Sometimes they may be right, sometimes wrong; but there is no review. In our system, the street cops are controlled by the lieutenants, captains and inspectors who make sure they do their jobs within the law. The DA reviews the arrests to make sure they are righteous. Then the judge reviews everyone else. In this way, the public has faith in the system. When you act outside the system, there is no control. Other vigilantes may be motivated by race, or some other prejudice. Maybe, they get this wrong guy. Who will control you? And who are you to decide who's right and wrong?"

"Don't think we haven't thought about it. I think now is the time for you to review our operation and get to know us. We want you to follow us around for a few days. We think you'll see how we always go on solid evidence or not at all. Plus, if we can clean up Germantown by intimidating dealers, we can clean up other neighborhoods. I mean, who suffers most by the extreme case we take in the justice system? The poor people - the Blacks and Hispanics whose neighborhoods are already riddled with drugs and gun shots. If we tip the scale in their favor, they win."

"But who is your conscience? Who decides if the focus on a guy is fair? Who decides if he is a bad guy?"

"First, we have two solid principles. We don't shoot people. We don't execute punishment. We identify dealers and we turn the evidence over to the cops. If they don't act, we embarrass the cops. We can conduct surveillance, drug buys, root out supply chains, better, faster, cheaper and with more certainty than the cops. We have the equipment, we have the best trained men and we have no bureaucracy, no politics. The whole thing is just a panel of four people who review the evidence.

"I can be convinced that you're better and faster than the cops. But who will be your conscience, who will issue the search warrants, who will decide who is the target?"

"We have an idea for that, but first we need to have you see how our operation works. Follow us around for three days and nights, see what we do. Then you can ask the question again. By the way, we've already paid the first semester of your daughter's school for this fall. In cash. Untraceable. Let this happen. If you don't like, you can quit."

"When does this start."

"We'll pick you up at 4:00 p.m. this afternoon."

I met the old clunker van on a street corner on Chelten Avenue in Germantown. Although shabby with a faded paint job on the outside and heavily tinted windows, it was pimped out on the inside with tan leather seats, and a high end sound system. There was a refrigerator in the back and microwave in the glove box in the back. The car was designed for long stakeouts in bad areas. As I got in, Joe drove and Hank was in the back with the fridge. Again, the blind fold. I knew this was for my safety as much as theirs. If I didn't know anything, I could not be expected to answer anything. We got to a beat up former Hertz rental truck, heavily graffitied. We climbed the small ladder to the rear. The rear door went down on what sounded like a slow almost soundless motor. With my blindfold off, I could see a small room jammed with electronic equipment of all sorts: Mostly computer screens, and several things I never saw before.

Joe explained. "This is the latest in surveillance equipment. Parabolic receivers can pick up sound from 150 feet away through brick walls. We can take videos shot from 300 feet with hi-def TV resolution. We can generate stills of portrait quality. The computers link up to street directories, motor vehicle records, arrest records, military records, finger print databases of all sorts, we can hack financial records, health records, credit card records, cell phones, you name it from this truck. We have similar more powerful systems back at headquarters. We are geared from instantaneous information retrieval and rapid response. The entire system cost less than $1 million – a donation from a devoted patron. With government procurement regulations, this would have cost over $15million and taken several years to assemble. Most of our stuff was acquired over the counter and assembled in less than a month. Much of it was bought on eBay second hand and juiced up for our needs. The programming and software was either hacked, "borrowed" or improvised by our programmers who work either at headquarters or from home. We are years ahead of security, firewalls, and deniability because we are a very simple organization with very few employees or contractors. We number eight in total: Two computer geeks, four experienced field men, a technical guy who does communications, commo-security, commo-intercepts, one forensic person who does lab tests of everything, and analyzes all crime data. We all get the same base salary of $50,000 with bonuses divided equally based on results. We maintain a list of 25 men trained by the military in different skills we can call on as a kind of SWAT team when we need them for heavy duty operations.

Because we are small and concentrated at this point, our operation is simple. We pick up junkies, scare the shit out of them, find their dealers, surveil their dealers' telephones, texts and conversations. Pick them up, scare the shit out of them, learn their sources. Surveil their sources, scare the shit out of their sources and locate their sources. We do everything the DEA does, without bureaucracy, but faster, and we can scare the shit out of our people with credible threats of torture. We tase them, and then we threaten them. None of these people are of very strong character or trained against interrogation, so they usually cannot resist us for very long. We never actually torture or harm people – just make very credible threats.

"We tape everything with body cams, zoom cams, or onsite cams. We tape confessions. We can assemble an entire arrest file in less than three days, complete with lab analysis, fingerprints, DNA, fiber analysis, etc. If we were the cops, we could put ten men in jail per week with irrefutable evidence.

"In the last month, we have taken into custody seven street dealers and seized 89 bags of coke, H or meth at a street value of $8,500 and taken $12,000 in cash. We have taken three of their sources, seized a street value of $270,000 in drugs, and $315,000 in cash. All ten have complete arrest kits. We have those sources under surveillance and have intercepted four mule trucks coming north and seized a street value of $1,200,000 in drugs. We currently have seven more street dealers under surveillance and expect to take them into custody within the week. We will have eliminated 14 street dealers in less than six weeks out of an estimated 37 dealers in Germantown. Nearly half of Germantown could be clean in six weeks, we have seized $323,000 in cash. Our salaries were about $70,000 for the month, our overhead was about $20,000 and we have paid back our patron $200,000 on his $1 million donation. We have been in business for six months.

"The DEA has used our arrest kits and developed their own cases on two dealers and two sources to make arrests based on their own independent surveillance and drug busts.

After six months, given startup costs, and some lead time, we will have netted after salaries and overhead, about $700,000, repaid our patron $650,000 and have in the bonus account about $350,000 or about $30,000 each net after six months. We project $90,000 per year a year. Obviously, this is without deducting federal taxes, FICA, unemployment, Medicare, state income, city wage, or Workmen's Comp. We do our own accounting in house and launder all of our payments either in cash or otherwise. Most of our people are retired cops or military, have their own pensions, and can figure out ways to receive our salaries or bonuses."

"That's all well and good. But you have committed some serious crimes. Robbery, theft, kidnapping. I've been through this before. If someone cracks your security, you are dead. Well, not dead, dead, but you could be in jail forever. Our country does not operate on the rules of private warlords conducting self-help police work. You have to see how important our safeguards are to the stability of the country. It is easy for unregulated police work to tap into anarchy or a police state. I mean you don't need to look further than Nazi Germany or the MKVD in Russia. In our country, we came dangerously close during the McCarthy era when we had communist witch hunts and the House UnAmerican Activities Committee. A vigilante system can be more dangerous to the country than the criminals themselves."

"Mr. Stern. We agree. We are technicians, we are capable of high level police work, we can fight battles of all kinds quicker, better and more efficiently than any government. We have no bureaucracy, no corruption. We have highly trained motivated employees who believe in our system."

"But what if you run off the rails and attack political dissidents or innocent individuals. What if you don't like someone's religion, or sexual orientation, or immigration status? Or if you just don't like someone."

"And you think that doesn't exist in our police or court system now?"

"Well, it does, but it is open and reviewable, not some secret body making secret decisions somewhere."

"We have an answer for that."

"You do?"

"Yes. You."

"Me."

"Mr. Stern We have selected you. After much investigation we have fully investigated a number of possibilities, but you had all the qualities we wanted. First, you don't need money. You are independently wealthy. Second, you have both legal and military training. You understand what we do and how we do it. But, mostly, you have a reputation as a fair-minded individual who can see through moral dilemmas, civil rights issues and human foibles. You will be our judge. You can make instantaneous, or, if need be, more thoughtful assessments of our goals and measure them against society's needs."

"Whoa! Me. I can't do all that."

"You will become familiar with the facts of each action we wish to undertake and have absolute veto power on anything you think is not proper. You will be the rabbi."

"There are two problems. First, if I know of any operation before it happens, I could be just as guilty as you. I explained this before. Second, as the only known member of your organization, I am an easy target for all these gangs you have antagonized. They'll go after me to get to you even if I don't actually know anything."

"At all times, you will have a bodyguard - almost always unseen - but at your beck and call. We can assemble a team of six to eight armed personnel to assist him inside of 30 minutes if he should request back up."

"Let's see how it goes."

CHAPTER 11

Hank picked me up at 6:00 p,m. or so and took me to the operations meeting blind folded, although I was beginning to suspect the factory building was in the lower northeast industrial section of Philadelphia. I was lead into a large room where a number of people- probably quite a few of them women - were dressed in black and wearing balaclavas concealing their faces and I was ushered into a chair near the door. Behind the speaker's table was a large screen set for a PowerPoint presentation. The speakers filed in - also dressed in black and dark balaclavas. Joe was the first to speak. He started without preamble or greeting.

"First, Mr. Stern is here as our lawyer. He is simply an observer and has offered no opinion on our activities planned for tonight. Any questions he asks must be referred through me - Capt.A or Capt. B. Please do not communicate directly with him."

My eyes were beginning to adjust to the dim light. I could see a large plain industrial room with concrete block walls, and windows and skylights covered with a dark material. The people in front of the door were sitting on simple folding metal chairs. A number of them had black travel bags at their feet.

The speaker, I recognized Hank's voice, began. "Tonight's mission is to protect Albert Haynesworth and capture those who would assassinate him. As you know, he was abducted by us and asked to give up his drug sources. He refused. We chained him naked to a fence on Chelten Avenue, and his transactions over several weeks with drug dealers has been amply recorded onto DVDs. Because he have been outed as a dealer, we believe either rival dealers may seek to kill him and take over his territory or his connection may do so to limit his ability to identify him. We intend to protect him and capture the hitmen for further interrogation. We believe it will lead to significant intelligence."

"Each of you has been given a map of the area surrounding Mr. Haynesworth's restaurant, complete with alleyways. Mr. Haynesworth usually leaves the restaurant between 11:00 and 12:00p.m. He has been induced to cooperate in this venture. He will be exfiltrated from the restaurant by one team and transported to safety. His family is being guarded by another team. Other teams will be stationed at strategic points around the restaurant to capture any hitmen who will attempt to assassinate Mr. Haynesworth's double. Each of you has already been separately briefed on your respective roles.

"We previously have captured a team of three men who attempted to place a bomb under Mr. Haynesworth's car. They have been mostly interrogated to this point and appear to be from a rival gang. They were three African-American males lightly armed with hand pistols in a stolen SUV. They had throw away phones, but had most of their hit money on their persons. The rival gang is a young black gang from the projects. We now know their leader's name, base of operation, and have begun conducting surveillance on it. We have identified six other gang members. We have circulated their pictures to you if the need should arise to identify them. We believe they will be only armed with hand guns."

'The sole basis of this operation is to gather intelligence by capturing the hitmen and interrogating them. Do not shoot to kill. You'll have Tasers. We want them alive and well. No police, no noise, no gunshots, no wounds, no hospital visits. Just incapacitated hitmen."

"Any questions?" Apparently the previous training and this briefing were sufficient. There were no questions.

"Let's roll." With that, the audience began to separate into different groups and head for the exits with little conversation or murmuring.

Hank took me to one of the group's vans. I sat in the back, but was outfitted with a bullet proof vest and night vision goggles, as they all had. We went to a corner and began the stakeout. No one spoke. The van had a separate radio system and a computer. Our

vantage point could observe two streets. The computer began to check all license plates in the area for stolen cars, or any suspicious ownership. One street was all commercial and had customers entering and leaving. The other was residential.

Most of the people in the van were either playing Gameboys or looking at their tablets, the others were on alert. Slowly, the commercial block was beginning to close down and the proprietors were pulling the steel gates over their front windows before leaving for home. That left only three cars on the block, which we had already checked out and belonged to apartment residents in the floors above some of the stores.

The residential street began to quiet down by about nine. All but three of the cars checked out for ownership by local residents. The street lights were on by now and only an occasional pedestrian passed by. They were either one or two people and checked out with our metal detectors not to be carrying.

By about 10:00, a late model dark green Chrysler with stolen plates parked on the street opposite Haynesworth's restaurant. Immediately, a parabolic receiver was aimed at the car by one of our vans parked across the street. Apparently, the driver called another cell phone to say he was in place. The telephoto lens sited on the car could only pick up images of two black males with baseball caps. The two received a telephone call from two phones saying they were also in place. We received a radio message from one of the teams saying that a black Honda Pilot was a block away with stolen Maryland plates, but a Pennsylvania inspection sticker. A parabolic receiver was directed at it. The men in the two cars were chatting back and forth. The name Haynesworth and his restaurant were mentioned more than once. This was it. Game on.

About 11:15, Haynesworth's double in full body armor hustled along with two men from his restaurant to a black Cadillac parked at the curbside. The real Mr. Haynesworth was securely stashed in the restaurant with two armed guards. The car across the street shouted excitedly into his phone and the black Pilot roared down the street into our block. Immediately a dump truck barreled down the other way and blocked the path of the Pilot. Another large truck blocked its rear. Two SUVs pulled into position behind and in front of the Chrysler. By now the street was filled with cars and the beams of flashlights. Men in dark gear, night vision goggles and carrying assault rifles were all over the street.

The two men in the Chrysler across the street tried to flee on foot. After about 50 feet, each crumpled to the ground with tranquilizer darts in their backs. Three men exited the Pilot with their hands raised. The five men were taken into custody and placed in plastic hand cuffs and leg restraints in several of the vans and given some chloroform. There were as yet no police on the scene. The entire operation had taken less than 10 minutes. All five were peacefully driven to headquarters and dispersed to separate cells. They were stripped naked and restrained around metal poles in the center of the cell until they revived.

The first to revive was one of the men from the Pilot. He had his wallet on him, with $1,000 in cash, and five bags of coke. He was Stephen Wilkes from West Philadelphia. A large beefy man of about 30 - maybe 6'2" and 230 pounds. A light shone down on him and an interrogator sat at a metal desk along the opposite wall.

"Who are you?" The interrogator asked.

"Huh!"

"Who are you?" Again.

"If you don't cooperate, it will be worse for you." At that, a woman in a white hospital doctor's robe came in and began to place several items on a table. One was a large pair of surgical scissors, then a car battery with jump cables was placed by his feet.

"Wha... what's that?"

"A little truth serum. It may hurt a bit."

"No... No... You can't do that... I didn't do nuttin... We were just driving."

"Name please?"

"Alphonse Greer."

"Not your favorite alias. Your real name. From 5916 Ogden Street, Philadelphia, PA 19137."

We, of course, had already been run through the computer.

"Wilkes, Stephen Wilkes", he blurted finally.

"Very good."

"What were you doing in the Pilot?"

"I want a lawyer."

"Sure you do. But we aren't police. We are the Blue Eagles. We don't owe you shit."

"You can't do this. We didn't do nuttin."

"No. Not yet. But we don't gotta prove nuthin. We know you were there to take out Haynesworth. We just know it. And that's all we need." The interrogator rang some kind of a buzzer. With that, two large men in green orderly outfits came in and put on latex gloves. One began to spray Wilkes' privates with a disinfectant and began to hook up an attachment to his balls. The other stretched Wilkes' arm onto a board and taped it in place. He then started to wipe disinfectant on the surgical scissors on the table."

"Whoa… Whoa… I know my rights. I want a lawyer. I ain't talking."

"Sure… Sure. We aren't the cops. We don't follow the law and you got no rights. Okay. Now, what'll it be, balls or fingers. You choose, balls, fingers or the truth.

One of the orderlies began to test the jumper cable. Sparks flew. He also plugged into a wall socket and began to test the wires.

"I don't gotta give you shit."

"No. That is entirely within your power. Now, which is it, balls or fingers?" Silence.

"I don't hear you. Balls or fingers."

Silence.

"Okay, balls it is." The orderly attached the wires to the apparatus on Wilkes' genitals.

"No balls, no balls."

"Okay, finger then?"

"No… no fingers!"

"Then truth or else."

"Okay. Okay, we wanted Haynesworth out. He had been made and was no longer any good. He wouldn't sell out. So he cooked his goose."

"Who hired you?"

"Come on now, he'll kill me."

"Okay then, balls, fingers or a free ride to Delaware and $1,000 in cash."

"What do you mean?"

"We'll drop you in Wilmington and give you $1,000 in cash to disappear." "Okay. Okay. It's Raheem. Raheem el Shabazz. He's the boss."

"From the Champlost gang. He wants to take over?"

"I was going to be a lieutenant here in Germantown."

"Where are his headquarters?"

"Tenth and Chew. In the shop... the automobile shop... the garage there."

"Now tell us the guys that were with you on this hit."

"I don't know them all. Two were from Germantown. They were brothers - Fat Boy and Squench. That's all I know. They were in the car across the street. Fat Boy is the skinny one. The others were Long, Toad and Tingle. I don't know their last names. They live around on Champlost sometimes with the baby mamas, sometimes not."

"How much were you paid?"

"A yard up front, two yards later."

"Who are the other guys in the Champlost gang?"

"I don't know the new guys. The main guys were Fonso, Hawk, Johnson and Jersey. I don't know the rest yet. I'm new to the gang."

"Okay. Mr. Wilkes, good job If we corroborate your story, we'll drop you in Delaware. So hang loose." The orderlies cut his left arm off the board and put the handcuffs back on, leaving his arms draped over an old steam pipe.

The interrogator got up, collected the surgical scissors and took his table to the next room. Similar procedure, similar result for the

Champlost gang. The Germantown boys were pretty new and didn't know much, but did give information of the drug sites in Germantown, and what they knew of the dealers.

It turned out that, of the five, three had outstanding warrants for pretty serious crimes. They had gotten bail and simply skipped. The bail was pretty steep and had not been sued out yet. Dropping these three off was worth about $27,000 in bail money. So we called a retired cop in Delaware and would drop them off with him to claim the bail. The other two were given a Blue Eagles sign on their backs and chained to fences in Delaware naked for the cops to pick up. Both were being sought by the Philadelphia cops and had APBs out. DVDs of excerpts of their confessions were sent to the appropriate detective division.

So it was Raheem el Shabazz, also known as DaVonte Taylor from Tenth and Chew, of the Champlost gang.

"So what did you think?" Hank wanted to know.

I had been thinking and knew my answer. "Very neat, very surgical, well planned, well executed. You, of course, had the right to protect Mr. Haynesworth, so your acts may be all justified. Technically, you did kidnap the hit men and the lookouts, but you are permitted self-defense actions. Since they confessed to their conspiracy and attempt, your arrest was probably justified. So I don't think I would add kidnapping, especially since they were sort of released. Since some were bail jumpers and you captured them, your acts were justified. Besides I don't think anyone would want to prosecute you, or convict you. You didn't actually torture anyone. Of course, you did touch them, so that could be a battery and the threatened torture was definitely an assault. Again, I don't think anyone would convict you. You could reasonably argue that you were acting on behalf of Mr. Haynesworth in self-defense, so you may have been justified. A bit too close to the border for my comfort, but I'd have to give it overall a pass. The execution I'd have to give A+. What's next?"

"Now we hit Raheem and make it look like Haynesworth's boss' mob. Very surgical. No shooting. No disruptions of the peace. We will kidnap his dealers in the Champlost area and his lieutenants, scare the shit out of them, drop off the ones with outstanding warrants on bail, leave the others naked on a fence with Haynesworth' s logo on their chest. Then wait to see what happens.

I got a call the next day from the Mayor's office. His appointments secretary, Martha Johnson-Caparello wanted to know if I would meet with the Mayor and the Chief of Police at 11:00 p.m. I knew something like this was coming. I, of course, said yes but insisted on a few things: 1) No recording of any kind of the meeting, 2) no reporters, no news media and no notes could be taken, and 3) I was appearing only as an attorney and not as a member of the Blue Eagles. Fine, fine, and fine.

Just to be on the safe side, I called Hank and Joe and told them about the meeting and asked for a device which could detect bugs, devices recording or transmitting data in a room the size of the Mayor's office. I had one delivered before I left.

I logged into the City Hall guarded entrance at 10:50 a.m. and went to the Mayor's office, signing in at his guard's desk. Ms. Johnson-Caparello escorted me into the waiting room. Philadelphia City Hall is an ornate building in the Second Empire style and is, after 120 years, falling down everywhere. The concrete floor is covered with 40 year old linoleum tiles but gorgeous crown molding is around the top of every ceiling. Back in the day, Italian plasterers had molds which they could press into wet plaster to create ornate moldings, and bas-relief impressions on the walls. In many City Hall courtrooms, rococo fluted columns rose from marble chair rails. The effect, of course, in the courtrooms was to make it impossible to hear as the sound reverberated off the many hard surfaces. With the heating or air-conditioning running it was even worse. The Mayor's Office was on the second floor, adjacent to the very ornate City Council Chambers where incompetent boobs elected to serve as Philadelphia's august and learned solons met to figure out how to divide up the spoils, both political and financial from each bill they encountered. I was never able to walk past City Council without feeling some slimy film had attached to my skin.

In all honesty, I can't say the same for this mayor. He appeared to be an honest straightforward guy who was sincerely dedicated to doing well. While he had twice been reelected, the public ignored him and City Council fought almost every measure he introduced. He was a conservative, soft-spoken black man who spoke like a liberal arts professor - a bit dry and careful with his words. The police chief was an old veteran who had made his way up through the ranks, learning the required education courses, the "old boy" network and voter apathy. He was also a black man, and had served in two other Eastern cities as chief with distinction. I felt I would be getting an honest response from these two.

Of course, I sat the obligatory half hour before being ushered into the Mayor's Office. There were two more people in the office I didn't like--the City Solicitor and the Mayor's Press Chief. The City Solicitor, Alma Dougherty, and I had crossed swords before and I didn't trust her. I had worked on a plea agreement for a client of mine to spill his guts and get a certain recommendation from the prosecutor whom I knew and trusted. Alma appeared instead at sentencing and in a mocking droning voice read out the plea deal that we had agreed on. Then she sandbagged me by exaggerating, misstating, and outright inventing facts about my client, which she did not have to prove. I, of course, was unprepared to respond to her ten minute hatchet job and tried to recall each of her so called facts and refute them. The judge was not impressed and buried my client. No.....Alma... Sweet Alma would not do.

The press guy was an old friend. We had played softball together, but I had said no media. Both had to go. They went.

Now, down to business. I first had to make a little spiel as to whom I was and where I stood. I was an attorney representing a client, nothing more. What I said could not be attributed to him, her or them and I would not betray any confidences. I would "proffer," that is, present in a hypothetical manner what they may have done and state their position. The Mayor and the Chief were down with it. I then used the device Hank had given me to sweep the room for bugs. There were none.

Now, it was the Chief's turn. "Mr. Stern, we can't have this. A vigilante force committing crimes and not subject to the rules, civil rights, proper criminal procedure, and deciding who they are after. It could easily spin out of control and harm innocent people. We know they must be ex-cops or ex-military and if we track them down we will arrest and prosecute. We can't have something like the Klan, or the Nazis, or Mussolini's brown shirts arresting people they don't like.

"Chief, Mr. Mayor, I agree. I have told them they are not a proper piece of a democratic society with a legal system which protects all parties.

"Let me describe what they may be doing in any case. First, they have identified a number of junkies and addicts and then have them wired and photographed making buys from their usual sources. So far they have committed no crime. There should be an arrest made on the basis of our tapes, DVDs, etc., but it is not acceptable in court because the court will not approve our evidence. Then the dealers are taken into temporary custody where they are encouraged to disclose their sources and what else they know about drugs in Germantown. They use scare tactics implying torture, but never implement it because the dealers are usually forthcoming. They also admit their sales on video. They return the dealers to their environment and take no further action against them. They then attempt to establish contact with their sources and follow the supply chain, to Mexico, Bolivia, Columbia, wherever it goes. Sometimes they take the sources into temporary custody. Sometimes they intercept their trucks or mules or boats, what have you. Of course, we hack the DA's files, the DEA's files, and have acquired our own vast amounts of intelligence just by concentrating on one little section of the City, Germantown.

"We have identified, taken into custody and debriefed 14 street dealers and gotten most to reveal their sources. We have identified, taken into custody and debriefed six of their sources. We have intercepted multiple pounds of cocaine, multiple kilos of heroine, and multiple pounds of meth, which we will turn over to you. Some we may retain to make deals with to trap other dealers. In short, in a two month period, we have done more than the police in Germantown have done in six years. The Blue Eagles are a known force in Germantown and have caused sales there to dry up. We believe we have eliminated 70 percent of sales and dealers."

"We have CDs, DVDs and other evidence to turn over to you which will implicate these dealers and their sources in drug activity."

The Chief was the first to speak. "Your evidence will not hold up in court. Without authentication, those recordings are worthless."

"Then we will dispose of the dealers in other ways. We will release the recordings to the news media and the DEA. We will let everyone know they are under our surveillance so that both their customers and their sources will avoid them."

The Chief was worried on another point. "If you disclose your members and your success to the media, it will make the police look terrible."

"True. We may also release evidence of your police, the detectives and the drug task force being involved with the dealers and their sources. We may tap their phones and show their connections to dealers."

"Okay, not good, not good. But you also realize that revealing those who control turfs of distribution may lead to wars among the competing parties."

"Yes. They may kill each other off."

"We can't have bloodshed in the streets, drive-bys, armed invasions."

"We already do. The highest death rate is among young black males in the drug trade, higher than heart disease or cancer. What have you done to stop it?"

"Homicides have shown a steady decline over the last six years. But more to the point, your clients have committed kidnappings, burglaries, thefts, torture, assaults and weapons violations in your operations. They have denied the dealers due process and the civil rights. In dealing with the drug problem, you threaten the very foundations of democracy. It is like a cancer drug that causes severe heart damage. It is totally against everything America stands for. We can't allow it."

The Mayor had been quiet all along and was deep in thought. "Could we deputize them?

Like privatizing the police somehow?"

The Chief was getting agitated and beginning to lose it. "Joe, we can't do that. If we make them our agents, we are liable for everything they do. That means lawsuits. It also means every arrest that violates someone's civil rights gets tossed, because they now are the police."

I had to calm down the Chief. "Mr. Mayor, I'd have to agree with the Chief. If we become deputized, we must abide by the same rules as the police. We couldn't do that."

The Mayor was still intrigued. "Well, then, what do we do?"

"Joe, we have to shut this down. We can take all their evidence, all their seized contraband, and use it. We can take everyone who has skipped bail into custody and sweat them into confessions with the evidence they have. We can get the task force to use the intelligence they've collected so far and use it to intercept shipments. Yes, we could do all that." "What do we get for turning over this to you."

"Immunity. That's it. What do you want, money, recognition?"

"No. Recognition is bad. Money - we would like to keep what we have already taken, with a release from you of no prosecution."

"Hmm. Well, we can't prove what you've taken or who you've taken it from. We don't even know who you are. I guess we could get something drafted that would say that."

"Since we already know where most of these people are, we'd like to bring them in and claim their bail. Some of these guys have posted over $100,000."

"We could agree to that. There's no law governing bail bounty hunters, you can violate their rights as long as you bring in a live body safely. But look, I don't want bloodshed, no harming of innocent bystanders, no public disturbances. Bring them in quietly in one piece."

"Where do you want them?"

"At the round house or at Holmesburg." He was referring to two jail facilities -- one was police headquarters, one was the main prison. "I'll arrange for you to call ahead, and guards will be available to let you in and receive them in a special section we will set aside for you. We will need you to have special IDs and we will need to identify your transport."

"How about if the prisoner has been tased or hit with a tranquilizing dart?" "Are they alive and well?" "Yes."

"No problem. I don't want any hospital cases, any medical conditions. Above all, I don't want any new crimes committed in my city. You got that?"

"Loud and clear. Now I want something from you. I am entertaining offers from other cities. I want absolute silence from you. We don't want you to interfere with any of our new business. We don't want you to testify about what we have done already or what we discussed."

"No problem. But same here. You do not disclose to anyone including the media what we discussed or what you've done here."

"Let's put all this in writing and get it signed."

"Wait. We don't even know who you represent."

"Just as well. I'll sign as the designated agent."

I knew Philadelphia would never buy a vigilante force. No police force could compete with an unfettered group of trained, motivated operatives like the Blue Eagles, and no democratic government would ever lose control of their police. I'd have to explain this to the guys. They wouldn't like it.

CHAPTER 13

As I walked out of the Mayor's office, I could tell that the Mayor and the police Chief had already been well prepped on the fundamental illegality of the Blue Eagle's mission. Although the statistics were enticing and drug trafficking had slowed to a creep in Germantown, the City and the nation were based on a system of laws which were far more important than an eradication of a temporary societal ill - the irrational desire of some members of our society to kill themselves by ingesting mind altering substances. Would we ever recover from this epidemic? Who knew? Nonetheless, I had to confront my clients with this firm decision of city government. How would they react?

I called. "Yo, Hank, I got some bad news..."

Hank and Joe were on a speakerphone and excited. "Pete, we gotta meet as soon as possible. Big development. Huge! We got picked up."

"But, the Chief of Police..."

"Forget that. Go to Cascelli's as soon as you can for lunch."

"Okay. Cascelli's, huh? On Ridge. I'll be there."

Cascelli's was a nice Italian restaurant on Ridge Avenue in Roxborough about two minutes from the gym. If I went out the expressway, I could get there in about 20 minutes. Traffic was light so I got there about 1:00 p.m., just in time for lunch. Joe and Hank were sitting in a booth in the corner. Cascelli's had a nice inexpensive menu that the Roxies (inhabitants of Roxborough) loved. I had discovered it years back and it had been on my list of favorites since then. Joe and Hank were already working away on some texts. I ordered the Mediterranean Seafood Special - clams, mussels and shrimp over linguini in a white sauce. I also hate to admit it, but I am not a big drinker. I ordered a glass of Zinfandel. Probably considered a girl's drink, but I wasn't proud. I liked what I liked.

I tried to go over the meeting with the Mayor and express my disappointment, but they had other items on the agenda.

"Pete, we got a line on some great work, down south. Can you go?"

"Whoa... catch me up... what's going on?"

Hank slid a cashier's check across the table to me for $25,000. "Report it, don't report it, up to you. Now..".

Joe butted in. "Pete, we got an angel from down south, wants his city cleaned up in the worst way... and fast."

"Okay. So I assume you're going to do the same things down there as up here. With the same problems, and in an area you don't know." It is a lawyer's job to be the eternal pessimist and rain on every parade possible:

Well, this guy owns a big business in Memphis, Tennessee and wants the drugs out. He has a huge investment in the area and if he can clean it all up, he stands to make out big."

"Memphis, huh. They have a big distillery, big timber, and I don't know what else." "Well, the town is a big trucking center too, and it happens to have a big infestation of drug traffic."

"But you don't know the south. You would have to hire tons of local help and train them. You don't have any local intelligence."

"Yes. But we have the secret cooperation of the mayor, the police and the prosecutor. This guy also has a sack of money and wants results - out of court, nothing official."

"Would we be deputized, or totally under contract, under cover."

"Under cover except that we would use the Blue Eagles brand to clean house."

"Although we make our money taking the drug proceeds, this guy will fund the entire operation out of his own pocket in offshore money."

"How will you train people?"

"We're going to take 12 people here from Philadelphia, and hire 10 ex-cops or ex-military down there."

"I hope you've got some black faces on this team."

"No sweat. We have already interviewed some great ones. Southerners, accents and all, but with military and police training."

"Okay, let's meet this guy and hear what he has to say. I can't promise anything but I need to think up all the problems."

"Have some tiramisu - homemade."

Yes the tiramisu was great. My mind was already spinning with ideas. "But guys. How about Philly?" I explained the deal on the bail money we could earn. They would be on it right away. I asked about Haynesworth. He wasn't cooperating with us although we saved his ass. They had explained he was at risk from other competitors. He said he would handle it. We didn't think so. But the word from the Philly Mayor was clear: No more.

If we weren't wanted, or even secretly encouraged and tolerated, there was no sense going on. Surprisingly, a coalition of criminal defense lawyers, drug dealers, and police would eventually demand an investigation. While our security was good, the feds would eventually penetrate it. No. Now was the time to get out while the getting out was good. The Blue Eagles were now a front. Maybe, it could strike fear. But Philly was not the city, maybe Memphis would be.

The Blue Eagles assembled all their files from Philadelphia and culled out those dealers with outstanding warrants. This was easy money. Generally when someone is arrested, they have a bail hearing at their arraignment. This occurs when they are first arrested, are told what charge they are facing and have filled out some paperwork to determine if their bail will be high or low, or "ROR." If the charges are relatively light and there are strong indications that they will show up for trial i.e., have a decent job, live with family, have other strong roots in the community, they may be "released on their own recognizance" ("ROR") or let walk with a promise to show up for their court dates. They simply sign a subpoena and walk. As the crime increases in seriousness and their ties to the community lessen, the court will require them to post monetary bail in varying amounts. One of the best ways to win a criminal defense case is not to show up when the case is listed for trial. There are two trials - a preliminary hearing and a final trial. They exhaust the patience of civilian witnesses, who often will simply give up. However, their presence is absolutely essential to get a conviction. With a stolen car or a burglary, for example, the civilian witness must show up to say he/she did not give permission to have the car or enter the building or residence. If they don't show up, the defendant walks, and he/she walks in a high percentage of cases. Of course, if the defendant is in jail, he/she must show up and the case is tried in a timely fashion. If they "FTA" or fail to appear, a bench warrant issues for their arrest and the bail money is forfeited. If someone captures the defendant, he can collect the bail money. Unlike with the police, a bounty hunter -someone who captures bail jumpers - is not restricted to the methods used to effect the capture, short of murder or serious injury. Bring in a warm body and collect your money.

The system, however, is very flawed and creates serious problems for the community. Because most criminal defendants are poor and can't afford high bail but commit serious crimes, the courts take pity on them and grant them low bail, which is an invitation to "fail to appear." Next, in the old days, there were "bail bondsmen." They would put up the cash necessary to release the prisoner for a large fee – between ten and thirty percent. If bail was $50,000, they would make $5,000 for keeping tabs on the defendant until the trial was held. If he skipped they owed $50,000 to the county and could afford to spend significant money to catch him/her and bring them in by whatever unsavory means were necessary. Bail bondsmen of course pushed the judges for high bail, and took collateral from friends and family to make up the $50,000 they might lose.

Instead, the City of Philadelphia decided to create its own bureaucracy for bail and offered bail at 10 percent which would be refunded if the defendant showed, less a small fee - about three percent. However, the bureaucracy was mostly political, no one cared very much, and as a result thousands of defendants didn't show, and roamed the streets freely. Many thousands of cases were lost due to lack of prosecution. At last count, the no shows in court exceeded 30,000 for trials and another 10,000 for parole or probation violations.

Worse still, there were many criminal defendants roaming the streets with serious warrants on their heads. If they were arrested for some other violation, they could not get bail again without a new bail hearing on the original charges, in which the evidence of their good faith promise to appear was lacking in credibility. As a result, there were hidden among the many people that police might come in contact with, potentially violent people with outstanding warrants. A simple traffic stop or shop lifting arrest could result in serious harm or death to the unsuspecting police officer who might check his computer.

As I explained the system to Hank and Joe, I could see independent sparks light up in their entrepreneurial minds. Of course, pick up bad guys and make money. Before we left for Memphis, we sat around for a few hours devising systems for bringing these guys in.

The first system was fairly cheap and held little prospect for violent confrontation. A complete list of fugitives was downloaded along with their last known addresses. A fancy letterhead was printed up and sent to the defendants at their addresses. A letter stated that they had won two tickets to a professional sporting event- the '76ers were the cheapest and best possibility but the Phillies were included as well. All the defendant had to do was show up on the date of the event with proper ID and claim his prize. In the meantime, a section of the stands were purchased with the full knowledge of management based on the number of people who responded by telephone to accept the award. On the four dates that the awards were to be given out a booth was set up outside the entrance for the "winners" to check in and buses were rented to round up those with IDs coming to the booth. About 80 were arrested on each of the four dates, resulting in a net collection of $400,000.

This money funded a larger search of Social Security, Department of Motor Vehicles, recent traffic tickets, child support - you name it. Another 200 were taken peacefully into custody at their residences. There was no apparent reason the city bureaucracy was unable to do the same thing.

These operations were repeated every two months with comparable results. Blue Eagle, Inc. was now a legitimate tax paying entity that could pay salaries to its employees, out of the bail money it collected.

As to Haynesworth, he still refused to cooperate with us. He must have made peace with his supplier who promised him further supplies and protection. Sorry to say, but he was killed about two months later, by a drive-by shooting along with two associates. The cops have not solved the case.

I had delivered the CDs and DVDs to the DEA. We were suspicious that someone of the local police might leak out some of the information. No arrests have been made as yet.

CHAPTER 14

Mr. Bowditch, the man who wished to hire us in Memphis, was most generous in his accommodations for our trip to Memphis - a town of about 500,000. As we had researched before, the town had a bourbon distillery which brewed a number of different brands of bourbon, from extremely fine and appropriately expensive to rot gut sold in pint bottles. Timber was also a major industry and all levels of maple furniture were made in town, some for its own brand, some as frames for other brands who merely upholstered them as well. Cotton, of course, was also a major industry.

Because industries all used farm commodities, there had been a large influx of slaves before the Civil War. After the slaves were freed, they at first began to have a strong political and economic influence, but then the poll tax - a fee charged for the privilege of voting - as well as other discriminatory practices, disenfranchised the large black population. The recently arrived Irish immigrants began to take on the manufacturing jobs, and, more significantly, became the police force and took control of the local politics. There were many violent confrontations between the Irish and the blacks, causing the older and wealthier anglo families to flee to the suburbs.

As a result, the blacks began to form violent gangs of their own to claim their share of the city's power. An epidemic of yellow fever further depleted the city and chased the remaining middle class from town. It has remained a largely poor population. In 1968 with the assassination of Martin Luther King in Memphis, there has been considerable although muted tension between the blacks and the white, primarily poor and primarily Irish populations. While the Irish still control much of the political system with a 60 percent majority, the blacks have gained to some small degree. At present, there is an uneasy alliance between the two in Memphis' government.

Unfortunately, in the power vacuum, the blacks have asserted their power by controlling the drug trafficking in the city with a particularly violent gang - the Sphinxes. The police, being mainly Irish, have little access or ability to prevent this activity and most gang members have grown up locally and are well-known by the gang leaders. That was to be our mission - to rid Memphis of drug trafficking and break up the gangs.

Mr. Bowditch, known as "AB" for Alpheus Bowditch met us personally at the airport in a decked out minivan. We all could sit in captain's chairs in the rear while his chauffeur drove. A tall thin man almost 6'3", he had light blond almost white hair, pale blue eyes and a red complexion. He actually was wearing a bolo tie with a silver and turquoise slide and a cowboy shirt with pearl buttons. He wore a gabardine jacket with a leather hunting patch on the shoulder, and ostrich cowboy boots. When he spoke, it sounded like he had gargled with tupelo honey.

"Welcome to Memphis, ya'll. Come on into the van and let's get something to drink. Ya'll bourbon drinkers."

Hank was delighted. A serious bourbon drinker up north, he would be in heaven. I had never been able to get into hard liquor especially before lunch and was a beer and wine man. I suspected that there were few fine wineries in Tennessee. Joe would try it.

As we went from the airport to the Peabody Hotel, we went through one ransacked neighborhood after another, but the Peabody was a delight. An old, old hotel with a magnificent lobby. We were back at least a century in time. One of those grand old hotels but in the 1920s when things were good. After checking in and leaving our bags in the rooms, we met at the lounge. AB was disappointed to hear me order some yuppie beer, but the guys accommodated him with sippinwhiskey on the rocks. He also ordered me one and told me I could not leave Memphis without it. I have to tell you he was right. Really good bourbon is really good.

As we were being told about the city, there was suddenly a commotion. As we turned around, a parade of ducks, yes, ducks, lead by a man in hotel uniform, waddled precisely down the red carpet to the fountain. There they flapped a bit and dropped quietly onto the water to a huge round of applause from the assembled hotel guests. I was beginning to tell I was no longer in Philadelphia.

The first dinner we had was in an authentic French restaurant in the hotel. AB promised us more appropriate Southern meals with a "meat and three" later, but for now he wouldn't explain. We'd see for ourselves as he chuckled. It was also apparent that AB was in no hurry to get down to business and either immensely enjoyed entertaining Northerners with his Southern hospitality or was very interested in buttering us up so we'd take on the assignment. He seemed to sense that I would be the hard sell.

AB was an old pre-war, he said "antebellum," Southerner. His folks owned plantations, that's plural with an "s." They grew cotton and harvested hardwood - mostly maple on what were probably zillions of acres in the surrounding counties. Cotton and lumber, of course, required vast numbers of slaves and his folks had their share and then some.

During the Civil War times were hard, but the Union hardly touched Tennessee and their holdings suffered very little damage. Col. Bowditch, his grand pappy, was probably not a colonel, but a few years after the war, everyone somehow claimed an officer's commission. The timberlands and cotton were too valuable to the Confederacy so there was no way his grand pappy would back down from the barrel of a Yankee rifle. Also, grand pappy was no dummy and stashed some money - France and England, and got some super bargains on things after the war. He lent money to all those damaged by the war and took a major piece of the action in the bourbon distillery, two banks, the railroad, and a lot of plantations and some river barges. AB's daddy and AB were not short of smarts. The family had attended Vanderbilt and paid attention in class. Now, AB was in his early 50s, and was the man to those who knew but he had no interest in politics, or power. Hell, he bought and sold these guys. So the hotel knew and the restaurant knew. The restaurant had at least six waiters hovering over us, with continental manners and service and I might add an excellent bottle of Chateau Margaux, and a dazzling sect from Czechoslovakia with dinner with dessert. The Caesar salad was exquisite, and the Canard á l'orange was superb. AB had ordered a chocolate souffle specially made in advance. Dinner left us in a pleasant but sated euphoria. And not once did AB talk business. We talked presidential politics, international issues, southern issues, southern football. He even made NASCAR sound interesting. AB was too much of a patrician to let business spoil a fine dinner.

Afterwards, we went down to Beale Street and stopped in a few of the blues clubs. I have to admit, I ordered "sippin bourbon whisky." The Rock and Soul music was live and great. I could see AB beaming as we got into it. As we rolled out of the last joint, AB walked us back to the hotel and said he'd be by about 8:30 for breakfast at the hotel. Still, no talk of business except to say, "Gentlemen, please dress casual tomorrow, ball caps if you got 'em, jeans and T-shirts if possible. We're gonna see some rough territory."

At 8:30 a.m. Mr. Bowditch came into the hotel looking like a farm hand, dirty work boots, straw hat, and an old Titans jersey. The food was southern breakfast food. We passed on the grits, and the biscuit with red eye gravy. Maybe later. The coffee tasted strange. We were told it was chicory. We went out to a battered pickup truck with an extended cab. We were in disguise, apparently to survey the neighborhood where we might be working.

It turned out to be the projects and the houses nearby in the black neighborhood. One house stood out, it had a large antenna on the roof and barbed wire on top of chain link fencing around. On the street in front were a number of shiny Cadillac Escalades and some Chrysler 300s. A number of men lounged on the porch of the house or sat in their cars smoking. No one seemed to notice us as we drove through. I took a number of pictures with my cell phone from just between the crook of my arm. We began to map out a number of ways we could bring this gang down. But first we had to know what the deal was with

AB, who so far had made no mention of what we would be paid.

As we were going back to the hotel, Joe couldn't contain himself any longer. "Okay AB, now what's the deal?"

Alright. AB was well prepared for this question. "First, I pay you and your men regular cops' salaries totally on the books, with benefits, Social Security, Workmen's Comp, etc. Second, I put an equal amount of cash, under the table into offshore accounts. Both up front on a monthly basis. I buy all necessary equipment, guns, bugs, tranquilizer darts, microphones. Give me a budget and produce receipts for any of your buys. Then I figure a bonus if the work is done completely. I was figuring $50K per man, and $500,000 for the Blue Eagles. Plus you keep whatever you get from the gangs."

"Well we need some more things. First, most of our work is illegal and we could be charged criminally. We need assurances from law enforcement that we have total immunity. Second, we need a secret headquarters to take our prisoners and interrogate them."

"I've already thought of that. You use the barn and stables on one of my farms outside of town. I'll get it fixed up the way you need. And if you say yes to all the above, we go talk to the DA and the Chief of Police."

"We're gonna need some vehicles-vans, SUVs.

"I got plenty. You can pick out what you need, or we'll buy some out of state." "AB, we'll have to talk and meet you at dinner. How's that?"

"Fine."

CHAPTER 15

Since Joe and Hank were getting the lay of the land and getting a positive feeling about the Memphis project, we decided that I would take an initial meeting with Bowditch, the Mayor and Police Chief of Memphis. At this point, we also decided that we would no longer be seen together and that they would operate totally underground, and I would be the only visible person identified with the Blue Eagles and that I would be able to claim attorney-client privileges.

So I called Bowditch and asked him to set up the meeting, but not at City Hall or some government location. I still needed to keep our existence totally in the dark. It was decided that I would go to the Police Chief's summer cabin on the river to meet everyone at 8:00 that night. I rented a car and got a Google map and got there early. Bowditch had arrived earlier and his driver stood next to a battered SUV as I drove up. I nodded hello to the driver and walked up to a nice log cabin with a deck looking out on the river. As I knocked on the door, I was admitted by a large beefy cop.

"Mr. Stern."

"Yes. That's me."

"Please come in. They're at the dining room table."

A rustic heavy wood oak table sat by a large plate glass window overlooking the river. Bowditch was sitting there with a black man and a white man in dark business suits. Bowditch stood up.

"Pete, this is Mayor Shawnessy (the white man) and Chief Faison (the black man). We're here to go over your proposal.

"Nice to meet you Mr. Stern." Each said. "Please sit."

Mr. Shawnessy was a tall man with graying blond hair. He had the earnest look of a high school basketball coach. He had been a local prosecutor who had worked his way up the electoral ladder by patient, careful good works. He was no genius, but he appeared to be reliable and competent.

Chief Faison was a large, very dark African American. He was immense, standing about 6'2" and weighing over 320 pounds. His voice could have been the entire bass section in the church choir. He had the look of a huge friendly bear, but his eyes seemed to scan everything. He was not to be messed with.

I sat across from them and pulled some papers out of my briefcase. "Gentlemen, let me first say that we had not yet finally decided to accept this assignment. My clients are still doing some due diligence, but I would say we are very positive so far in what we think we can do. That is why I am here. As their lawyer, we are assuring ourselves that the project will be resting on a firm basis with local government and law enforcement. We absolutely must assure ourselves of a high level of cooperation."

The Mayor said, "We would not be here if we were not prepared to give you whatever assurances you might need. Our city, especially the black wards, are being strangled by drug gangs and it threatens this city's very existence. Mr. Bowditch has agreed to fund your operation and to ensure complete security for whatever you might undertake. There will be no paperwork linking your clients to government.

At this point, the Police Chief spoke up. "We will maintain absolute security. You will communicate only with me. We will not see, hear, or acknowledge the presence of your clients. Only you and I will speak. Are we understood so far?"

"That's essential. Yes. Now let me outline what we do and what we may require.

"First, we do not intentionally kill, or cause bodily harm to anyone. We may be forced to act in self-defense, but our actions will be totally deniable by the government or the police Department. We may engage in kidnappings of drug dealers and may use strong interrogation techniques; however, as I said before, we will not cause serious bodily injury. Most of our techniques use psychological intimidation or threats of violence. No more. We will identify the persons to the police department and offer them the opportunity to set up buy-busts or other means to establish their guilt, but we will not testify as to any of our acts or participate in your investigations, except give you DVDs of our buys.

"In addition to kidnapping and interrogation, we will retain the proceeds of any of our work, including money, drugs or guns. We may use the drugs as bait for transactions to identify those dealing in drugs.

"We may occasionally discover 'dirty cops" during our investigation. We expect you to take measures to see that they are fired or prosecuted. We will set them up as best we can.

"We expect you each to sign documents which will remain secret setting forth what we discussed here. We don't believe that we will become vulnerable to arrest, but expect complete cooperation with the judiciary and the Feds to ensure our immunity in this operation."

At each turn, I was receiving positive nods.

"Look, if you can free this city from the drug gangs, we will cooperate." The Mayor had a various but tired expression on his face. "You will not receive any recognition."

"We don't want or need recognition. Only a positive reference from Chief Faison, and complete backup from you as we proceed.

"Please remember that I am a lawyer. I do not know in advance what my clients will be doing, and I cannot be compelled to give information against them.

"Understood," rumbled out of Chief Faison. "But a couple of things. First, do these men have criminal records?"

"They are not all men and no, they don't have criminal records."

"Are they foreign nationals?"

"No. They are American citizens."

"Do they have any bankruptcy or are they persons of interest in any criminal investigations?"

"What are your references?"

"The City of Philadelphia. Our work was successful in shutting down major drug activities in the area of Germantown. We had no publicity or major repercussions from our work. The Mayor and the Police Chief felt that we were impinging on the drug dealers' civil rights, or that we might provoke open violent drug wars. They asked us to cease work, but agreed that we could keep the proceeds, money and drugs. They agreed to give us full immunity for our past work. There were no hard feelings. We were permitted to pursue a search for bail jumpers and recover their bail money. We have been successful in this, but we ceased our interdiction of drug traffic. We turned much of our investigation materials over to the police department."

"Okay. I'll be in touch with Philadelphia Police Chief. If everything checks out, I'll be on board with it." The Mayor nodded as well.

"Good. Then I will contact the Chief only through a burn phone and advise him from time to time of what is going on."

Bowditch got up. "Gentlemen, we may have the beginning of an interesting relationship."

CHAPTER 16

I left first, giving them a chance to review what we had discussed and got into the rental car. I switched on the GPS and went down the entrance to the cabin. When I got back to the local road, I made the left as indicated. About 200 yards down the main road, deserted at this time, I saw the parking lights of a car go on, and begin to follow behind me. My bodyguard jerked in his seat and hit a button on his phone. I went another quarter mile and another car turned on its lights ahead of me. It turned on the road and was now ahead of me. Then, I started to slow down, as the car behind me closed to within a car length of me. From behind, the car beeped and struck my bumper. The car in front slowed down and crossed diagonally across the road and stopped. Men in ski masks with automatic rifles got out of each car and started to shout something. I was now boxed in. I raised the windows and locked the car. The men began to pound on the windows telling me to open up. There were four men. I raised my hands inside the car and shouted, "Don't shoot. I'm not armed."

The man at the driver's window gestured for me to get out or he would shoot. I certainly knew that getting out of the car was a bad idea. I had little money on me and the car, while new, was not an expensive rented one. A Nissan Sentra. A bit too much firepower just to carjack a Sentra. No, they wanted me and I was no good dead. They wouldn't shoot me. Although I guess that somehow the Blue Eagles' work had become known here, I did not know anything specific. Someone had tipped off the Sphinxes. As the lawyer, I was not part of the operations team. Whoever this was would beat me up and try to get information. No sense giving them a clear shot at me. They then banged on the window until the two front windows shattered spilling glass shards over me and the front seat. Two men began to open the doors, reaching for the buttons inside.

About then, I heard the squeal of tires on the pavement as several new SUVs came to the scene from the back and the front. The two men around my car silently wobbled and fell to the ground as a number of men came running up to my car. Others ran up to the SUVs blocking me in. There were two men seated in the SUVs blocking me in. The one in my rear tried to reverse out, but rammed into the SUV behind it. The one parked diagonally in front of me tried to plow off into the woods along the roadside. First it went about two feet down into the roadside ditch and then sideswiped a tree and came to a halt. The drivers were motioned to get out with guns pointed at their windows. They got out.

All six men who rescued me had on black balaclavas over their heads. They had the two drivers lie on the roadway and asked them who they were and who sent them. They said little that was intelligible. Each was shot with a hypodermic needle and carried to the back of the SUVs. The four men lying on the ground were still twitching from the Taser shots with wires sticking out of them. They were also given hypodermic needles and carried to the SUVs.

Hank came up to my window. "Sorry we were a little late."

"Thank God you're here."

"Go back to the hotel for now. You may want to hear what they have to say tomorrow. They won't be ripe until then."

By this time, other men got into the SUV in the rear and were turning on the engine. The one in the woods was hitched up to the towline on one of our SUVS and was pulled back on the road. Just as they had come, they took off quietly and disappeared down the road. The whole think had not taken more than 20 minutes. I could feel the waves of adrenaline coursing through me and I had the shakes. It would be a few minutes before I could drive. I turned up the radio and got a country station. I'm not usually partial to country but now it was very calming. Some guy still wanted his girl back, but he was drinking again and she wouldn't want him like that. Poor fellow. Then, the fastest car in the country was bringing a guy to his high school sweetheart. My shakes began to ebb. I could turn the radio knob and get another station. Finally, I got some church music. It sounded like old rock and roll. But it was more soothing. I started the car and followed the GPS back to the hotel. The windows were down (not by my choice) and I could feel the sweat on my back and armpits go cool. But I was out of danger. I could calm down now.

I walked up the steps to the hotel still a bit wobbly and right into the fancy bar. I remembered my days in the military when a guy named Sanders introduced me to Wild Turkey. Tonight was a night for Wild Turkey on the rocks.

Ah! It went down smooth. Sour mash, smoky flavor. I could feel a slight shiver, but at least my hands had stopped shaking. I leaned back into the barstool. I somehow had sensed people were looking at me. I had on a decent business suit. My shirt probably had sweat stains, but not enough to go through the suit jacket. I was glad I had not peed myself.

I turned around on the bar stool to see if I was right in feeling eyes on me. Sure enough, two well-dressed black men and a very attractive light skinned black woman were talking and looking over at me. They seemed animated. Should I ignore them? Or walk by and say, "Better luck next time?" No, discretion is the better part of valor. I sipped my drink and looked around the room. Nothing else stood out. A second Wild Turkey definitely calmed me down and I knew I could sleep. When the ballgame on TV ended, I went to bed. I couldn't wait to find out what had happened to the men we reverse-hijacked overnight.

CHAPTER 17

About midmorning I got a call on my burn phone that I was to go down to the rear of the hotel and look for a red Yaris. "Yo, dude, a red Yaris. Not an SUV or a Lincoln. I'm a lawyer."

"Does the Yaris get you from point A to point B?"

"Yeah."

"Did you almost get kidnapped last night?"

"Okay, Yaris it is."

The man who was to be my driver standing by the Yaris was built like one of their mixed martial arts guys, at about 5'10" and 175 pounds, but he was built lean and mean. "Call me Sam. I'm supposed to look after you from now on. Most of the time you won't see me. If you go to bed or don't want me around, just call me on your burn phone and I'm gone. Otherwise, I will follow every move you make." Sam had a southern accent. He was local.

"Good to meet you, Sam. Are you ex-military?"

"Yes. Ex-Seal. Now retired."

"Okay. Stay close."

I got in the red Yaris and went out to the Bowditch farm about 45 minutes out of town. When we got inside the barn, I could see major changes had taken place. The side had been made into six soundproof cubicles. In each, the prisoner was handcuffed to the wall and naked as a jay bird. In front of him were the large surgical scissors and a car battery with cable running up to each man's testicles, which by now were sprayed bright blue.

In front of each man at the rear of the cubicle near the entrance door was a desk and several office chairs. In front of each desk chair was something that looked like a microphone with a cone around it. The desk and chairs were in the dark and a bright light shown on the prisoner who was wriggling in the handcuffs and a few inches off the floor.

I put on a Halloween mask, (I chose President Carter) and took a seat at the desk. The woman to my right began the questioning in a dull monotonous tone. Speaking into the microphone, her voice was altered and sounded a bit like Darth Vader.

"Who are you? What is your name?"

No response.

"I see. Well, you have a few choices. First, I can fry your balls with electricity. Second, I can begin removing body parts with surgical scissors. Third, I can starve you slowly while you hang in the cold. Now, you have thirty seconds to make up your mind and select what you want. In the meantime, the nurse will spray your penis with salt water to make sure we have good conduction. Nurse, if you will."

A large woman in a nurse's uniform wearing a Halloween mask of Daisy Duck brought over a mister bottle and began to spray the man's genitals.

"Okay. Thirty seconds are up. What is it? Talk, balls or fingers."

No response.

"Nurse, more salt water. We'll be back."

All of us got up to leave. The nurse touched the jumper cables together and produced some sparks as we left.

We made several visits to each of the cells during the course of the morning. After we left each cell, we played excerpts from a few movies. The favorite was the scene from "Taken" where Liam Neeson questions an Albanian while raising and lowering the electricity on his genitals. We also piped in screams from horror movies. But most of the time, we just played loud heavy metal music, and blew cold air at the naked men.

After visit number three to one of the drivers, he continued to refuse, but as we went to the door the man spoke.

"Darnell, Darnell Mathis."

"Ah, what's your street name?"

"Pirate."

"Pirate?. That's it."

"Yeah. I don't know why. Jus' Pirate."

"Who do you work for?"

"The Sphinxes."

"Where are they located?"

"Eighteenth Street next to the Projects." This was information that was well known. At least, he was telling the truth so far.

"When do they get the drugs in?"

"I think I want a lawyer."

"Very funny. We are not cops. We are the Blue Eagles. You don't get a lawyer. You don't get civil rights. You don't get shit. You talk or you suffer. Got it?"

"If I say anything, I'm a dead man."

"Or maybe you talk, don't suffer and cooperate with the cops and get a reduced sentence."

"Okay. The drugs don't come into the house. They go somewhere outside the city. I don't know where. I don't handle that part. I just ride shotgun on the deliveries."

"You mean, when you deliver to the dealers, you carry a gun and protect the vehicle."

"Yeah. That's it."

"Look, we got you for attempted kidnapping, attempted carjacking, gun possession. Have you got a record?"

"A few minor beefs." By now the computer had gotten his name.

"We got armed robbery in 2002 (two to five years), domestic violence (two years probation with anger management) and drug possession (2009). Is that it? Minor beefs."

"Yeah."

"This would be strike three. Life imprisonment. So your choices are jail, the boss kills you or you cooperate and get a reduced sentence."

"I guess so."

"Now here's what you're gonna do. We're gonna give you a burn phone. We want to know when and where the drug deliveries are gonna come in. Got it?"

"Why would I do that?"

"Then, we send your boss excerpts from this little interview. He will kill you then. Now who are the bosses?"

"There's Little Jimmy and Fat Marvin and Garcia. They all the boss."

"Garcia? Is he Hispanic?"

"He got a Mexican daddy, but he grew up in the projects with us."

"What does each boss do?"

"Little Jimmy, he kind of handles the money. Fat Marvin is a big mean mother fucker. He keep everyone in line. Garcia, he buy drugs."

"How do you know this?"

"We be inside the house. Sometimes we ride with Marvin, sometimes we ride shotgun for the drugs."

By this time, the computer had found the pictures of three bosses. They were flashed up on a TV monitor. "Is that the three guys?"

"Yeah. Marvin on the left, Garcia on the right."

"Now when you use this burn phone, you don't call anyone. You just press the call number for Tanya, let it ring twice and hang up. Got it?"

"Yeah, but if I get caught, I'm dead."

"Then you better be careful."

"Now show us where your car goes to deliver the drugs."

He was released from his handcuffs and given a map of Memphis and a magic marker. He drew three simple routes through the poor neighborhoods and designated the day for each route.

"Now, put an X at each stop." He did. He then was chained to a chair on the floor and food was brought in for him: eggs, bacon, toast and coffee.

As we slowly worked our way through each of the prisoners, we got each to corroborate what the others had said. It was slow work. Sometimes we got lies. Sometimes, we got a different story. But, we got the names of the bosses, their respective duties and most of the drug routes. These men were not the drug dealers, nor were they the shiniest pennies in the pond. These were the muscle, the gun men and mostly stupid. They were trying to be macho, but were obviously scared and bewildered. We had captured six of the armed guard. We had a few choices.

Turn them over to the police for prosecution. Each had major prior arrests and were looking at long prison terms. But then, I would have to testify, they might reveal their interrogations and our entire plan and operation would be out in the open.

We could expose them to their bosses along with the CDs of their statements. Then they were surely dead.

We could hope that they might actually use their burn phones and become informants. Not likely. They were bottom of the barrel guys who couldn't be depended on for anything. But it didn't matter, as long as they kept their free burn phones. We could trace their movements. We didn't need them to tell us where they were.

Besides, it was now obvious that there was a leak in the Police Department or the Mayor's office. We knew we were alone, and we would have to act accordingly. Someone had warned the Sphinxes of our mission.

The best thing was intimidation. We kept the men in isolation until the early hours of the next day. Then we loaded them naked in a van and drove them down to a playground in the midst of the projects. We handcuffed each man, by his ankles and wrists in a squatting position to a chain link fence. We sprayed their genitals bright blue and used a stencil to spray the Blue Eagle icon on the back of each man. Each man's clothes and burn phone were left in a shopping bag in the front of him.

At dawn we called the media, the police, and the Sphinxes drug house, and alerted them to go to the playground fence. The media and the police arrived about the same time and began to take pictures. When the gang bosses arrived a bit later, they were photographed as well as they sawed through the handcuffs and drove the men off. Everything was videotaped along with the reporters asking questions of the men.

The game was on. We were in town. We took down your best men, and we would take you down too!

To the Sphinxes, it was confusing. Who were these new guys? Cops? Why didn't they just arrest those guys instead of showing them up – naked on the playground fence? Were they a new drug gang? Hey, this is our turf. Someone's looking for a fight.

To the public, it was total confusion. Were they cops? Shouldn't someone be arrested for something. But who? The men tied up or the guys who did it?

To the cops, not in the know, something big was about to happen. A drug war? But you didn't mess with the Sphinxes and get away with it.

Another shoe fell that night on local TV and some on national TV. An e-mail was sent to a local station. Photos of the six men were posted and their criminal records were detailed, some with two or three felonies. Portions of their coerced confessions from the previous night were shown on the screen – obviously well edited to conceal the circumstances.

At the end of the e-mail was an advertisement, posting a reward for information necessary to the arrest and conviction of any Sphinx member. An 800 number traceable to Washington, D.C. was posted for any calls.

A few calls trickled in, but nothing of importance.

Now, it was time for the intelligence and research team to take over.

CHAPTER 18

Nora Johnson, a diminutive black woman with a Masters in Computer Science lead the team. She was one of the Blue Eagles and an equal partner. She had been given access to codes to the local police files and had begun to identify everything known about the Sphinxes. Arrest records, police reports, FBI and DEA wire tapes. Junkies of all sorts were interviewed to determine where and from whom they bought their drugs. They were mic'd and body cam'd to make new purchases under the eyes of the Blue Eagles armed as well with parabolic receivers.

Soon a comprehensive list of names of dealers and locations began to evolve. Each dealer was then surveilled to determine his source of supply. Twelve dealers were ID'd and four delivery routes. The delivery vehicles were traced to a farmhouse outside of Memphis. SUVs would drive up, collect their inventory and start their route. There was a driver and a shotgun heavily armed. They would make about four different stops each day dropping off drugs, picking up money, serving each location Tuesday, Thursday and Saturday; and another on Monday, Wednesday and Friday. They would all return to the farmhouse at the end of each day by about 6:00 p.m. with the cash.

The farmhouse was surveilled now with a coverage consisting of cameras and parabolic microphones. Some bugs were even posted on the first floor windows.

On occasion, Little Jimmy and Fat Marvin would visit the

farmhouse, but Garcia spent most of his time there, buying the drugs, observing the distributors of the drugs to the SUV drivers, and collecting the money on the return trip. Much of the time, he would leave the farmhouse and return with the rental van carrying a new supply of drugs. Although the house near the projects appeared to be the center of the Sphinx's operation and was heavily fortified, the farmhouse was surprisingly open. Guards patrolled the grounds on paths made for golf carts. There were two men on the golf cart, heavily armed which swept the area every 15 minutes. There were cameras on trees which covered spans of the open fields, but only up to a depth of 20 yards. The Blue Eagles' over-the-counter microphones and cameras could easily conduct surveillance from 200 yards away and identify license plates, individuals, even labels on boxes with high definition optics. Soon a delivery picture began to emerge.

Rental trucks would arrive in the driveway driven by Sphinxes. Garcia was often on these trucks. They would carry beer boxes into the farmhouse. About noon each day, some middle aged black women would arrive by a long retired school bus in the driveway, usually between 10:00 or 12:00 a.m. and leave about 6:00 p.m. These women would be re-rockers. Usually cocaine or heroin or other drugs come in nearly 100 percent pure. The women then would come in, strip completely naked and begin to cut the pure drug with a variety of white powders to reduce the potency to between 50 percent or even 25 percent. They then bagged the results after carefully weighing them in plasticene bags printed with a Sphinx in varying amounts and bundle them in sandwich bags ten each. At days' end, the women would shower – rinsing off all drug residue and put back on their clothes for the return trip to the city.

Photographs of the women were especially valuable and were taken with a telephoto lens. These women would make great witnesses. Although well paid for their "re-rocking" work, they had families. They would be easy to flip – be offered immunity and describe the entire drug operation at the farmhouse and ID all the participants.

By now, a picture of the entire operation was clear; but here were a few nagging details. Who had tipped off the Sphinxes to try to kidnap me after I met with the Mayor and the Police Chief? Where did the rental truck get its supply of drugs for delivery to the farmhouse? And how to take down the entire Sphinx operation as surgically as possible. Should we seek arrests; should we just irrevocably disrupt the entire supply chain? While we, and I should say Ms. Johnson and her crew, collected and verified the operation's patterns, the Blue Eagles board discussed the alternatives.

The first thing on the agenda became the identity of the leak that had gotten me almost kidnapped. Could we depend on the local cops? Was someone in the Mayor's office connected? How much cooperation could we expect? How suspicious should we be?

The next step would be for me to meet with the Mayor and the Police Chief again. A meeting was again arranged at the Chief's summer cabin on the river. This time I insisted on bringing along my own bodyguard. This was for show. I knew a gang of kidnappers would easily overpower one bodyguard, but it would demonstrate my claim that I had been nearly kidnapped because of some leak in the Memphis government from either the Mayor's or the Chief's office. The bodyguard was amply supplied with communication gear to alert the Blue Eagles team to drop and protect me as before.

In the meantime, we had tapped all lines of communications from the Mayor's and the Chief's offices after the initial request for a meeting was made. Had we done something illegal? Yes. Were we justified and would any jury convict us after the previous confrontation? No. We instructed the Mayor and the Chief to keep particular note of whom they told.

I arrived at the cabin at 8:00 p.m. as planned, this time in a rental vehicle from a different rental company. The previous company I had used was not happy about the broken windows and scratches around the door frames. I don't know why. My own insurance covered it because I had elected the exorbitant $9 for the one day's coverage on the rental form. But they still were not happy with me when I returned the car.

Once again, as I walked into the Chief's cabin, his immense bodyguard let us in. My bodyguard asked for and got permission to sweep the cabin for bugs under the close supervision of the Chief. Result: no bugs.

"Please have a seat. Can we get you anything?" The Mayor was being a gracious host.

"Ice tea would be great." My bodyguard motioned for his also. The Mayor's wife came out of the kitchen. This was a welcome sign. The Mayor knew his wife could not possibly be in on anything like the Sphinxes, and her presence was a sign that there were no other people in the house to compromise security.

It was my turn. "Gentlemen, you may or may not know that as I was returning from our last meeting, some muscle from the Sphinxes attempted to kidnap me. Those were the six men you saw handcuffed naked to the chain link fence at the playground. Fortunately, the Blue Eagles had foreseen such an attempt and provided me appropriate security. The six men were neutralized, captured and interrogated. Since we did not wish to disclose our presence or our operations in a criminal matter which might reach trial at least a year from now, our recourse was to release them in a way which would embarrass the Sphinxes and make the public less wary of testifying against them."

"We have learned that, from information we provided, two of the men were wanted on outstanding warrants, were arrested and released on $50,000 bail each. The $50,000 bail fee was posted within hours by their attorneys and they are at large once again.

"But the point I wish to make is that someone knew in advance of our meeting and probably the purpose of our meeting, and alerted the Sphinxes. Since we only contacted each of you individually, the leak must be traced through either of your contacts back to the Sphinxes. So, I need to see who in your offices has the connection."

"We will set a trap for that person. We need to do this before we can take further action which may be jeopardized by a leak." Of course, I didn't believe that what we planned to take down the Sphinxes could be jeopardized by the leak. Neither of these men would ever again know of any of our plans in advance or have the slightest inkling of our methods. But we could not tolerate leaks in any operation and had to send that message out. As a side note, I was hoping that neither the Mayor nor the Chief were dirty. "So, I have to ask you to try to recollect everyone you may have talked to about our last meeting from the time Bowditch contacted you and explained the purpose of the meeting. If you need to consult your phone records, e-mails, texts, what have you, please do so."

The two men looked at each other and shrugged. The Mayor spoke up first. "Mr. Stern, we will have this for you in 24 hours. We will meet here tomorrow. No one else will know of the meeting except us. Not even my staff."

"Same here," rumbled the Chief. "I feel ashamed that this has happened to you."

"Don't worry. We don't get mad. We get even. Now, I have another topic for you. Quite a few of the people we can identify as associates of the Sphinxes are bail jumpers. They have either violated parole or probation or failed to appear for court hearings for all of which they posted bail. There is over a million dollars of bail money which could be collected if we brought these people in. We do not need to be police to arrest these people. We do not have to observe civil rights. We can arrest these people any way we see fit, as long as we do not cause serious bodily harm. We intend to use Tasers or tranquilizer darts. We need to know where we can bring them in to some service building. We expect to arrest about 30 people to start. The people we will use are not members of our company, but are paid on a contract basis. We feel this will weaken the Sphinxes before we begin operations on them."

The Chief said, "We have a large detention compound at Jefferson Street Prison. You could bring them in there. I will have a clerk ready to process them when you give us the go ahead."

CHAPTER 19

The Mayor and the Chief asked for another day to review their lists for suspects. On the second day, I went to each of their offices. The Mayor's list was there: his secretary, his bodyguard and the President of City Council. He vouched personally for his secretary and his bodyguard. We decided to take this at face value for the time being. The Chief also listed his secretary and his bodyguard, for each of whom he enthusiastically vouched. He had run the idea past the local chief of the DEA and felt he could vouch for him as well. By the way, the DEA apparently knew us from the Philadelphia adventure and said we were "professional." He also said that he consulted with the inspector in charge of Drug Enforcement for the city. We felt we could focus for the time being on the President of City Council and the Inspector in charge of Drug Enforcement. Of course, we immediately wire tapped both men and put a discrete tail on their movements.

About six hours later, we placed a call to the Mayor and another call to the Chief. We were warning each man that we would be arresting (or kidnapping) a drug dealer along a route. Each dealer, however, was at a separate location and different time. We, of course, told the Mayor and the Chief not to reveal this information to the other or anyone else. One takedown would occur at 9:00 p.m., one at 10:00 p.m. So whoever was the leak had at least eight hours to warn the Sphinxes. The 9:00 p.m. info was given to the Chief, the 10:00 p.m. info was given to the Mayor.

With the permission of the Mayor and the Chief, we tapped all phones they or anyone in their offices might use. It didn't take long. A male voice using the Mayor's office land line called Harmon Prestwick, the President of City Council and a prominent lawyer in town. "Beware the eagle Friday at 10 at Brookfield." That was it. Then he hung up. Aha! We had a link; but to Prestwick. No! It couldn't be possible.

Harmon Prestwick, a distinguished lawyer, had handled cases of all sorts over the years, usually criminal and personal injury. He was the acknowledged leader of the black voting faction in town. But he had a law firm full of lawyers and paralegals to handle estates, divorces, union hearings, Workmen's Compensation. He drew his clientele from all over, but a majority from the black community. He was a tall handsome man in his 50s and was enjoying the hell out of life. He was separated off and on from his wife of 27 years, who bore him three sons, each of whom had gone to the University of Tennessee. Harmon drove a big Lincoln and frequently used a driver. He lived in an expensive high rise downtown and his wife and sons lived in a mansion in the suburbs. He had been a basketball player at the University and used his scholarship to get an education. He used his signing bonus with the pro basketball team in Spain to get his law degree over five years as he took law courses in the off season. He was well liked and well respected. He and the Mayor had to work together and their relationship was cordial enough for a white mayor and a black city council president in a southern city. Harmon wanted to be mayor, and possibly a senator. He had everything going for him. Why work with the Sphinxes? We wanted to know.

We hacked his bank accounts, brokerage accounts, checking accounts; we even checked his medical records. He was definitely a high liver who had saved almost nothing. His credit cards were replete with bills from fancy restaurants, bars, resorts, travel agencies, tailors, men's stores, decorators, gardeners and college bills.

As it turned out, he was paying rent in two different locations aside from his own high rise. One was in a town about 50 miles away and the other was local. The airline tickets were for himself and two different women. His school bills were for two different children and one of the women had her car paid for. For a high flying guy, he had some bad spending habits and a possible vulnerability to the Sphinxes for a source of funds. He had to support two mistresses and two children, and spent lavishly otherwise. From what we could tell of his taxes and tax payments, it looked like he was spending more than he made. This meant he was receiving unreported cash. We could see the monthly deposits by check from his law firm – about $250,000, but his expenditures by check, credit card, online payments were $150,000 more per year. So it was probably that he got $12,500 a month in cash from the Sphinxes over and above whatever legal fees they paid. Since it was illegal to have gotten this information, we, of course, could not divulge it to law enforcement. We could, however, direct them where to look and have them retrace our steps. The text message also was illegally obtained and could not be used as evidence. Of course, we could also alert the police to retrace our steps, but they did not even know of my kidnapping, could not react quickly enough in my case.

Plus, there was the problem of Prestwick himself. He was a high profile guy, a major pillar of the black community as well as a major pillar of the entire Memphis community. Bringing someone like that down was not done lightly or with tainted evidence. And did we really want to bring him down? It was certainly bad that a man of his achievements was beholden enough to the Sphinxes to dime us out. But if we brought the Sphinxes down, we would be eliminating his major source of outside income. We had to bring the Sphinxes down outside the legal system. There would be no need for prosecutor evidence, testimony, civil rights hearings. They would, as far as the public was concerned, disappear like a thief in the night. Maybe some could be prosecuted and get heavy jail time if it could be arranged. But mostly, the drug traffic and the intimidating presence of the Sphinxes would be excised surgically from Memphis. Did we need to take down Prestwick with it? This might require an exposure of our organization in lengthy trials and disclose possibly our illegal collection of evidence.

Perhaps we could use our evidence against Prestwick in other ways. As their lawyer, he couldn't testify against them. As their lawyer, he couldn't divulge confidential information. Maybe, he could set them up for a trap, just as he had set us up. We'd have to think about that.

CHAPTER 20

By now, everyone but me from Blue Eagles management had moved out of the hotel to a rented estate well outside of town. I still had a very nice room and remained the only known contact with the Blue Eagles. The Sphinxes obviously knew who I was since they had tried to kidnap me earlier. The Mayor and the Chief could always reach me, but there would be no further contact with anyone else. I, of course, had a bodyguard discretely out of view and could walk around in public places, but to be on the safe side, I didn't venture too far from the beaten path.

Tonight, I decided to try one of the spots on Beale Street. It had a southern menu and a continuous show consisting of southern blues and rock for which the city was famous. So I sat down quietly in a booth in the rear and ordered.

The restaurant was a large open room and the focal point was a small well lit stage. The rest of the restaurant was dimly lit. The audience were all seated at large wooden tables facing the stage. The wait staff bustled back and forth to the kitchen. A huge bar lined the back of the room. As the next band came on, hoots, whistles and yee-haws greeted them.

The service was not fancy. I was given a roll of paper towels and a service of silverware. A heaping plate of half rack of baby back ribs, a leg and a breast of fried chicken, coleslaw and baked beans, with a frosted mug of beer came to the table. As the music played, I could hear different arrangements of "Gimme Two Steps," "Keep Your Hands to Yourself." I was definitely getting into this mood of the syncopated beat of the crossover southern sound.

About half way through dinner, a gorgeous woman ambled up to my booth. I thought she had been one of the three people who had been so interested in me the night before. She was a very dark black woman with dark, shining eyes in oval slits that seemed to sparkle as she talked. She had one of those amazing bodies only black women seem to have. Long legs with muscular thighs and high rounded butt with an impossibly small waist. I could see all this in the tight knitted skirt she wore. Her small upper body was in a loose silk blouse of light tan, dare I say ecru color, which fluttered as she moved. Her makeup, while light, was precise. She was wearing high heels with straps around the ankles. But the most amazing part of her presentation was a large star opal. It must have been at least 10 carats and was a dark musty brown color with sparkling star formation in a bright amber in the middle. It was set in a heavy gold mounting and hung on an intricately woven gold chain around her neck which fell to the middle of an exquisite cleavage. The opal beckoned me perilously.

"May I join you, Mr. Stern?" Uh oh! Red flags all went up. I was a man on a mission, but my libido struggled with my frontal cortex, or should I say my little head was winning the battle with my big head. I didn't know how James Bond was always so cool.

"Please, Ms.   " I gestured to the other side of the booth. "What can I do for you?" I was a bit nervous. How could I ask such a stupid question? But I couldn't summon up anything else brilliant.

"It's Fontina. Fontina Fitzhugh."

"Can I get you a drink?"

"That would be nice. How about a Crown Royal?" I waved to the waiter who not only had already focused on Ms. Fitzhugh as she – what, I don't know how to describe the walk – came over to me. A kind of stroll with a roll in high heels. I don't think humans were designed to walk like that. We don't have enough bones or joints to execute that maneuver. The waiter snapped to attention and with something between a smirk and a smile took the drink order. He was half congratulating me on my .... my what? My choice, my possible conquest, and was expressing his personal jealousy.

I mean this was a real southern laid back restaurant. People wore jeans and tee shirts or plaid shirts with ball caps. Even the women had ball caps with their pony tails hanging out back. I had even managed to blend into the southern funk. And here came this creature from another dimension to my table as the band played some Credence.

"Ms. Fitzhugh...."

"Fontina, please."

"Fontina, what brings you here?"

"You don't know?"

"Well, somewhat."

"You're the Blue Eagles' attorney and you're in town to take down the Sphinxes."

"Ah. Well, I guess that's true."

"I'm their lawyer."

"You're the Sphinx's lawyer?" The beer I was trying to sip casually made a few attempts to come through my nose. I was not cool. Ah, but a great play by the Sphinxes! Sending this gorgeous woman to discombobulate me.

"Yes, we need to talk, but not here. It's too noisy."

"We can go to my hotel."

"The Peabody?"

"Yes, just around the corner." My senses were returning to me. I knew she and two men had been looking over at me the other night. She was hard to miss. Now, she was denying she knew I was staying at the Peabody. But she obviously knew I was having dinner here. Was she playing games? Or was her cover a bit messed up? Hard to tell. "Shall we go there?" The Peabody had a gigantic lobby with as many alcoves and cocktail tables.

"Fine." I was almost done my dinner, but I could not finish what was left, especially now. I flagged the a-bit-too-attentive waiter. "Check please." He pulled a folder from behind his back and laid it on the table, and gave me another congratulatory-bemused-jealous-smirk as

I flipped my credit card on the folder. I could hear him humming the last lines of "Dixie Chicken" as he picked up the tab. "If you be my Dixie Chicken, I'll be your Tennessee lamb." Since he was probably right, I was neutral on my tip – I couldn't be upset at the warning I heard.

We walked slowly back to the Peabody. I caught sight of my bodyguard about a half block behind. My head was racing. Was I going to be kidnapped, or was this some lawyer's confab? During the walk, Fontina said she was with a local law firm and had looked me up on Google. She had grown up with a single mom, been good in school and gotten a scholarship to the University of Tennessee, and its law school. She was a trial lawyer, but had a business practice. All very mundane coming from the otherworldly creature to my left, who was sauntering – was that it? Sauntering? Next to me. The rolling hips and firm butt had distracted me from the star opal. I "uh-huhed" through the conversation.

In the lobby of the Peabody, I at least had my wits about me enough to pick out the exact spot Fontina and her companions had observed me from the other night. She was unfazed by my choice.

I began the conversation on my terms so she could change it to make whatever proposal she had in mind.

"You seem to know about me and my mission. How did you find out? It was supposed to be a secret."

"The Sphinxes have a lot of connections." I'll bet. "You do know that I am just their lawyer. I don't know about their operations in advance or take part in them. I simply am their external source of communication."

"So I've heard." No sign of a belief in my words.

"How does a reputable firm represent the Sphinxes? I mean they seem to control the drug traffic in this town."

"As you know, everyone is entitled to representation and my firm is extremely careful to avoid ethical pitfalls in the representation – the same as you."

"Alright. We seem to represent parties in strong opposition to each other."

"Maybe we can reach a middle ground."

"I can't see the Sphinxes pulling out of Memphis."

"But the Eagles are only here for a short time on a contract. You're not pro bono (meaning doing this just for the public good) and you did embarrass them with the men naked on the chain link fence."

"How do you know we did this?"

"Come on, let's not be too dense?"

"So you knew about my kidnapping?"

"I learned about it."

"So you know these were the men who did it?"

"I've been told. Why didn't you just have them arrested?"

"First, they didn't give up enough information about the Sphinxes and it would compromise our presence."

"Are you doing this for money or pro bono?"

"You'll never know."

"We do know you are pretty well off and don't need to do this work. We know that you did some work in Philly for free. So who are you?"

"Me. Just an ordinary guy."

"With quite a few bucks. An ex-wife with a seven year old daughter who you've called twice this week."

"True enough. Are you threatening my daughter?" I could feel the silken threat. "If anything happens to her, you'll be the first to go, believe me. She better not have a hang nail or a scraped knee. I'll be looking for you first." I was thundering now and drawing some attention from around the lobby. I could see she was rattled. She was not used to violence.

"No. No. Nothing like that. We never harm family."

"Except if it's necessary."

"No. We don't do business that way. We are much more sophisticated."

"Yeah, like a bunch of street thugs kidnapping the lawyer to squeeze him for information, confidential information, which by the way, I don't have and never will. You can't get to them by squeezing me. We are too careful for that. How stupid were they to think that would work?"

"They never knew you were so prepared. They underestimated you."

"So what is this now?"

"They think you want in on the deal. They want to know your price."

"They think we want a percentage or a payment to back off our investigation?"

"Sure, back off. Take some regular payments and go to another town and shake them down."

A good lawyer always listens. A deal offer is never rejected, but must be communicated to the client, however ridiculous. Listening should never be a sign of weakness, but a sign of good lawyering. Besides, the offer itself may be a source of information.

"Okay. What's the deal?"

"Twenty-five thousand dollars per month. You leave town. Simple as that." "Well, two obvious problems. What if you stop paying? How do we collect if you decide to stop? Do you have any security or collateral? And two, not enough. You are taking in millions from our limited investigation so far. Three hundred thousand dollars a year is peanuts."

"We can discuss the numbers."

"How 'bout if you give us enough information about the Sphinxes so we or the feds can do serious damage if you don't pay."

"Like what? Offshore accounts, Mexican sources., names of the organization's members." We already knew most of the names, but why tell her?

"No way we could give that up. You could squeeze us for more."

"Well, that's a problem then for a smart UT law school grad to solve. Give us some security."

Any information of that sort was a bonus. She would have to reveal things we might never learn otherwise, and in negotiation there would be no guarantee we would not use this against them now.

"But I have another idea. Let me be blunt. What are you worth?"

"What do you mean?"

"You're not very old. You can't have gotten a total free ride at UT. You have student loans. You have information worth millions to us. You could get enough money to move far away and live comfortably for the rest of your life. You're a smart girl. You could practice law anywhere or go into business."

"Ha! First, I would be killed and second, all my information is protected by attorney client privilege. I'd be disbarred, sued, you name it."

"Look, we are not government. We are independent contractors. We can keep a secret. We can give you guarantees backed by collateral. We can keep this silent until the Sphinxes, and I mean, all Sphinxes are long gone – in jail or dead. We can make any secret arrangement you want. The Sphinxes are illegal. Their power is limited to Memphis. We have funds and backing all over. You name it. I could arrange it.

"No one would ever know where we got the information from. You'd have guaranteed money."

"Nice try! I do alright here and I'm no rat."

"The Sphinxes are evil. You'd be doing good."

"Like I said. Nice try!"

"Okay. I'll talk to my clients and get back to you." "Nice doing business with you." Handshakes.

Alas, I wasn't enticed by some cheap sexual encounter first. I mean, who needs cheap sexual encounters. At least they could have tried to soften me up with a cheap sexual encounter.

Something primal was leaping in my body as Fontina sauntered away.

CHAPTER 21

Prestwick's test message had notified the Sphinxes, "Beware the Eagle Friday at 10 p.m. at Brookfield." There was a vulnerable dealer at the Projects in a building known as Brookfield who was the obvious target. The Sphinxes would assemble their muscle to protect this location at 10:00 p.m. and ruin the bust. They would not want to screw up this time so they would over man and lay in wait for our takedown. Now was the time to lay the trap. Time for the Feds. We guessed there would certainly be at least one gunman inside the Project apartment with the dealer. The dealer's stash had to be within easy reach for his customers. Outside the DEA would post a contingent of armed men waiting to attack the delivery SUV as it got to Brookfield. The delivery SUV would hold cash and drugs. Everyone would be dirty. We expected the Sphinxes to post their own contingent around the location to attack whoever they thought would be our man, who tried to take down the delivery vehicle and the dealer inside Brookfield.

A discrete call had been placed to the local DEA and FBI as to the confluence of these drug operations. This call was from what would be known as a reliable source from our organization well known to the Feds. As a result, the source did not need to be revealed in court, and would be sufficient for a search and arrest warrant. The Feds could come loaded for bear. They were more than happy to get a major collar laid in their laps even though the Blue Eagles had done all the work. They would get all the credit.

By 8:00 p.m., FBI snipers were on the rooftops of the surrounding buildings. A helicopter with big light beams was ready for takeoff ten minutes away. Anonymous, bullet proof black SUVs were stationed several blocks away. A photo of the delivery SUV had been dispatched to the FBI and the DEA, along with photos of the dealer and the two men in the delivery SUV. The feds had been forewarned that these men should be taken alive because they were looking at major federal sentences, but could receive significantly less if they rolled over on the top three of the Sphinxes.

The apartment on either side of the dealer was now occupied by DEA men. There were no Blue Eagle men involved in this ambush. It would be all DEA and FBI – all clean. All capable of full prosecution in federal court.

At about 10:00 p.m., the red delivery SUV rolled up to the Brookfield Building. It did not appear that the delivery man who was carrying a cardboard beer box into the building knew that a raid was imminent. After a few minutes, he returned to the SUV and was getting back in when two black bullet proof SUVs from the DEA hemmed him in both fore and aft. At that point, three SUVs from the Sphinxes rolled up and hemmed in the DEA vehicles. The Sphinx men got out and began to fire at the DEA's SUVs. DEA and FBI men wearing jackets identifying their agency fired tranquilizer darts at the Sphinxes' men. Then the helicopter flew over and hovered flashing light beams down on the area around the building. The DEA men in the apartment adjacent to the dealer's ran down to his door, smashed open the door and threw flash bangs on the floor. They smashed in the door of the apartment and tased the dealer and his bodyguards.

Within seconds, shots rang out from the areas around the Brookfield Building. Dozens of FBI and DEA men fired tranquilizer darts and tasers at the Sphinx men. There were two men from each side now rushing up to the dealer's apartment firing away at the federal SUVs and the apartment. The federal SUVs were soon covered in red and blue smoke to conceal their location, while the FBI snipers on the rooftops directed tranquilizer darts at the Sphinxes' men outside the red and blue smoke. A few began to fall. Tasers felled some of the older Sphinxes and eventually, the last two surrendered. As the smoke blew away, the helicopter called on a loudspeaker for all residents to remain in the apartments. They did not need to be told twice. Most had sought refuge under their beds. Unfortunately, they had heard gunfire often before and knew the risks of a stray bullet.

News crews from several TV stations showed up but were blocked off from the scene just far enough so they could film men in DEA and FBI jackets bustling around the scene and carrying automatic weapons, but the crews were promised the footage from the government who had taken extensive shots from several different angles.

The men lying on the ground were handcuffed and left where they were until a van could come in and pick them up. The dealer and the armed Sphinx member were walked out of the apartment and handcuffed. As it turned out, Fat Marvin had been one of the hitmen tased and lay twitching on the ground face down – all 300 pounds, with a snarl on his face. A big wounded bear – one leader down along with eight Sphinx men all involved in drugs, guns, attempted murder, etc. A federal prison sentence would be at least 25 years apiece minimum.

Out came the cameras for the crime scene. In the dealer's apartment the drug stash was photographed next to the gun in the living room drawer. The Sphinx man inside was photographed holding the AK-47 in his hands, next to his now subdued body.

The delivery SUV was photographed with the men inside with their hands up. The cardboard box with about $40,000 in cash, and another box with 40 bundles of drugs was also photographed. Each of the fallen Sphinx men who had been tased or darted was photographed with their guns still in their hands as they lay on the ground.

Soon vans showed up to whisk the men away for questioning at the local field office.

By previous arrangement, the Blue Eagle people were allowed to participate in the questioning. The films were rushed to the technical department to be reviewed before they would be passed along to the TV station.

Ten more Sphinx men were in custody with solid criminal cases against them, lots of drugs, lots of money, many guns, and attempted murder. Under federal law, these guys were looking at life, unless they rolled over on the others, but even then at least 25 years. A good haul and no one was hurt. The DEA and FBI got all the credit for clean arrests. None of the Blue Eagles were involved.

CHAPTER 22

fter the raid on the dealers' apartment and the capture of the Sphinx operatives which we all watched with great interest on closed circuit TV, I went back to the hotel and sat in the lobby. Calls began to pour in on my cell phone. I moved to a back booth in the lobby and ordered a Wild Turkey on the rocks. I wanted to calm down, and ease into bed, but the calls wouldn't stop. Since I was the only known contact for the Eagles, I knew I couldn't just duck out of sight.

The Mayor and the Chief, of course, congratulated me on our triumph. They had been under fire for the crime in the city for several years and needed a bit of good publicity. This raid would go on their resumes and give each great credibility in the years to come. In front of the national media, the DEA, FBI and local cops had taken down ten members of the drug gang which had plagued the city for years. Of course, the local cops had never been in the loop and had only been advised of the takedown an hour before. The Chief of Police, however, got serious face time on the media as he explained to a massive local TV audience and a national link that the Sphinxes were now on the run. The DEA and FBI men played their parts and shared the credit since they had no local political aspirations and their bosses well knew what had gone down. No one really knew or could conceive of the real machinations behind the whole operation. While publicity is a good thing for some, it does the Eagles little benefit. At worst, it exposes us to investigations and civil rights inquiries. It destroys our ability to operate under cover. The very basis of our existence is that we produce results for those in the limelight, without having to disclose our methods. The Mayor and the Chief had made the right move, they hired us. We did the job, they got the credit and we got paid.

Bowditch called. He was ecstatic. He did not need the credit in public, but had earned the undying gratitude of the Mayor and the Chief who alone understood his involvement. He had their ears whenever he needed them from now on, and had clout and political power, neither of which he really needed. However, his modest investment in our organization made his city appear to be safe and, now relieved of a major crime syndicate, his investments in real estate and business in the area would massively increase in value. Bowditch wanted all of us out to his resort home in the Bahamas for a party to end all parties and he declared a double bonus.

I knew that our work was not done. Yes, we took down in very public fashion Fat Marvin and quite a few of his thugs, and one dealer, but the organism was still alive. There was more to do. We had to get Marvin and the other thugs to roll over on everyone else. This would take months. They all needed lawyers – all of whom needed to be shown vast amounts of evidence to convince them that a trial would be a disaster; but no lawyer advises his client to plead guilty and cooperate unless he has explored all other avenues. While it was time consuming, the process of negotiating cooperation should not be hard. The armed confrontation had been captured on cameras from various angles and the men were armed, firing assault weapons on a public street in defense of a drug dealer and his supplier who were in the process of being arrested by men in the DEA and FBI jackets. What more was there to prove?

The crimes would be prosecuted in Federal court under sentencing guidelines. These guidelines were a catalog which analyzed the elements of each crime and awarded points based on the severity of the conduct. These crimes consisted of attempted murder, resisting arrest, use of a firearm in the commission of a crime, sale of drugs, conspiracy to sell drugs – I mean the list could go on forever. Suffice it to say that these men were all looking at life in a federal prison without the possibility of parole.

There was only one game left – cooperate with the feds. Only by cooperating could a criminal defendant avoid the heavy prison time of the guidelines. The federal criminal code provided that the U.S. Attorney – the prosecutor could make a motion to the federal judge that the defendant had provided cooperation in the prosecution of others and was therefore eligible for a lighter sentence than the guidelines. This motion was vital to reducing a sentence. Once the motion was made, the judge was free to consider a lesser punishment. And there was an unspoken rule – usually followed – between the prosecutor and the judge that the judge would follow that recommendation to prevent the court from wasting time by unnecessary trials and to encourage guilty pleas. But mainly, it gave the prosecutors great power in investigating crimes. Make nice to them and you got much less time.

There was another rule – He who rats first, rats best. When the arrest was made, the clock started ticking on who would roll over first. If you ratted out more people, sooner than anyone else, you got the best deal at sentencing, and the prosecutor was sure to tell the judge. Those people who could do little more than corroborate what other people had already said would get less of a bargain because the prosecutor would let the judge know exactly that.

But the whole plea bargain negotiation dance of the seven veils was costly and time consuming. Little Jimmy and Garcia still had a viable, although somewhat crippled operation. Obviously, the men they lost in the raid might rat them out, and obviously, someone had penetrated their inner workings enough to be able to set up and time the raid. They also knew that our organization was not to be messed with. They couldn't kidnap me, and I was all they knew of their enemy. But they were still taking in barrels of drug money so they could not stop, but they had to tighten up on security.

I was discussing all this and the next plans on the burn phone by which I and the rest of the Eagles communicated when I got a call on my other phone from Fontina. She wanted to know what was going on and wanted to meet. Tomorrow at breakfast turned out to be a good time.

I had a lot of work to do. I had to assemble a convincing case against Prestwick and possibly the law firm and do it for a preview the next morning.

In the meantime, the smooth sour taste of Wild Turkey would have to be put aside as would be pleasant fantasies of Fontina. I went up to my room and assembled the documents I had to take down to the business center at the hotel, complete with copier, computer, scanner and fax.

CHAPTER 23

I had assembled a discreet file which I brought with me to breakfast. I ordered a massive southern breakfast to celebrate the raid last night, and was waiting for Fontina at 8:30. I did not know what to expect.

She came into the hotel. Uh oh. Gone was that liquid saunter of the other night. She was wearing a business suit of brown with a floral silk scarf of tans and pinks. She carried a slim briefcase. Her heels clicked smartly as she swept across the tile floor of the lobby. No saunter. All business. She looked mad. My turn to play it cool.

"Mr. Stern," she started as she came up to the table about to launch into what was to be the beginning of a tirade. Apparently, I was no longer Pete.

"Please, sit. . . have some coffee or juice" I rose and pulled out the chair next to me.

"Mr. Stern . . . about last night."

"They have an excellent breakfast here." I signaled for the waiter. "Please have a seat and let's talk."

She reluctantly sat in the proffered chair. "Mr. Stern."

"Pete, please." The waiter came up. She ordered some coffee and a sweet roll. "Okay, Peter." The waiter smiled at her angry tone and rolled his eyes. Was I gonna catch it! Only my mother called me Peter! "That bogus raid. We know you did it."

"Who? And where were we? Not one of our people was within blocks of it. And we didn't bring the guns." Actually a man had filmed the entire takedown from a nearby apartment.

"You were behind it."

"I believe that was an undisclosed confidential informant, if you'll check the government's 302s (the FBI and DEA official versions). They should be available in a few weeks."

"And when they come out, we'll show your kidnappings and torture sessions for what they are. That's how you got the information you passed on to the DEA."

"Now Fontina, let's talk like lawyers, and not drug lords. All the DEA knew was that drugs were being dealt out of Brookfield and a delivery vehicle would supply it that night. They were also told that the Sphinxes had been tipped ahead of time."

"First the court does not need to force the government to reveal its confidential source. The DEA knows nothing of our methods, they only used our information. We are not government, we don't have to comply with the Fourth Amendment. And, we never used torture or caused physical harm to anyone. We may have scared the crap out of them, but we never harmed them, not one. They got information for a simple drug bust."

"The DEA's raid on the drug dealer was all based on your information and how did the snipers get there."

"First, you don't know that. They may have had previous information. That makes the raid legit, no matter what we told them. By the way, we didn't "kidnap" anyone, they were all legitimately under arrest and taken into custody when they were interrogated."

"We'll see what happens when we file motions in court."

"No you won't. These men will have plead out and cooperated long before we get there. Don't forget, no matter where the underlying information may have come from, your men attacked DEA and FBI men with assault weapons while they were making an arrest. That's a life sentence and we got it all on videotape. If they want a trial, they'll get one. Besides, Fontina, your law firm may be in this a little too deep."

"What do you mean by that?"

"Prestwick is the one who tipped the raid!"

"How do you know that?"

"We had a phone tap on the tipster."

"And he called who?"

"Prestwick."

"Prestwick was set up."

"No. The tipster was, and he tipped Prestwick."

"Can you use that?"

"Of course. He was the only source."

"Besides, the tipster will roll over on Prestwick, if we need him or her." At this point, we knew it was a male, but why tell her.

"Which was it?"

"Ask Prestwick." She was starting to shake. The coffee cup rattled as she held it in the saucer."

"You'd try to take down Prestwick?"

"It's a possibility. You want to talk?"

"These are just your words. You're accusing the defendant's lawyer without proof." More rattling of the cup.

"Okay. Here's the tape of the tip." I played the phone call of the tip on my recorder, then flipped the cassette to her. Now she and Prestwick would know that we knew who the tipster was, but of course they already know. Now they knew we knew.

"Here's a list of the cases in which your firm has represented the Sphinxes. Some of the Sphinxes may rat you out further."

"What do you mean?"

"Subordination of perjury, conflicts of interest, obstruction of justice."

"You mean some of these guys will say we told them to lie, or conceal information."

"Very good!"

"You'll never get Harmon. He's too slick."

"Well, not so fast. He has lead a very high life style. He is supporting two mistresses, and pays for their rents and credit cards. He supports two other children, and pays their private school tuition and he takes them all on separate vacations. He has no other assets in brokerage accounts or otherwise and seems to get cash payments tax free from the Sphinxes of $12,000 per month that do not go into the law firm account. Without the Sphinxes' payments, his life style crumbles and he can't pay his debts. Even now, he bounces checks and is late on his credit cards and mortgages.

"How do you know all this?"

"Do you doubt our methods?"

"But you just admitted you had information that you had to get by hacking into his private computer or other illegal sources. How do you know I didn't just record you?

"Fontina, you were swept for bugs as you passed."

"But who . . .?"

"I waved to the large man two tables over. He looked like a rube from Texas with a plump country wife. "Say hello to Sam."

"The man who bumped me in the entrance."

"The same."

"Well, what do you want from Prestwick?"

"We don't know yet. We'll let you know. Have some eggs."

Those beautiful almond shaped black eyes flashed at me. She squinted, took a deep breath and stared off into space. Then, "Order me some pancakes and syrup. Lots of syrup. I have to make a phone call. She turned around and went into an alcove to talk. Sam signaled to the man at the end of the lobby with the parabolic receiver. At least we would know one side of the call to Prestwick – all perfectly legal. You talk in public, we record you in public. All admissible in court.

CHAPTER 24

Fontina came back from her phone call just as her pancakes showed up at the table. Her crisp clip clop of her heels on the tile floor had disappeared. She was walking with a heavy tread and her shoulders drooped.

As she got to the table, she said, "I… I… don't think I can eat … I'll have to go." She looked like she had been crying and had obviously gotten some bad news. I could only guess what about.

"Fontina, please, relax. Have some breakfast and coffee."

"No… No… I…" The chin quivered. Gone was the sexy self-assured lawyer. I got up and gave her a pat on the shoulder and a few strokes on the back. I heard a few shuddered sighs, and saw a few tears. Something about a woman crying always gets to men. They become totally helpless and inept.

"Please, sit." She sat and looked at her hands. Silence. A few deep breaths… Silence…

"You don't know what it's like!" She finally got the energy to say.

"Relax. You don't have to say a thing." Somehow I didn't want to hear.

"No… I… I… That bastard… That bastard!" Uh-oh, now I wanted to hear.

"Who?"

"Prestwick! The dirty mother fucker… that snake… that… that…"
Ah, I knew it!

We were not talking law now, we were not talking plea bargain. This was love, and a woman scorned. Egad! She was Prestwick's lover and she had just found out about his other women.

Now, there are some wives that can forgive a peccadillo as long as their husband is good to them and the family. There are even some that can forgive a mistress. In some cultures, a mistress is a way of life. But a mistress can never… never… forgive being cheated on. Then the man is a pure bastard, through and through. Fontina was expressing that anger. Not knowing, I had given her the information about Prestwick's other women, and now Prestwick was screwed, blued and tattooed forever. She couldn't hide it, not now.

She ate her pancakes in silence. She took a few sips of coffee. A sigh or two was mingled in every few bites or sips. She stared into space. Finally, she looked up.

"Peter, they're coming after you. In force this time. Get the hell out of here. They are going to hold you for ransom and cut off a finger a day – or some such bullshit. Get the fuck out of here. And do it now. I was supposed to set you up. I didn't know I was, but I see it now. They knew you'd meet with me. Then they'd get you afterward. I know what they'd do."

"But I'm just a lawyer. I don't know anything."

"But they'd send a message. That's what they want. They can't lose face" "Fontina, what are you doing in all this?"

"Now, I don't know."

"Look, I can have a dozen armed men here in fifteen minutes. Come with me. I can protect you."

"No. I couldn't do that."

"You could salvage your career. You're a bright young lawyer. You could work anywhere. Don't go down with these scum."

"No. I can't. I just can't. Don't ask! Now get the hell out of here. Now. I'll be okay. Prestwick won't sell me out, he'll just … never mind. Get out of here now"

I signaled to my bodyguard, and the man with the parabolic receiver. I gave the danger signal. I made sure to stay in a public place until I got the sign to leave. I stayed with Fontina until she left. Then I walked to the reception desk where I could see in all directions. Eventually, my bodyguard signaled for me to leave by the rear. There was a dark blue Yaris waiting for us with a driver. Jesus, another Yaris. At least I should get a Camry.

"What is this with a Yaris again?"

"Who's gonna guess you're in a Yaris."

CHAPTER 25

We drove away without incident. I expected something. Of course, two Jeep SUVs followed us at a discrete distance. No need to guess who they were. We were met on the outskirts of town by Hank and Joe. I explained to them my whole meeting with Fontina. I explained that I had tried to develop her as a source. They were still high from the DEA takedown. So far no one was talking, especially Fat Marvin. I was generally satisfied that we really didn't need his help and might expect the government to reject it in the future. Maybe they preferred a big noisy trial which once again would trumpet their exploits and get major, major sentences in federal court.

Now the time had come to clean out the farmhouse where the drugs arrived from Mexico or wherever. This part of the operation had already been designed and put in motion. Soon, the rental truck which had delivered the drugs before from probably Texas or Arkansas would leave to purchase the drugs at a remote location. There would be a suitcase full of cash, a driver and two armed men, possibly Garcia, from what we heard. They would hand over the suitcase and pick up the coke and drive the coke to the farmhouse where it would be re-rocked and bagged for distribution. We would first take down the truck then grab the cash. Easy peasy!

At the same time, the road was already thick with our SUVs ready to pick up the Sphinx SUVs coming back from dropping off the drugs and picking up the money. We already knew the incoming routes, so it was easy to waylay them and grab the money, the men and the cars.

Mo' money!

The Sphinx SUVs surrendered quickly. They were well aware of the violence from the night before. With a black SUV coming in front and a black SUV coming up from the rear. When they heard a loudspeaker telling them to exit with their hands up, they did so. Four Sphinx SUVs were taken down, their men in handcuffs and the cash safely in our possession – the total haul for an entire drug ring for two days – over $200,000.

The van sent to receive the drug delivery also surrendered peacefully. The two armed men were taken into custody and the Eagles put two men in the car and told the driver to go to the pickup point. In the meantime, of course, the suitcase filled with cash was emptied and filled with newspaper. The driver at gunpoint took them to a roadside parking area, where they waited. The location was remote. Two Eagles' SUVs had followed the car to the site and were forced to park a mile away at some forest dirt road. The men hustled back and each took a walk around the parking area.

In the meantime, the DEA had been alerted. They were to have two functions: a) arrest the men from Mexico or wherever at the delivery point. They had to move fast, but were well prepared to move quickly; and b) take down the farmhouse.

First things first. The truck from the farmhouse, now with the Sphinx's driver but two of our men riding shotgun – literally – took a very slow route to the delivery point. The DEA was contacted and began to track us on their GPS as we drove to the delivery site. Soon, they signaled they were within five minutes of us and had a helicopter on alert. (Great to have government money.)

As the truck delivering the drugs rolled up, it flashed its lights and got a return flash from our driver. He appeared to be cooperating with us and we were betting that he had not flashed a danger signal. The rental truck pulled up about 20 feet away and three men got out of the truck – two with guns and one other to open the rear of the truck. The driver of our car got out and brought out the suitcase while the two Eagles stood nearby. At this point, no words had been spoken.

The driver of the rental truck was stacking boxes at the rear of the truck. Our driver handed the suitcase to one of the armed men. At that point, both of the armed men fell to the ground as if they were marionettes whose strings had been cut. All guns were now focused on the man at the rear unloading boxes who slowly, deliberately raised his hands.

"But…. but…." He was shocked. This had become a routine trip where he made easy money. He never suspected that the buyers would jeopardize a large source of regular supply.

There was a million dollars of drugs on the ground, and a million more in the truck. Man, oh man, would they be pissed when he told them back home he had been robbed, but they would be in the slammer looking at an eternity in prison unless they ratted out their bosses.

The rental truck driver had a cell phone on which he was supposed to call in anything untoward. They would be awaiting his call to say that he was alright and the deal was done. He couldn't get to his phone now. A car who had trailed the delivery truck would be just behind with two armed men. How long would they wait if they didn't get the signal? In the meantime, the DEA stepped in and whisked the men and the drugs into custody and drove off.

It was decided to stake out the empty delivery truck to see if the following car, whoever he might be, came up to investigate the lack of communication. Off the roadside, the woods were thick with agents. After an hour, a new gold Cadillac pulled up to the truck and a few men got out and walked up to the truck. When they got to the truck, they opened the doors and began to look around. They found a few empty boxes in the rear and began to speak on their cell phones. At that, the DEA turned on search lights, hurled flashbangs – loud explosive devices which gave off a deafening noise and a shock of an explosion but no fire. The men in the immediate vicinity were stunned as the men swooped in and threw them to the ground.

The next step would be to see if they could trace the men back to some distribution point in the U.S. or even into Mexico if possible. But that was a job for the DEA, not us. Our job was pretty much limited to Memphis.

We had now closed up all the main drug dealers who serviced Memphis. We had taken the funds for a week's delivery and funds from a week's pickup. We had captured their dealers, 14 of their enforcers, and Fat Marvin; the last step would be to take down the farmhouse. We set this up so that the DEA could surgically cut off the farmhouse and capture its inhabitants. We had given them camera footage, a diagram of the area, and an entire briefing on the operation. They took over our positions in the woods around. They waited until the re-rock women arrived for the day. Arresting them would ensure two very important things: that there were drugs in the house, and that there was an ample supply of witnesses who could implicate everyone in the farmhouse operation. No one wanted these women to do time. They would readily cooperate with the government and sew up any chance that the Sphinxes might win at trial.

The takedown started shortly after noon. As the buses delivered the women and they were safely inside the house, a loudspeaker blared out the news that the house was surrounded, the DEA was on the scene with enough men to defeat China and the firepower to back it up. When the doors still did not open, tear gas canisters were launched through the windows of the upper floors. As the gas descended through to the lower stories, a mix of people began to stumble out of the building, coughing and rubbing their eyes. They were told to lie down in the grassy area off the front stairs. They did not need to be told twice. The chief prize of course was Garcia, but he was accompanied by the naked re-rock women and ten men with automatic rifles which they laid meekly on the ground.

The DEA team advanced to the house cautiously with metal shields with a Plexiglas bullet proof window. They went up the stairs and into the house to ensure there was no further danger. When they came back out signaling all clear, a team of forensic specialists went in to photograph, dust for prints and box up the drugs. They would take their time and get it right. All prisoners were whisked away. The re-rock women were each given a baggy jumpsuit and taken in a bus to a local police station for questioning.

That left the remaining Sphinxes, Little Jimmy and a house full of armed men as well as possibly a large stash of money and drugs in downtown Memphis. The DEA and local cops took over this responsibility. They needed to make sure they could prosecute everyone with absolutely clear evidence. To be completely sure, they waited until the first man under arrest decided to cooperate and give them enough of a statement to answer all the requirements of a valid search warrant. Fortunately, this did not take more than a few hours.

The DEA then set up a major military force around the Sphinx house and alerted the surrounding neighborhood. They did not need to be told twice. Again, a loudspeaker announced that the house was surrounded and there was no hope of escape. The search warrant was catapulted through the front window attached to a brick.

For some unknown reason, Little Jimmy decided to fight it out. A few sporadic shots came from automatic weapon fire inside the house. The DEA had brought in the local military base personnel who retaliated with an anti-tank 50 millimeter gun, and three rocket propelled grenades, very nearly simultaneously at pre-arranged parts of the front wall. Soon it was possible to see through the plaster dust of an almost completely disintegrated front wall. Men were arranged about on their backs; they were completely inert. A few men still were armed with automatic weapons and lay on mattresses facing out. In the silence which followed the initial blasts, the loud speaker again told everyone to surrender. This time, the men meekly came out what was left of the front door or the front wall with their hands up. They were told to lie prone in the street. Another team of forensic people came into the building and began to photograph everything on site. They were able to open two safes in the basement and take out several large boxes of drugs and large garbage bags full of money. They would fingerprint all of these.

By this time, the TV stations had arrived and were filming every move by anyone that looked remotely like law enforcement. There were no Blue Eagles in sight. The DEA and the police chief were happy to accept congratulations for the operations. The cleanup and the camera crews were there well into the night. The Sphinxes were no more. The Eagles had earned their fee. Of course, the Mayor and Police Chief showed up for face time on local TV.

CHAPTER 26

As the dust settled on the raids at the farm house, I got a call from Fontina. She wanted me to come to the Prestwick law firm's office for a meeting with Harmon. This irritated me immediately. First, Prestwick did not have either the stones or courtesy to call me himself. He had to send a flunky with a message. Second, his clients had already tried to kidnap me once based on a leak from the Mayor's office and I had no desire to put myself in jeopardy again. Did he think I was naïve? While I was sorry Fontina was in the middle, I was even a bit fond of her now that I saw her vulnerability, I had to decline and I told her why. If Prestwick didn't have the courtesy to call me himself, I was not going to go like a beggar to his home field. I am not in favor of these macho displays, but I had sound reasons.

About ten minutes later, I got a telephone call from Harmon himself.

"Mr. Stern, this is Harmon. Can we talk?"

"Harmon, we can always talk. I just don't like being kidnapped."

"No… no…. I'm sorry about that…." (He better be, he set me up.) "Can you come to my office." (Ridiculous. He already knew I knew he set me up.)

"Not possible. You've already set me up once."

"No. I think you're mistaken about that."

"Come now, Harmon." (I still had not asked him to call me Peter.)

"I'm sure Fontina gave you the tape from the wiretap of the Mayor's office. Are you suggesting I should believe that you knew nothing about that?"

"Perhaps we should discuss this in person rather than on the phone." He was telling me he would admit it in person, but was afraid my line was taped and he might be admitting it in a way that could be used in court.

"I am not coming to your office. I thought that was clear." "How about if I come to the hotel? We can use one of their conference rooms. I'll have the room swept for bugs when I get there."

"I could do that. I'd be interested in what you have to say."

"Fine. What's convenient?"

"This evening at 5:00 p.m."

"I'll be there."

Prestwick showed at 5:00 p.m. with Fontina in tow. She might turn out to be an adverse witness to me, but I thought she should hear with her own ears what Prestwick had to say to my evidence. I was secretly enjoying watching their interplay when I proved the existence of Prestwick's two mistresses. Also, not to be outdone, I had a man with a parabolic receiver 50 feet away to record the conversation. These babies were amazing. For under $500, these receivers could pick up with reasonable clarity a conversation within 900 feet. They also could not be detected as a bug might. They weighed two pounds and could hear through walls. I had not heard of law enforcement using these with any regularity, especially for obtaining evidence to be used at trial. I hoped to lure Prestwick into a few admissions.

Prestwick was directed by the hotel desk to a small conference room off the lobby. I sat at one end of the table. Prestwick and Fontina pulled up chairs at the other.

"Mr. Stern, glad we could meet. Fontina has told me about a few interesting ideas you have about me." He was smugly denying what I told her.

"They are not just ideas, Mr. Prestwick, they are provable facts. Shall I start with one?" I pulled out the cassette tape of the call tipping our raid at the Brookfield and slipped it into the handheld dictation device. A man's voice was clearly heard dialing Prestwick's private number, and tipping off the time and place of the DEA raid.

"But that's illegally obtained and it's not me. You don't tape phone calls without a warrant."

"Not so. We can tape a phone call in Tennessee if we have one side's consent. We also did not tape your voice, but someone else's who may not object to admitting it in court and not raising the issue of an illegal wiretap. Once this case gathers a little momentum, he will roll over on you fast to get a more lenient sentence. Do you still want to play that game? He also may be in the process of ratting you out as we speak that he got word of my meeting with the Mayor where the Sphinxes tried to kidnap me. You set me up for that. Which game do you want to play?"

"I'm not playing any games. I'm just the Sphinxes' lawyer. I don't know anything about this set up. Besides no judge in Tennessee would let me be convicted. After all, you know the definition of a lying witness; one who has made a deal with the government. Nobody will believe him."

"I won't go into the proof we have. But I can tell you we know much more than you think we do."

"Who is we?"

"I should say 'they'. I am just their lawyer. Unlike you, I do not participate in their actions. I give them advice. I receive information and I deal with the outside world."

"From what I hear, they commit numerous violations of civil rights."

"That's possible, but we are not government. We are not bound by the Fourth or Fifth Amendments. If we develop evidence, it is not thrown out by the court."

"You can't do that."

"I'm afraid we can. Now would you like to hear what we know about you?" "Alright. Go ahead."

"First, you are supporting in addition to your wife, two mistresses. You are broke. You are about to lose the $150,000 per year the

Sphinxes pay you in addition to the legal fees your firm bills them. You are participating in an illegal conspiracy and criminal operation that makes over $20 million per year and sells over $50 million in coke. You are paying three mortgages. You spend over $400,000 per year, yet your firm pays you only $250,000. We obtained all this from public sources without the necessity of hacking or obtaining data illegally." I shot over to Prestwick a file of papers.

I looked over at Fontina as I said all this. I had told her this before and she had told Prestwick because the parabolic receiver had picked up her end of the conversation at the hotel. I ran through what evidence we had. Fontina was staring intently at Prestwick. Could he deny it? Could he refute it?

Prestwick sifted through the papers slowly and carefully. He certainly recognized the papers, but was stalling while he plotted the next move.

"How did you get this?" he said at last. (Not exactly an admission.)

"Some came from your trash."

"You can't do that?"

"Once you abandon it, anyone can pick it up." More deep thought by Prestwick, more sorting through papers.

"You rooted through my trash? That can't be legal."

"Look it up. You have no expectation of privacy once you abandon it."

"Okay. Mr. Stern what do you want?"

"I don't know yet."

"Is it money? Are you just impressing Fontina? Do you expect an admission, a guilty plea? What do you want?"

"I don't know what my clients want. It is, of course, up to them." Fontina, by now, had started again to tear up. Her very impressive boss and mentor had been laid low before her eyes. But more important, he had not refuted the mistress charge. Several of the documents on the table were letters from the mistresses, his name on leases for their fancy apartments, airline bills for their trips to exotic resorts. Photographs on vacations, photographs at restaurants. For her, the goose was cooked.

He was a triple cheat, a sleaze, words were coming to her mind – a cad, a bounder, a serial whatever. The tears were a bit more visible now.

"Tell me what you want, damn it."

"As I said, I don't know yet. Maybe, you should make an offer."

"Is it money? I got money stashed."

"Where?"

"Nice try!"

"Do you want testimony?"

"Are you kidding? You are their lawyer. You can't reveal confidential information."

"How about if I reveal it between the two of us?"

"No good. We can't do that. Why don't you sit and think for a few days? You might also wish to rearrange your finances – the Sphinxes' money has dried up." Harmon got up and left. He was so disturbed that he didn't take the file of documents I had so carefully collected.

As the door slammed shut, Fontina she began to sob and shake. The lip quivered again. No man could resist that. Somehow my inner knight came out and I got up to pat her gently on the back. "Can I get you a glass of water of something?"

"I want a double Jack Daniels on the rocks."

I dialed room service.

"I can't stand to look at that file and I don't like this room"

"Shall we go into the lobby?"

With that she got up and put her head on my shoulder. I could feel the warm tears on my neck. No man can ever withstand that. I hugged her and patted her back. Then I could feel warm lips on mine, not harsh, just soft and full. I could also feel the shudders as the sobs came through her body.

What was I to do? She was vulnerable and sad. A man doesn't take advantage of a situation like this. More soft kisses, a firm embrace. And then the defeat of all men. An erection. An undeniable healthy erection. You dirty dog! What were you doing in this scene? Very unknightly.

Bad boy! Down! Down! Think about baseball. She did not seem to object and wriggled for a closer hug. Then she murmured, "I want it. It's okay." By then I knew I could not go through the lobby. I opened the door and kept my briefcase squarely in front of me and my errant member. We staggered to the elevator and somehow got to my room. I do remember a long heartfelt embrace in the elevator. I don't know how I got the keycard out of my pocket. Then I certainly remember and will remember forever, how soft and silky her skin felt on her breasts and thighs. I fondled the star opal. It seemed to be gleaming at me and then: sighs, sobs, shudders, grunts, tears, more sighs, more sobs. In fact, I can remember vividly everything, every detail after that, until we were both bathed in sweat, sweetened by the exotic scent of her perfume. After a long silence, she said, "I've got to get away."

"What can I say, I'm sorry."

"No. Not you, dummy! I've got to get away from Prestwick."

"Sure. Anything I can do to help."

"No. It's me."

"Well. Look, you've got some insurance. Leave that file and the tape with someone and let him know it's hidden. I'd have a healthy fear of him."

"Yes. That's good."

"Well, he's not your client. You've got to put some distance from him. Besides you could get a new start anywhere."

"I know. I have to think. By the way, did you make some money on this whole thing?"

"I guess so."

"You're not married, are you?"

"No, divorced. I have a seven year old daughter."

"Have you ever been to Rio?"

"No. Well, spend some of that money and take me to Rio. I want to dance and I want to swim on the Copa Cabana beach. Can you do that?"

"Sure. Let's do that."

"And I have to learn to like nice guys. I'm too old for this."

I may not understand women that well, but I knew it was my time to shut up. Rio it was.

CHAPTER 27

Rio with Fontina was great. I had received a nice bonus from Hank – every one of the team and all the subcontractors got initial cash distributions before all the final calculations were done. We were obviously aware about spending too much too fast so that we would not draw suspicion. But Rio was a great place to spend a pocketful of cash.

Rio is a fascinating city. The actual city proper of Rio is a bit old and shows wear and tear, but the beaches – Ipanema and Copa Cabana are fantastic. Two huge half-moon shapes of sand are filled with Brazilians and tourists enjoying year round sunshine. There are volleyball nets with the young men playing volleyball with soccer rules – they use only their feet and heads. The women have wonderful butts and wear thong type bathing suits so skimpy they are called dental floss. Meanwhile the Brazilians are a melting pot of many races -- skin colors of every known type and mixture of black, brown and white, pass freely and happily. The beaches are ringed by tourist hotels and have wonderful restaurants, bars and shops. As a mixed race couple, we drew little attention; but Fontina drew her share of lustful glances.

I could see Fontina's eyes sparkle when we went to the jewelry shops. Brazil is the leading source of colored gems. Unlike southern Africa, which monopolizes its diamonds and keeps the prices high, Brazil has a variety of stones which are much cheaper. Sapphires, opals, topazes, citrines, amethysts, emeralds and tanzanites are sold from dozens of shops and even flea markets along the beaches. With the cheaper labor costs for jewelers, it is possible to get amazing designs of settings cheaply. In fact, it should be a question of concern for women: Why is it that they desire diamonds from a monopolistic, repressive regime in South Africa, when for a tenth of the price they could have wonderful colors and settings from free market Brazil? Perhaps that issue will one day be raised among politically aware women, but not now.

The food in Rio is also amazing. Seafood of all sorts is cooked in styles both domestic and foreign to Brazil. A certain type of restaurant for meat lovers is the Churrascaria. From the moment you sit down, after electing from huge salad bars, waiters walk by with all sorts of cuts of beef and pork on skewers, from which they slice off pieces as selected by the diner, all you can eat. As long as you select, they keep coming with filets, strip steak, flank steak, top sirloin, pork loin, you name it, some new waiter will bring it. With a bottle of Malbec wine from nearby Argentina, this culinary adventure was a treat.

And then the music. The Brazilian samba is not like the pallid version we hear in the United States. Every city has its own variation and savvy natives can easily identify each region. The further north you go in Brazil, the greater the African influence. In the United States, during the end period of slavery, we imported 700,000 Africans. During the same period, the Brazilians imported 7,000,000. With the dominant white culture, much of the African culture was lost, but in Brazil, it flourished. The rhythms, the melodies and even the languages have remained strong over the centuries. Many songs still exist in the Yoraban language of West Africa and are incorporated into their folk and religious music, although the singers have long forgotten what the words mean. You must select your night club to find your music and your dance. Fo ho is a light popular form of dance music and varieties up to heavy percussion with evocative, compelling rhythms which bring out the beast in you. It also does not matter whether you know the steps or the movements. We were able to get through with all the old American steps: the Monkey, the Frug, even the Mashed Potato, the Bristol Stomp and the Watusi. I used the Funky Chicken to great advantage. No one looked askance at us as we mingled on the tiny dance floors of the boites. I say no one looked askance, but I must also say Fontina was a knockout – our girls can dance and Fontina was magnificent. Fortunately, part of my misspent youth involved listening to the music from the '60s. I was able to throw in some MC Hammer, some Michael Jackson especially the Moon Walk, and lots of funky chicken. No one looked or cared about me, but Fontina was a star, just like her opal.

I could tell that some healing was going on inside Fontina's head. She would sip her coffee in the morning staring off into the horizon over the South Atlantic, or lapse into silence at the pool. She was healing. At that point, I knew my job was to shut up.

Alas, the trip was over too soon. I had already gotten five phone calls from Hank. I was needed at a meeting in Philadelphia for a huge job. I dialed him back, set up a date on the first Monday back.

As we settled in for the long plane ride back, Fontina took off her sunglasses and stared at me.

"I've got it. I've got what I want. I am very thankful for all your files and the tape of the telephone call to Harmon's office tipping off the raid. I am going to get a very nice severance package from the firm and get another job."

"That's great. You could get a job anywhere."

"Thanks, but it's not that easy. But, I'll be alright."

"I'm sure."

We both fell asleep and only roused as the plane prepared to land in Miami. We went our separate ways after immigration, but I kept her on my speed dial. I know we could use her in the future, but she would be in my heart as well.

CHAPTER 28

Gentlemen, I can spick some englis, but I heff brought my interpreter so I meck myself more clear. So pliz, Oxsana.

While in many spy movies, the translator is a gorgeous young girl who becomes a love interest, our Oxsana was a squarish women in her mid-50s dressed in an ill-fitting grey suit and sturdy black oxford shoes. Her hair was cut short with bangs, but dyed an odd red color, but from the first words out of her mouth, her English was perfect, with a slight accent, but perfect in grammar, vocabulary and even mixed with accurately chosen slang.

Meester Stern, and you other gentlemen. I am sorry but I am not allowed to know or say your names. We are pleased to meet you. May we present our proposal?"

"Yes, Dmitri and Oxsana, please proceed."

"Our client is a businessman from the Ukraine who has very substantial business investments in the Crimea. He has lost a great deal for which Russia will not compensate him." Oxsana smiled proudly at the placing of the preposition at the beginning of the clause.

"He wants to provoke Russia to give it back to Ukraine or at least honor interests. He believes you can do this."

"How? Putin is overextended financially. He spent over $50 billion on the Sochi Winter Games. Between the drop in oil prices, the effect of sanctions on Russian trade, the drop in values of the Russian ruble and

Russian stocks, the fear of foreign investment in Russia, all have caused the net value of Russia to be bankrupt. Yet he continues to pursue old Soviet style economic fiascos. He has expanded the military, spent heavily on military hardware, expanded the reach of his offensive and defensive influence to Syria, Turkey and the Baltic. He spends heavily on sports in which he instructs his coaches to use illegal performance enhancing drugs. Yet, the spending on the domestic economy – health, housing, roads, bridges, transportation is minimal as it was under the Soviet Union. The people do not see this yet, but eventually continual financial setbacks and hardships will enflame the people.

"Our interest is solely in the Crimea, but, as you will see, my solution will cause tremendous economic setbacks for Putin. To begin with, Crimea was always a money-losing proposition for the Ukraine, and it continues to be so for Russia. It produces very little, cannot support itself and requires many subsidies from the parent country. Currently, Russia pays $4.5 billion in subsidies. It has also had to construct a bridge over the Kerch Strait at a cost of $4 billion to replace the very inadequate ferry.

"Plus, the Crimea gets both its electricity and water from the Ukraine. In addition, Crimea's only real industry is tourism and vacation travelers have dropped to ten percent of what it was.

"In a way, Russia, by taking Crimea off its hands, has done the Ukraine a favor. The only benefit Russia gains is to secure a port at Sevastopol which can house submarines and navy vessels. It may have some minimal use in the Middle East.

"In short, the taking of Crimea was an economic disaster for Russia. It cost billions and will cost billions in the future, for no other purpose than for Putin to flaunt his ego. It is difficult to see how his oligarch friends permitted this. One can only suppose that the paranoia left from Putin's day in the KGB saw the NATO treaties with the old Soviet satellites were steadily encircling Russia and the Ukraine was next to follow.

"From a financial point of view, Putin has placed Russia in a downward spiral it will take years to recover from, if ever. Meanwhile, Putin chooses to follow the path of the rogue nations of the world – North Korea, Venezuela and Iran, rather than deal with the West.

"The strategy is precise. We want Crimea to cost Putin dearly. We want to destroy valuable economic targets, but avoid loss of human life where possible. We want Putin to have to expend tremendous sums to create security in Crimea.

"We want a discrete band of saboteurs to damage or ruin targets of high economic value in guerilla operations. We want these operations to take out, if possible, the Sevastopol fleet, Russian airplanes and airports, the Kerch Bridge, the port and the ferry, police stations, military computer networks, oil tanks. We want as few as possible human casualties in the first strike. We want the first strike at these targets to occur, if possible, simultaneously.

"We will pay you to train saboteurs, infiltrate them into Crimea and design the attack on their targets and then disappear. Can you do this?"

Hank and Joe had sat at the table, taking notes in longhand. Occasionally, they exchanged looks and mumbled to each other. Then they whispered to me. "Tell him we have to do some research and have many questions, but it is in the realm of possible."

I told him. He grinned. "I thought I had the men for the job, but I have several rules: No one can attribute your acts to me or the Ukraine, or the United States. No one can be captured. You, Mr. Stern, will prepare a letter to Putin after it is done explaining that Russia must surrender Crimea or we will attack human targets."

Joe whispered, "Understood." I repeated it aloud.

"Now, you men will be well paid and well-funded. We will need to see a budget and a full military plan. I will provide you with all my research to date on the different targets."

We were already flush with funds from our Tennessee adventure and the team was well rested. So we gathered up Dmitri's files and went back to the large conference room on Venango Street. The whole project had excited us. For once, we would not be hamstrung by legal constraints – now we were totally illegal. We felt morality was not an issue since Russia itself was acting in an illegal and irrational manner.

CHAPTER 29

We got our computer expert, Nora Johnson, busy doing research on Crimea. She was a tiny black woman in her forties, but an IT whiz. She came up with mounds of reports.

As we reviewed the entire geopolitical picture, the map of the Crimean Peninsula was remarkable. About 80 percent of the land mass was not heavily populated – only along the south and eastern coastline was the population concentrated. Immediately behind the eastern coastal area was a range of mountains, most of which were heavily forested and not heavily populated. Except for two targets, all lay within easy striking distance of the mountain range. There were only three possible targets of interest that were located outside. One primary target was the city of Kerch.

The only way to enter Crimea from Russia was through Kerch – a small city on the far eastern, and northern edge of Crimea which provided five ferries – all old, slow and dilapidated, to the Crimean Peninsula. Once the Russians started the takeover of Crimea, they began a $4 billion bridge project to replace the ferry. At least one of our efforts would be to damage thoroughly the beginnings of the bridge project, knock out the decrepit ferry and discourage as much as possible the flow of traffic through Kerch. All other means of entering Crimea were either over water or through some very narrow roads from the Ukraine which had a heavily guarded border on each side. Cutting off any easy means of Russia's supplying its forces would be a permanent goal. The task of designing the attack on Kerch was assigned to Joe. He was an ex-marine and could evaluate the naval bombardment to take place.

The next area of importance was the military base in Sevastopol. Since World War II, this had been a port for diesel powered submarines and the Russian Black Sea fleet. It had been long neglected during the Cold War years. After 1991, the Ukrainians and Russians had shared the port and done little to maintain or upgrade it. Only once since its takeover of Crimea, Russia had decided to bring a few modern ships to the port, mainly as a display. Currently, the base had no nuclear submarines or aircraft carriers, and only a few rusting World War II smaller ships. Since Sevastopol, and in fact all southern Crimea, was on the Black Sea, Russia had little power or influence in the area which was also bounded by the Ukraine at Odessa to the north, Turkey to the south, Georgia to the east and Bulgaria and Romania to the west. Of primary importance was the fact that Turkey controlled the pinch-point at Istanbul at the southern end and was heavily allied with NATO. There was little mischief Russia could mount in the Black Sea. Shore batteries could bring down most ships and submarines. For most purposes, the port of Sevastopol was of little strategic importance, yet for no apparent reason, Russia had lusted after it. For purely psychological purposes, it would be important to demonstrate the vulnerability of Sevastopol and force Russia to spend billions to defend it against guerilla attacks. In fairness, if it had access to Russian goods, it could be one of Russia's few good warm water ports for Russian commerce.

Not far from Sevastopol on the southern end of Crimea, lay the very nice city of Yalta. It was where Churchill, Roosevelt and Stalin met in 1945 at the end of World War II to decide the fate of Europe. It had little strategic importance militarily, but was a center or tourism and commerce for Crimea. Since the Russian takeover, it had fallen into a deep recession. Any guerilla activity in this city would have a negative effect on the civilian population. Russia's incompetent and corrupt administration was already having a severe impact on those ethnic Russians who might be expected to support the continued Russian occupation and control of Crimea.

About the only area of interest would be the town of Simferopol.

With a largely third world economy and level of development, Simferopol was the site for international airplane traffic. It is centrally located in the middle of Crimea and is also the main hub for Crimea's rail and bus transportation and commerce. The placing of the airport so distantly from the cities of Sevastopol and Yalta was an obvious Soviet planning error. There was a two or three hour ride to the only areas of importance on the east coast. Yet, the airplanes and airport itself presented delicious sites for guerilla attack. Its effect on communication with Russia would be substantial, and the rich expensive targets of commercial and military airplanes, as well as the oil and fuel tanks would have a significant effect on the cost for Russia to occupy Crimea. Also, the cost of defending and fortifying the airport and Simferopol itself would be costly to the Russians in the future.

In fact, in reviewing the entire Crimean affair, it is a mystery why it occurred at all. The Ukrainians and Russians are a very closely related ethnic group and have for at least the last 100 years freely intermarried. Crimea has no economic advantage to offer whatever country happens to control it, and is in fact a population that requires substantial subsidies to survive. Although Sevastopol may have been strategically important in past wars, it has been neglected as a military or naval base for years and had a minimal fleet of smaller naval vessels including a few World War II diesel submarines, but no nuclear submarines or aircraft carriers. With the presence of Turkey, a NATO member, controlling the southern end of the Black Sea – at Istanbul, there is no prospect of Russia utilizing this port for any naval operations.

As a result of the takeover of Crimea, Russia has suffered devastating financial losses, sanctions, and a loss of credibility in international relations. The only explanation ever offered for his absurd move was that Putin feared that NATO or Western influences might encircle Russia. Recently, the Ukraine's largely puppet ruler whose corruption and profligacy was well known provoked a rebellion and had fled to Russia. Putin felt he or Russia had been embarrassed.

The consideration then for the operation was to be just what could be accomplished. Ethnic Russians by far outnumbered the ethnic Ukrainians, about 70 percent to 25 percent. Despite all the hardships they now endured, the Russian population still sided with Putin.

Their affections would only change when their hardships became unbearable and Russian administration could be shown to be its usual ineffective and corrupt self. This was a long term prospect. There was no point then in "conquering" Crimea and taking over the burden of its economy and government. The sole point in this operation then was to embarrass Russia by a series of high value attacks on economic targets, which would compel Russia to provide very expensive security measures in a country which was already a financial millstone around its neck. If human casualties were low or non-existent, international opinion would not disapprove of the action and Russia would be further embarrassed. If Russia really was at the end of its financial rope, it might seek peace and cooperation with the West as Gorbachev did prior to 1991. This relatively benign action could be a tipping point in the conflicts Putin had generated with the West.

The inner circle of the Blue Eagles got to work immediately on the Crimea Project. After a brief review of the map of Crimea and some of the military sites, a lively discussion ensued. It first began with a short briefing by Nora Johnson, the diminutive black accountant whose wizardry with the computer was legend.

"The geography of Crimea is unusual. Along the south and east run several mountain ranges known collectively as the Crimean Mountains. They called some of the ridges by different names, but you don't need to know them. Between the mountains and the eastern and southern coastlines are almost everything that is important in Crimea.

At the southern tip is Sevastopol – an ancient city that was a functioning military and submarine base during World War II. It had become obsolete and neglected under Ukrainian sovereignty because the Ukrainians had enough economical problems of their own, and they always looked to Russia or the Soviet Union for protection. Today, about 30 modern interceptors, SU-27, equivalent to our F16s are based at Belbek military airport nearby. Apparently, the Russians feel the need for some early warning protection for aggression coming from the south. These planes might be our prime objective. They are extremely expensive and are a big psychological prize if destroyed.

While Sevastopol is known as a submarine base, the subs are all the now obsolete World War II diesel variety. There are some smaller destroyers, cruisers, tenders in port that occasionally patrol the Black

Sea and little else. It might be nice to torpedo a few of them.

The next priority is Kerch. There is a narrow strait that connects Russia with Crimea in this strait which currently has five old ferries that slowly ply the trip back and forth. Russia would have to appropriate $4 billion to replace this ferry line with a modern bridge. This connection is an extremely valuable target.

I would place low priorities on almost everything else. The town of Simferopol is a rail and bus hub that is situated in the geographic middle of the peninsula, but has little of strategic or economic value. The international airport for all of Crimea is situated just outside of town, but air traffic has dwindled to very few flights. There are few old military transport planes and several ancient passenger planes on the ground.

The rest of Crimea, about 80 percent of its land mass is low, flat, and sparsely populated. There are a few farms, some forest land and little else.

For our purposes, the west coast of Crimea is ideal. There are a few small scattered towns along the coast. With some investigation, it should be easy to land small boats of men and material without any trouble. The area is sparsely patrolled.

Between Ukraine and Crimea, there are two long narrow routes into Crimea. We do not know the status of the border patrol or customs, now that the Russians and the Ukrainians are at odds. We should probably research the locations and preparedness of the Russian border controls along this route.

"We need to get men with military expertise on the ground to evaluate each target, determine how far from the target we can set up shop, and what type of weapons we need."

"Very good, Nora." Hank said. We would have to deploy our own men into Crimea. Who and what target was now the issue. I can see that targeting the Sevastopol naval base is a naval operation. We need a good navy man, maybe a sub specialist. We may want to torpedo some of the ships around subs.

"Okay, Joe, we need to do lots of research here. We will get Dmitri to give us some upfront money to develop a plan and he will have to get us some secure connections in Crimea so we can evaluate the targets. Otherwise, I think this is doable."

CHAPTER 30

Hank, Joe and I were invited to dinner with Alexei, Dmitri's boss, at the Ekaterina Restaurant, a five star Russian restaurant in Northeast Philadelphia, an enclave for Russian and former Soviet Union ex-patriots. As we walked in, we were overwhelmed with the décor which passes for Russian high fashion. The walls were papered in a gold brocade and hung with heavy gilt framed artwork of Russian scenes, or portraits of some of the Tsars. The windows were draped in heavy gold curtains, also in heavy brocade. We were ushered to a private room where five people were seated at a round table. Alexei, in the middle, introduced himself in a very passable, only slightly accented English. He was dressed in high New York fashion. A cable stitch cashmere sweater in different shades of tan, and razor sharp tan gabardine slacks with tasseled mahogany loafers. He was a handsome guy in his 40s with a very professional haircut. He was the man who silently had attended as Dmitri laid out his proposal. Alexei was the boss apparently and had taken over the discussion. Two hefty men on either side of him were introduced simply as Piotr and Valeri. They wore the usual ill-fitting suits, and had immense shoulders and no visible necks. When they heard their names, they simply nodded. On Alexei's left was a tall thin, but athletic looking man in an American style dark suit and striped tie introduced as Ilyosha Popov, and a small, blond woman introduced as Sveta Agoritsova. She was dressed simply in a white blouse, and as she rose to shake our hands had on a straight dark gray skirt. Ilyosha and Sveta were introduced as "people we may be working with." The two hulks were noted as "my bodyguards."

Joe, as was always his custom, took a receiver out of a small satchel he carried and began to clear the room for bugs or radio transmissions. He nodded at us to assume our meeting would be private. One of the bodyguards did the same and nodded to Alexei.

Waiters came in carrying an array of hors d'oeuvres. Alexei said, "I hope you gentlemen will sample some Russian fare. Perhaps, you will sample more of it in the future." There was some black caviar sprinkled in sour cream on miniature blinis, gravlax with capers on toast, red caviar in cream cheese and sardines with lemon, an assortment of pierogis filled with different cheeses or liver. The waiters also brought in full bottles of vodka and bottles of sekt – a sweet white carbonated wine, and Georgian red wine. Alexei again said, "I wasn't sure what you men drank so I ordered a bit of everything."

We passed the platters of hors d'oeuvres around and each filled our glasses. I had always heard of Georgian wine and was very pleased with my first sip – full bodied and smooth, but not so sweet, more of a hearty rich taste. Hank and Joe tried some and filled their drinking glasses with sparkling water just in case. They were a bit wary of the menu, but did dig into the hors d'oeuvres with gusto.

As we settled back, Alexei started. "Gentlemen, I am an ethnic Ukrainian some of whose family comes from the Crimea. I was very shocked to see the ease with which Putin and the Russians came in and simply took over Crimea and started a war in Eastern Ukraine. Many people have died.

"I cannot understand Mr. Putin's actions. They are devastating for both Russia and Ukraine. He is driving his country into bankruptcy. The Sochi Winter Olympics cost an admitted $52 billion. The invasion of Eastern Ukraine and Crimea cost billions more. The very foreseeable imposition of sanctions by the West has cost billions more and caused both NATO and Russia to expend billions in defense to respond to Mr. Putin's provocations.

"The ruble has sunk in value. Russia's only real source of foreign income, oil, has been severely rocked by an oil glut and price drops. In short, Russia is a disaster because of Putin's policies, and will be for generations to come."

"First, before we do business, I must ask you if you agree with me so far in what I have said."

Hank, Joe and I looked at each other briefly and nodded. I answered. "Mr. Kirilenko, we can easily say without further conference that, not only we, but virtually all Americans are appalled at Mr. Putin's actions, and feel his new aggressive position in the world is very dangerous. You may proceed."

"Good. Good. Tonight, I do not wish to discuss business especially in this environment and so public. I would like to get to know you. I have, of course, become familiar with your careers and have used my many contacts in the U.S. to evaluate your activities so far. I must say, I consider your work histories to be exemplary. But enough of this for now. Can we meet in a more secure environment of your choosing?"

Again, Hank, Joe and I looked at each other briefly and nodded. It was my turn to speak. "Alexei, we too must rely on complete security for our own protection. It is only by your reputation that we were induced to meet here in public. For our next meet, I propose that we pick you up at an agreed location and take you to our headquarters. You will have hoods over your heads and have loud radio music playing so that we can conceal our location. We must ask that your bodyguards be left behind and that you come unarmed. When we discuss matters, we and the rest of our staff will be seated in the dark and you will be seated under lights. Some of the staff may speak into voice altering machines. Our headquarters are not posh and you will be seated at conventional conference tables and sit on ordinary desk chairs. Our session with you will be recorded. Can you accept these terms?"

"I would not have it any other way. I admire your need for security and hope that our business can be conducted that way."

After that, the dinner broke down into both side conversations and general ones including the entire table. It turned out that Sveta had been a gymnast with Olympic dreams as a teenager, but developed as she put it "the unfortunate female malady of breasts and hips." The hormones had not done her a disservice, if I might observe, and she was quite attractive, and still looked petite. Hank, Joe and I being inveterate gym rats invited her to our gym in Roxborough the next day to work out. Ilyosha was also invited and became enthusiastic when he discovered we had a sauna, a hot tub and a swimming pool at our disposal.

Hank seemed to have become involved in long stretches of conversation with Sveta. Joe and I looked quizzically at each other as we heard snatches of Hank referring to Russian novels and Chekhov. Where did he get all that from? Did he actually have interests we didn't know about? Sveta was obviously pleased with his interest and had a grin that glowed. What was happening to our Hank? Sveta had gotten a college degree in something called "World Culture" and had a background in liberal arts – very rare for a Russian-style education, but not apparently for an aspiring gymnast to be appearing in international contests.

Alexei also explained his rise in the post-Soviet environment. He was trained as an engineer as many men in the Soviet Union were, and just after Perestroika used his ingenuity to design machines to make wire and pirated more than a few items from the factory he was working at, and scrounged some loans from friends, to assemble a factory line in Odessa. Basically, he bought copper salvage, sometimes ore but mostly salvage, heated it up, and put molten copper through molds which extruded the cabling copper into wire in precise widths which were then fed through machines which put different kinds of insulation around the copper, mostly wax and plastic. His labor and factory space were cheap and he sold the wire for a very nice profit. Now, he was visiting outlets in the U.S. to sell his wire, but had been rejected because the wire did not meet U.S. standards of safety. He was here to learn how to meet those standards. He was now into all forms of metal products and had expanded tremendously in a few short years.

He had been born and raised in Crimea and had many relatives and friends there. As an ethnic Ukrainian, he had seen some discrimination growing up, but felt it made him stronger. Now, it was his vision to move some of his factories to Crimea under a friendly regime protected from Russian corruption and politics, and welcomed by a possibly autonomous Crimean government under Ukrainian control and hopefully NATO protection. He was anxious to engage the European Union in commerce.

Ilyosha was a former Ukrainian military officer, trained in all sorts of NATO and Russian weapon systems. When the Russians moved into Crimea, he moved out and tried to join the Ukrainian Army in their fight in the Eastern Ukraine, but because of the confusion within the military his papers were sitting on someone's desk. He was working now as a policeman in western Crimea. His family knew Alexei's family going way back.

The waiters meanwhile had been bringing in platters of "traditional Russian food" I can't say I was a big fan. The hors d'oeuvres had been great, but the overdone stuffed meatloaf with heavy tomato sauce, the roast suckling pig with porridge and the chicken Kiev were dry and somewhat tasteless. I did like the potato pancakes and the blini with cherries. Fortunately, the Georgian wine was really good. So the dinner passed nicely.

The next day, we picked Ilyosha and Sveta up at their hotel and brought them to our gym. Ilyosha was more than content with the swimming pool and sauna, but Sveta wanted to pump iron with us. Generally, the free weights section of the gym is testosterone territory with a lot of men grunting and talking sports. Sveta, petite and muscular, was a welcome addition. We greeted our usual crew of suspects in the heavy iron section – Fred, the guy who worked produce at the local supermarket – who benched twice his body weight at 165 pounds; Pluto, the maintenance guy at the Marriott, with the booming voice who was the "pep" coach for the lifters; Garrett, the huge young Irish kid who weighed 320 and benched 500. I was the oldest of the crew, but held my own in the bench, not quite getting twice my body weight on the bench at 175 pounds. Sveta had her own warmup – something Russian gymnasts do, then at a body weight of about 120, maybe, benched 170 to great rounds of applause. She then bowed, stretched and did a running double somersault in layout position – again to rounds of male applause, I could hear the women grumbling. Now, she was one of the guys, the workout continued for another hour and a half hitting different machines and free weights. Then, lunch time. Perhaps we hadn't noticed, but Hank had carefully followed Sveta around while we were pursuing our own workout routines.

As we debated lunch, somehow Sveta and Hank slipped off to the salad place around the corner in the shopping center. Salad Place! What was happening to our Hank? He went a good 250 and was 6'3". Salad was rabbit food, not for a mega-bruiser. But as we passed them in the gym, we could hear a conversation about seeing Balanchine performed by the New York Ballet that night. God! Hank with salad and ballet! No way!

Joe and I took Ilyosha to a really good taproom with great

hamburgers and roast beef sandwiches. It was heartwarming to see Ilyosha really appreciate good. American beef. It was a bit disconcerting, however, when he asked that his draft beer be put in the microwave to heat it up to room temperature. That seems to be the way Slavs drink their beer. They must all have some congenital brain dysfunction. Beef and cold beer is what made America great – not odd chicken parts and warm beer.

We dropped Sveta and Ilyosha back at their hotel and told them we would pick them up at 6:00 for a meeting of our directors along with Alexei.

CHAPTER 31

Alexei, Sveta and Ilyosha were picked up, fitted with hoods and driven a devious route to headquarters in North Philadelphia to the heavy masking sounds of Shostakovich and Stravinsky – a misguided effort to make them feel at home. They were guided up a ramp onto a loading platform and ushered to their seats at a long, battered old conference table bathed in spotlight. They blinked for several minutes while they adjusted from the dark blindfolds to the bright lights.

I welcomed our new guests and offered a brief explanation to the assembled board. "We have been asked to undertake a new mission by Alexei Kirilenko seated in the middle. Two of his operatives are seated on either side. The woman you may address as Sveta, the man as Ilyosha. We have been briefly told that Alexei is a successful businessman from Ukraine with family in Crimea. He has expressed a strong dislike and mistrust of the present Russian government of Vladimir Putin and his corrupt oligarch friends. Alexei had once been in the inner circle of this group, but has been deeply upset by the turn of events in recent years: Putin's taking over the Crimea, the financial disaster of the Olympic winter games in Sochi, the foreseeable sanctions against Russia by the west, the heavy investment in military expenditures, the many aggressive provocations against the NATO countries. . . need I go on, Alexei?"

"No, that is fine, but only a partial list." Alexei's clean but lightly accented English rang through.

"Alexei is now interested in finding a project for us to undertake and wishes to outline his proposal today. Please proceed if you are ready."

With that, Sveta placed a small carrying case on the table and stretched out a screen above it. She switched on a computer and took her seat. Alexei got up with a laser pointer and pushed a button on a remote. A map of Crimea was displayed on the screen, with the city of Simferopol in the center, Sevastopol on the southern tip and the city of Kerch on the northeastern side. The map showed points of Ukraine including the city of Odessa in the west, and the Russian port opposite Kerch on the far east. The Black Sea was a large expanse to the south.

"Ladies and gentlemen, (at least I believe you are there, I can't see you) my object is to engage against the Russian occupying forces in Crimea. I seek to achieve the following goals:

1. To embarrass Putin and the Russians by demonstrating their inability to provide security in Crimea to protect their new territory.

2. To cause the Russians large economic losses by these acts of sabotage. Russia is already on the verge of bankruptcy. Its only profitable product is oil which is only very marginal in the profit it is contributing to the Russian government. The western sanctions have created great scarcity in many items and drained the Russian coffers for goods they must import. The ruble has tumbled from about 30 to the dollar to about 90 to the dollar. As a result, nearly all countries demand payment in U.S. dollars or Euros, which puts severe drains on all import-export operations. Simply put, Russia is being gouged in exchange transactions. Large losses of financial assets in the Crimea will cause severe economic consequences for Russia.

3. Already Crimea is a drain on Russian cash flow. It requires major subsidies in oil, pension and welfare benefits which Ukraine no longer supplies. Ukraine also no longer supplies water and electricity which Russia must supply at great expense from Kerch (pointing to the Strait of Kerch in the far east of the map). Its investment in conquering Crimea has gotten Russia a very expensive and useless bauble for its (or should I say Putin's) ego.

4. A well-orchestrated attack on strategic economic assets in Crimea will compel Russia to invest further in men and material to protect its new asset. An investment the strained Russian budget is ill-prepared to make.

5. Already, Russia is planning a $4 billion bridge over the Kerch

Strait to connect Russia to the Crimea. This is the only possible connection except for the present ferry. If Russia is required to commit this much money to its expensive ego bauble of Putin's, it will drive a huge hole in the Russian budget and may never be undertaken.

6. I have selected a number of tentative targets for you to explore and advise me on the possibility and cost of sabotage of them. These are in brief: 1) the submarine base in Sevastopol, 2) the military airport in Belbek, near Sevastopol, 3) Simferopol City, 4) Simferopol railroad depot, 5) the Kerch ferry. I want a team of your military experts to accompany Sveta and Ilyosha on a reconnaissance team of the signs and determine the feasibility and cost of causing massive expensive damage to these sites in a coordinated series of attacks which will take place at nearly the exact time to demonstrate the skill of the organization which will oppose the Russian forces. I will ask you to prepare an estimate of the cost of such a reconnaissance mission. I will, after the mission's report, expect you to define the parameters of each attack on each target as well as the cost including weapons, men, material and supplies for the mission.

7. Now, the most important caveat of my presentation: I want to incur no, repeat, no loss of life in any of these attacks, and as few injuries as possible. Where possible, the attacks will take place at night when as few military and civilian personnel are present. I want to use the most focused fire power possible to cause the least collateral damage to humans. I want to limit as much as possible the psychological reaction by the Crimeans to this attack. Many are ethnic Russians who still side with Putin despite the suffering they have endured under Russian occupation. I want them to understand that these attacks are directed at Russia and not at the Crimean citizenry.

8. It must also be obvious that I want the perpetrators of these attacks to be a total mystery. If someone in power were to believe that the Ukrainian government initiated these attacks, it would further provoke the fighting in eastern Ukraine. If they believe it is either NATO or the U.S., it will increase

tensions to the point of a break out of an all-out war. In all events, unidentifiable ammunition and weapons must be used. The personnel involved must not be captured, killed or in any way identified so that they can be traced back to a specific organization. Unlike other terrorists, no one will claim credit for these attacks.

I am acting alone. I am funding this out of my own pocket. The only ones who know about this are Sveta, Ilyosha and my two bodyguards who are not here. I will expect updates from time to time directly or through Sveta and Ilyosha.

I have many contacts in Crimea who will support this operation in any way. Just advise Sveta and she will provide the contacts.

The room was silent for several minutes as the members of the board slowly digested the points Alexei had made.

The first to speak was Nora Johnson, through a voice altering device. The diminutive black lady sounded now like a tubercular Britney Spears. "If we do the reconnaissance mission and don't like the prospective outcome, what then"

"You may take your fee for the reconnaissance work and go home. No questions asked, but all reconnaissance notes, maps, strikes belong to me."

"If we, as Americans are captured, what do we do?"

"You claim you are tourists or journalists and never deviate. You will have no government back up. I will pay your attorney's fees, but you will be disavowed by every possible organization."

"Will you pay for expensive equipment such as a submarine or a missile system?"

"If that is the most feasible alternative, yes."

"Do you stand to profit personally from a relinquishment of Russian control in the Crimea?"

"Me personally, yes. My business prospects will improve very substantially. I also feel I can better protect myself and my assets if I should no longer be in Putin's inner circle.

"Do you have any contacts in the Russian occupation force that we can rely on?"

"Yes. At the appropriate time and on a need basis, I will use my contacts to your benefit."

"Can we trust them and will our leaders be able to evaluate their reliability?"

"On a need to know basis, yes."

"Do you have access to Russian weapons that we can use in the operation?"

"Yes. Outline your needs and I probably can get you what you want. I have sources."

"Do you have an interest in the Tatar community?"

"Interesting question. Simple answer, no. More complicated answer: the Tatars as you know were longtime residents of Crimea since the early thirteenth century when Genghis Khan and his horde rode through Russia and Europe. A remnant remained behind since then. Stalin, for security purposes had a vast number relocated forcibly to distant locations. As a result, they hate the Russians and can be expected to oppose Russian occupation. As a result, some tactics I expect to use may point to Tatar involvement as a distraction. It is also my intent to strengthen the Tatar community to join with the ethnic Ukrainian community in the formation of an anti-Russian voting bloc in an autonomous Ukrainian province. Although Tatars represent 12 percent of the Crimean population today at about 250,000, possibly 150,000 were forcibly relocated to Uzbekistan and Turkey by the Soviet Union during World War II. They could represent a significant political bloc in an autonomous Crimea. They have an inveterate distrust of Russia."

"Do you have the funds to carry this out?"

I have given my confidential financial records to your representatives. I believe they will be more than satisfied with my ability to compensate you for your efforts."

"We may need ethnic Ukrainians to carry out some of these attacks. I am thinking snipers, mortar experts, frogmen and support personnel in Crimea. Do you have access to such people?"

"Yes. Absolutely. They will need to be integrated into your training and made aware of your plans. But, the answer is yes."

"Where will we train?"

At an isolated base in the Ukraine, which I have been given access to."

"When can we start?"

"Now, if possible. As soon as your reconnaissance and evaluation is complete. We will start planning and training. Hopefully, the entire process can be complete inside of three months."

No further hands were raised so Joe stood and thanked Alexei for his presentation. Hoods were placed back on the guests' heads and they were driven back to their hotels.

The lights were turned back on and the board assembled around the table. There was a universal air of excitement After a brief 15 minutes of discussion, a unanimous vote adopted the plan for Joe, Hank and I to proceed with reconnaissance.

CHAPTER 32

Nora Johnson and the others got busy on working up an estimate for an exploratory reconnaissance mission into the Crimea. Alexei would of course supply Sveta and Ilyosha at his own expense. He would supply the van and all fuel. Everyone was fitted out with their own cameras. Except for food and lodging, tolls, and a delay here and there, the entire initial phase came in at less than $200,000 minimum with a maximum of $500,000. Alexei, to show good faith, put up $1 million into our offshore account. This, of course, would not cover the contingency of arrest, injury, or even death of one or more operatives, but Alexei agreed to fund all such contingencies up to $10 million.

In the meantime, Hank took Sveta to see the New York City Ballet performing some Balanchine on its tour through Philadelphia. Of course, Hank could not escape the centuries old ritual of abuse by one's comrades for his interest in romance. As we were working out the usual time at the gym, it was not possible to avoid the tidal wave of testosterone that overtakes you in the free weight area. I didn't start, but Joe couldn't resist. He began lightly as Hank loaded the bench bar for our warmup.

"So, Hank, when did you get an interest in "the dance?" (pronounced the daunce). I hadn't seen you stretching at the gym."

Hank, who can best be described as a big lug, raised his eyes to the ceiling; he knew what was coming. "Well, in college, I did some musical comedy as "Big Julie") in "Guys and Dolls" and had to take some dance."

Now, that was not going to deflect anything. Joe, on the attack and smelling blood. "Oh, so did you date the choreographer?"

"Well, no, but we were friendly."

"So, ballet, huh? How was it?"

Hank still played it straight. "Very nice. Sveta hadn't seen any American ballet companies. You know, that Balanchine created a whole new American style." He was still trying to take the high road.

"No, no. I hadn't known that. And did you point out the finer nuances to Ms. Agoritsova?"

"I did not have to say much. She took it all in and loved it."

"I'll bet. And did she show her appreciation?"

Uh-oh. Now it was getting a little too much, but Hank was a big lug, but a gentle one. Guys are never supposed to kiss and tell, especially if they are really smitten.

"Now, Joe…" The big lug was showing the results of a few hits. I had to interrupt, after all I was the lawyer and I couldn't leave them fighting. "Now, Joe, I think this is good to have a little fraternal connection going here, with those on our mission."

"Ah, fraternal. Is that what is going on?" from Joe.

"Now, Joe…" from Hank.

"How flexible is she?" Way too close. At that, Sveta came into the gym in her Ukrainian team warmup – pale blue and bright yellow. This set off her pale blond hair and her vivid blue eyes. She smiled at Hank. Joe was a bit cowed by her presence. She was cut – she had some delts and traps pushing through her blue tank top and a six pack. She stretched and then slipped some weight on the bar – six reps at 125. Joe had little to say.

"Great, Sveta." Said Hank, now beaming. "Not bad, huh? Joe?"

"Yeah. Great."

"So Sveta, what do you want to do today?" I had to ask.

"I want four reps at 155, then I'll see how I feel." Since she weighed about 120, doing more than her body weight was great for a woman, but four times 155 was equivalent to 185 one time. At her weight that was competitive in national meets.

We reloaded the bar each time for our lifts. In between hers, Sveta was stretching. She left briefly to go to the basketball court. We could see through the glass, she was doing some cardio. Then, after a short rest, she started doing some tumbling runs – a one-and-a-half with a twist, a double, and one-and-a- half full pike. All perfect technique. Her little body forming clean tight spirals. She came back in to do her lifts. Four at 155 – bam! all clean.

Hank looked over at Joe. "Any questions?"

"No…No… very good." We were impressed. Hank had found a gem.

It was now Hank's turn for his set. He put his usual three wheels on the bar (three 45 pound weights on each side) a total of 315 and cranked out four clean ones. Joe and I got four each at 275. It was a great day for a workout.

We overheard Sveta and Hank muttering over by the side. She seemed to be calling him "Medved." Ah-ha. Hank was not out of the woods yet. We'd have to look up Medved. Was that a new pet name? Had to be.

After the bench, we all split up and did our own variations on the machines – bis, tris, delts, lats and chins. Somehow, we were all persuaded to go to the salad place around the corner from the gym. Salad place! What was happening? She wasn't Yoko Ono, was she?

What was happening? Had someone put estrogen in the water? To make up for this departure, I asked for an extra helping of ham in my chef salad with bleu cheese. I had to admit the salad wasn't bad. Hank had a perpetual smile on his face and Sveta was pleased to have shown she could be one of the guys. The whole episode had silenced Joe, who would not tease Hank anymore. Sveta was now a fixture. At least until we could look up "Medved."

CHAPTER 33

There were several targets that had to be assaulted by land. As we looked at the map of the Crimea, there was the Belbek airfield just outside of Sevastopol, the Simferopol train station, the military base in Sevastopol, both sides of the town of Kerch, and the fuel depots throughout the countryside.

The aim, as defined before, was to cause the most economic damage to Crimea without incurring any human casualties including especially the loss of human life. The object was to cause Russia to realize it had to expend much more money, men, and material in defense of Crimea and leave the rest of the world alone. The attack would be closely coordinated so that, as near as possible, all targets would be hit at once, and all forces withdrawn from apprehension as soon as possible.

The Belbek air base was an obvious target. Many expensive airplanes were parked there, including the 28 new TU-27s which Russia had only recently sent. They were primarily interceptors and not bombers. The Russians obviously wished to protect Crimean air space from attack or surveillance rather than attacking any targets elsewhere. The jets' presence eliminated the possibility of a surprise bombing run, but since that was not in our game plan, that idea was irrelevant. We just wanted to cause as much economic loss as possible. These planes were the most expensive things on the peninsula – at a cost of about 20 billion a pop. Knocking out some of these on the ground would be a major blow to Putin's defense budget. The problem was to find locations from which land based weapons could blow up the planes quickly, and from which escape could be effected quickly.

Next in priority, would be the two sides of the Kerch ferry which was the only way to access Crimea from Russia without going through Ukrainian territory. Same issue. Where to place what weapon to cause the most damage and escape quickly. The Russians were committed to spending an estimated $4 billion on a new bridge to cross the narrow strait but that would be at least three to four years in the process and would be way over budget.

Fuel depots were an easy target, but they had to be located. A few mortars, or even a rocket propelled grenade into one take might ignite the whole depot.

Simferopol by itself was of little value. While the capital of Crimea, it had little industry and little of economic value. However, it was a transportation hub for the whole peninsula – bus routes and train tracks were located in the center of town. The airport was on the outskirts. Blowing up a few commercial Russian planes had some attraction. Cratering the rail lines would set up transportation back in the country for months while the Russians repaired it at substantial expense. However, there could be a negative aspect. All those Crimean residents inconvenienced would be mad as hornets and hate the attackers and not the Russians however drunk, slow or incompetent they might be in repairing the lines. Better to save this for later. Maybe blow up a few local oil depots – easy enough.

The naval base in Sevastopol was a tempting site, but it was full of Russian enlisted men. Not our first priority. Taking human life had negative consequences. It also could be dangerous and difficult to get close enough to targets. Better leave this for later.

The next issue was who would locate the targets and what was the best way to attack them, and then, how to get the necessary equipment into the country. Joe and Hank both had long military experience with weapons. They were the logical guys. Would they get fake passports and drive round as tourists, or just enter illegally through the long coastline of western Crimea, get a vehicle and a translator and check out the various sites. If they were caught, they would get heavy sentences as spies. If they entered on a fake passport and were caught, it would not take long to unravel the fake passport. A fake passport meant a border crossing – Joe and Hank did not speak Russian. Possible trouble at the border.

The best bet was an entry along the large unpatrolled western coastline to a nice sandy beach to be met by a car and a translator. They could carry fake passports with fake entry stamps to get through possibly a cursory scrutiny, but not anything competent. Maybe they could be British men on a tour of the escort and prostitution services in the many beach communities. Very thin cover, but maybe useful in a pinch.

Alexei and his military advisor were called into a conference in Odessa. Retired general Amitov was a Ukrainian who had made his way up the ranks in the former Ukrainian National Army. At present, the military forces were a mess. Many ethnic Russians sided with Putin and were security risks within the ranks of defense forces. Amitov was ethnically Ukrainian and had supported the "Orange" party. He had been carefully vetted by Alexei. He would now consult with us in the Crimean attack.

Hank and Joe stood up in front of the map on one side and a PowerPoint screen on the other. The various targets were pinpointed. Alternately, Joe and Hank presented our ideas on each target. Alexei and Amitov were busy taking notes. The entire presentation took a crisp 45 minutes. Amitov took a few minutes to conclude his notes and then began checking and underlining them. The room was quiet. Finally, the General rose and took the laser pointer and cleared his throat.

"I have been in the infantry and tank forces for 30 years. I was stationed in the Crimea for only three years, but I am very familiar with Sevastopol, not so much with Kerch or Simferopol.

"I have to agree that your best and most valuable land target is the Belbek air base. There are 28 brand new TU-27s there just arrived from Russia. They were interceptors, and yes, they cost over $20 billion each. They are not well covered in armor and use speed almost exclusively to escape danger. A well-aimed shot at the fuselage or fuel tank areas would destroy the plane. Anything from rocket propelled grenades, 50 caliber antitank weapons or mortars could do the job. It depends on the available range. The closer the target, the greater likelihood of damage. I suggest as a rocket propelled grenade the Russian-made RPG-29 or RPG-30. It will give the attacking force complete deniability as to the country of origin, but for your purposes, almost any RPG will do. Penetration of the target is not an issue. All RPG models are light and portable by one man. However, they only have a range of 200 meters. I doubt you could get that close to a military jet at Belbek. RPG7s claim to have a range of 900 meters, but I don't believe it can be accurate from anywhere near that distance. The weapon itself weighs about 15 pounds and the projectile about five to nine pounds. Accuracy at 200 meters is supposed to be about 50 percent.

A Russian made PTRD-41 antitank rifle may be better for you. It has a range of 2,000 meters, weighs 38 pounds, and uses 14.5 millimeter shells in single shot mode. It is fired like a rifle and can be much more accurate. The latest version of this model is a V-94. It is a bit cumbersome – it is 67 inches long and weighs 24 pounds.

The best option is the Czech ZVI Falcon – with a range of 1,600 meters, weighs 27 pounds and has a 12.7 millimeter shell. They are difficult to find, but are very effective as sniper rifles for hard targets. This could be your best option.

Lastly, there are mortars. They can fire multiple rounds quickly, but not terribly accurate. You can cover large areas of terrain quickly though. The U.S. version weighs 46.5 pounds, and has a range of 2.17 miles, over 3,000 meters and can fire 30 rounds per minute. The M120 has an effective range of 7,200 meters, weighs 320 pounds and delivers a 120 millimeter shell.

"I consider this a preliminary briefing. It would be best to examine the targets from all angles and determine where it would be safest to launch an attack with the greatest chance of success and the highest chance of escape. After you have toured the area, we will discuss this further and permit you to recruit and train men for the job."

CHAPTER 34

Hank called me for the meeting with our proposed new advisor on naval matters. We would all be wearing our masks for the interview to preserve our anonymity. I was e-mailed a number of papers including his resume and a few letters from Navy personnel. He was highly recommended, at least on paper. He was Commander Henry Stoudt, retired. He had served for 27 years in the Navy and had tours almost everywhere in the world, Asia, the Mediterranean, the Indian Ocean and had been in combat for about eight tours as far as I could tell from the resume. What struck me was that he had never been on a staff; he had always been a front line officer and in the last several years in submarine operations. Hank told me he had been briefed slightly on the nature of our operation and asked to be prepared to discuss it at the interview. This was going to be interesting. Hank and Joe were former military – but Army and mostly in land-based combat operations. I was only a staff man. I had only worked a desk in the CIA, but had received class work instruction in covert military operations. None of us had any naval training, although we had done a number of covert beach landing exercises. I say exercises, not the real thing. Commander Stoudt was by training, then involved in covert submarine operations. He knew the drill.

We arrived at the old factory building from different directions and entered different parts of the building until we all assembled in the main conference room. I put on my mask. I always chose Jimmy Carter. He had been a good man. The others had masks ranging from Goofy to Vladimir Putin. We all sat at a long table in the shadows. For this interview, there were six, Hank, Joe and I, as well as Nora Johnson, our computer expert, and two men I vaguely recognized.

Commander Stoudt was lead into the room with a black hood over his head and positioned at a chair facing us in the light. Behind him was a map of the Black Sea and the Crimean Peninsula. His hood was removed and he sat blinking into the light for a few seconds.

He was not an impressive looking man for a naval officer. He was short, stout and balding. However, he had grown his hair long in back and tied in a short pony tail. I had expected a trim, spit and polish guy with a salt and pepper crew cut and a jaw chiseled from granite.

Joe began. "Commander Stoudt…"

"Call me Hank." His voice was gruff.

"Okay, Hank. You've been brought here to be interviewed for a very sensitive position on which we need a huge level of expertise in naval or port operations."

"Yes. I have been briefed on what you want and signed a confidentiality agreement. So okay, let me cut this short. I'm 62; I've been in practically ever navy situation you could ask for. I've been briefed on what you want and I know how to get there. I don't waste time and I don't screw around." Excellent, this guy was used to command and obviously impatient with amateurs or staff people. It felt like we had a miniature Patton.

"Okay then. We need to plan to have a guerilla attack on two areas in Crimea and we need someone to plan and conduct the operation. Can you do it? Remember, we need to do this without any casualties or captured men on our side, and a minimum of casualties on the other side and no deaths. We need total deniability by the U.S., the Ukraine and NATO. We need this to be coordinated timewise with other land-based operations we are planning. All have to occur within an hour of each other. And then, we have to disappear fast. Got that so far?"

"I was aware of this in the beginning and I have studied the options. I am ready to lay them out for you."

"Okay,   shoot."
"You have two targets I looked at. The town of Kerch and the base at Sevastopol. Kerch is relatively unfortified and is only important because it is the point at which Russias can get into the Crimean Peninsula. See here on the map." He pointed to the narrow passageway in the northeast part of the Crimean Peninsula. "Currently an ancient ferry takes passengers, cars and trucks on a 45 minute trip across the strait. It does not run currently on Sundays. The Russians have started to build

a bridge across the strait which will not be completed for four years according to the Russians, more likely seven or eight years according to Russian past performance. The bridge will only have four lanes, so the ferries will have to carry at least half the traffic."

"I have two solutions each with sub points. Both are no-brainers. First, we get a sub to torpedo the ferry, the docks and the infrastructure on each side."

I could hear a few gasps. "A sub? How do we get a sub?" Commander Stoudt continued on like a quarterback barking signals at the line. "A sub you wonder? Yes, a sub. Believe it or not I could buy a sub for about $150,000 or less with six torpedo tubes which have torpedoes having a range of five miles at least. These are old diesel subs left over from World War II and are now used by civilians for exotic playthings. They could be retrofitted and operational in about six months. For a short mission, I would need a crew of six to operate it. Me, a radar guy, a sonar guy, a torpedo man and an engineer. We could easily hit an undefended, stationary target with four torpedoes and be out of sight in less than ten minutes, and get lost in the bottom of the Black Sea for a few days. These subs travel at four knots per hour and can be anywhere in the Black Sea within two hours and out of sight.

Okay, here is the list of problems to solve:

1. Reconnoiter Kerch by air, land and sea. We will need to be able to pinpoint areas at each port, the Crimean side and the Russian side. It may be impossible to fly over discretely, but it could easily be diagrammed by a man on foot. Worst case: a quick view from a pleasure boat going past the strait.

2. Possible mortar sights: This may be difficult. Russian security around the port may prevent getting closer than 600 to 700 meters, probably outside the accurate range of most mortars.

3. Hire and train a crew. No sweat here. I could assemble some of my old retired guys to man and operate this. Training time, about one month.

4. Buy and refurbish a sub. No real problem. About two to three months depending on wear and tear on the vessel.

5. Where to put in port. Looking at the Black Sea, and the

depth of the areas around the coastlines, probably no sweat. Arrangements would have to be made with countries bordering the black Sea. Suggest Georgia, Bulgaria or Turkey. Always probable. Ukraine. However, you want some deniability for the Ukraine. This sub could tour the Black Sea comfortably for six months without being detected. You would need to do some serious diplomatic work to arrange to dock the sub after the attack.

6. How to get out into the Black Sea. The only passageway in is the Dardanelles, off Istanbul. Probably will need full cooperation from Turkey. Difficult. This is a heavily monitored passage.

Now, Sevastopol: Sevastopol has an aging and neglected fleet of small to medium sized warships, all severely neglected and of little or no strategic importance. Sinking them has little value except psychological. Russia has transferred two larger vessels into the region for very little purpose other than to threaten the area. They are extremely vulnerable to air attack. But, if you want a meaningless trophy, you can get it easily.

Everything I said about the submarine for Kerch, I would repeat here, except that it is easier. Four to six torpedoes could sink ships, or subs, or severely damage the port. Once again, I need a sub, a crew of six, a port in the Black Sea and a place to hide afterward.

After a few minutes, while everyone finished up their note-taking, Commander Stoudt was thanked and lead out the rear door. After he left, we looked at each other. His approach did not hold much promise. Too much contact with foreign governments, especially Turkey. Too difficult and risky from a security point of view.

CHAPTER 35

After making arrangements through Alexei, Hank and Joe were fitted out for a reconnaissance mission to explore land targets in Crimea. I was to remain safely in the U.S. with full deniability. After much debate, a general consensus was reached that Hank and Joe would take a small boat at night from the southern coast of Ukraine, several miles east of Odessa and the mouth of the Dnieper River. There was a short dock off of an old seaside hotel where an innocuous pleasure boat was loaded with an inflatable raft and two waterproof bags for the men's gear. The entire trip was to be no more than 50 miles and take no more than two and a half hours. Near the western shore of Crimea, there were a number of small rundown beachside towns dotting the northwest coastline of Crimea. Once contact was made with a Crimean agent, the raft would be put in the water a mile off shore and sent onto the beach. The two men would hastily deflate the raft and load it and their gear into a waiting van with a much battered exterior. In fewer than twenty minutes, the men would be on their way inbound to a small farm house about 20 miles off shore. They would stop there and sleep for the night.

With the landing completed in short order, the following morning they came in for breakfast and met Iloyosha, the translator and guide, and contact from the night before. Over the breakfast table, they spread the map that showed the places they needed to visit. Ilyosha, a long time Crimean resident, was very familiar with the area, especially the back roads. He was a tall, soft spoken almost shy man in his late forties who had kept a military bearing and good physical conditioning. He had already driven to a few of the sites and done his own work finding targets. He was, of course, fluent in English and had served for 20 years in the Ukrainian Army. Like most of the inhabitants on the western side of the Crimean Peninsula, he was very upset about the Russian takeover and needed no extra motivation to harass the greedy and brutish

Russian occupiers. His wife, Oxsana, a sturdy but attractive blond had short hair and a Crimean native, was also an ethnic Ukrainian who needed no one's prompting to have her give an opinion on Russian government. The Ukrainians had always been treated as second class citizens and got little attention from Moscow during the heyday of the USSR. They were more than familiar with the deprivations, shortages, mismanagement and corruption of the Russians, whom they viewed as drunken, brutish bullies. She was proud Ilyosha had something he could contribute to the cause. Alexei's very generous fee for services did not hurt either.

Hank and Joe were dressed in the ordinary work clothes of a Crimean laborer. They carried no weapons. If captured, they would simply go into custody. There would be no fire fights. Their excuse was that they were adventurers looking for excitement, but were there to sample the local prostitutes. They carried Irish passports with the appropriate forged stamps to pass at least ordinary scrubbing by the local police. Ilyosha would do all the talking if they were stopped and explain that the two men were religious men seeking converts. There were several piles of religious pamphlets in the car.

The next day, early on, Ilyosha drove the two hours over bad back roads in the van down toward Sevastopol. First stop, Belbek Airport – the site of all the new interceptors TU-27s Russia had recently sent down. As they approached the area, a turnpike sign directed them to T2707, a road which skirted the airstrip. Ilyosha stopped the van and lifted the hood and looked quizzically at the engine as if the ancient van had engine trouble. Hank and Joe could see directly into the airport. The main airstrip was a long slab of concrete running from the Black Sea on the west, inland in a northeastward direction. The planes were parked on the other side of the terminal no more than 400 meters away. To their backs were some heavily wooded areas which could serve as good cover if they were to launch some mortars. They would be no more than a half mile from the airfield.

The other side of the airfield looked even more promising. They circled back on T2707. They made a left, back to the Black Sea and found themselves among some neatly laid out farmland. In fact, the farmland ran directly up to the runway. The planes were parked no more than 50 to 100 meters away with their tails pointed at a slight angle at them. A sniper well positioned could easily dispatch virtually as many planes as he wished. The only question was how long he could take before the police arrived. There was some cover. A number of grape vines were situated on the north side of the runway with the planes parked just east of the position. It would be difficult to locate the direction of the muzzle flashes and the sound of a sniper rifle from in there. In fact, it would be possible to create a lightning joint attack on mortars and sniper fire for about 15 minutes. The result would cause heavy damage to the planes and crater the runway. They noted their observations on the aerial photographs they had received before.

After Belbek Airport, they crossed over Sevastopol Bay into Sevastopol proper and drove toward the naval base. There, the fears they had about the target were realized. There is a very narrow inlet at the southern tip of Crimea which runs eastward for several miles. Buried down in the walls deep inside this inlet with submarine hatches, there were thick concrete tunnels protecting them. Although there are steep hills on either side of this inlet, there is no foliage or cover. Immediately to the south is the town of Sevastopol itself which is an active commercial town, densely populated, and old ruins from about 200 A.D. occupied a large area. At the mouth of the inlet is a very narrow opening that would prevent any type of vessel in or out without complete naval scrutiny. Sevastopol harbor itself was a no-go. But there might be a better idea. Because of its relative invulnerability, the harbor was only sparsely patrolled. A few discretely placed mines could do considerable damage to any warship. With a few small modern boats, several dozen mines could be devastating. Something to be researched and discussed. This would have to be weighed against the lack of any real naval targets. Most of the ships and submarines were aging World War II era old rust buckets of no real military concern. They were not fitted with any real fire power to threaten anything on land except the immediate Black Sea neighbors – Bulgaria, Moldova, Romania or Turkey. A sea war in the Black Sea could be easily extinguished with a few air strikes. Sorry to say, but Sevastopol offered little of strategic value. A few covert hits could have significant value to demonstrate Russian weakness or vulnerability, but little economic value. It is a wonder that Putin had considered this a valuable military asset.

So they went north to Simferopol.

CHAPTER 36

After leaving Sevastopol, they took the main road north to Simferopol Along the roadway, it was possible to see the signs of poverty and dislocation everywhere. By the side of the road, people of all kinds were trying to hawk meager piles of goods. Old babushkas (elderly women) sat behind piles of pumpkin seeds or a block of slowly melting butter, or a blanket in front of a disheveled man had an assorted collection of old shoes, broken watches, and odd pieces of silverware. Another had a five gallon can of petrol he was willing to siphon into a car. Some were hitchhiking. And there was little traffic on the route. It looked like a world that had come to a standstill, and its faces were grim.

Simferopol was little better. The city was ringed with some ugly-looking high rise apartments. The sloppy workmanship of the buildings was evident. Cement seeped randomly from between bricks, rows of bricks stuck unevenly out at the edges, and the windows were out of alignment. The Soviets had built these slapdash housing units years ago in a manner which showed how little they cared for the domestic wellbeing of the people. While huge sums could be spent on the military, sports teams, and international displays such as space programs, little of the budget was allocated to the domestic economy.

Getting out the map, Ilyosha drove from one potential target to another. For the most part, the neighborhoods were depressing third-world scenes with walls of deteriorating concrete, trash, graffiti and drab people moving about. The buses and trolleys were pre-World War II vintage and the few cars were elderly Ladas, small Soviet-made vehicles renowned for their unreliability. As they surveyed the different sites, it seemed a shame to heap any further misery on the indigenous population. While the percentage of ethnic Russians was over 70 percent and Ukrainians at about 20 percent, the Russians were reportedly staunchly in favor of the Russian takeover despite the severe downturn in their prospects. Markets were closed, banks and ATMs were idle, credit cards were useless, daily life was at a standstill, unemployment was high and the people ambled around the streets with little purpose. Drunks even in midday lurched along the sidewalks. Although this was a city of over 300,000, it had few, if any, valuable targets.

The main transportation hub at the center of Simferopol had trains, buses and trolleys which connected much of the country. The trains dated back to almost the World War I era and the trackage was shoddily repaired over the years. It would have been easy to blow up the rail lines or crater the tracks and bring the entire country's transportation system to a dead halt. In a way, it would have been a mercy killing. Modern buses could easily be brought in to replace the rail lines. The interim dislocation would do little more than make the largely pro-Russian population even angrier at someone who was not Russian – whoever the attackers happened to be. Putin would likely seize the opportunity to blame the U.S. or NATO. Russians as well as Ukrainians were used to hardships and would shrug off one more inconvenience or outrage. The purpose of our mission was to cost Putin and the Russians dearly for the takeover of Crimea, but angering the already pro-Russian ethnic Russian population against some third party would be counter-productive. Sorry, old, deteriorating Simferopol would have to be scratched off the target list. It had no strategic, tactical, economic or psychological value. So they would report to Alexei. Better to flood the internet with happy cheerful views of the now reconstructed countries of the former eastern European bloc after the freedom from Russian dominance. Alexei would have to figure out a way to penetrate the internet blackout of Crimea and show these sad Crimeans a happier life.

CHAPTER 37

Before going east to Kerch, they decided to take a look at Simferopol airport. Since the Russian takeover, all international flights had been suspended except those connecting to Moscow and a few other Russian cities. There were approximately 23 flights arriving and departing each day, mostly on the Aeroflot schedule. After 10:00 p.m. until 6:00 a.m. each day, the planes were parked on an unguarded single runway until taxied up to the terminal for loading. The planes were the smaller model jets and were of an ancient vintage. It would be possible to blow up a number of them in a swift sniper or mortar attack and devastate the very light traffic in passengers each way. It would have little effect on the Crimean economy since the tourist traffic had come to a minimal trickle since the takeover. However, the surgical removal of a number of passenger planes (without passengers) would make for some large international headlines and draw expensive security resources from Russia. It was something to consider.

CHAPTER 38

The trip on the major highway from Simferopol towards Kerch was uneventful. They picked up Sveta since this might be her portion of the mission. Traffic going east was sparse and, once again, even though the road had limited access, there were bands of people by the roadside hawking meager piles of goods at some of the turnoffs. Since they had time, they decided to test some of the back roads along the peninsula to see if they might serve as escape routes. What they saw was not appealing. Many of the roads were not paved, and if paved, had been long neglected. They were rutted and heavily ridged. Worse still, the entire peninsula leading to Kerch was very flat and sparsely treed. There would be no cover for a getaway vehicle if one became necessary. Any patrol vehicle could spot and chase any vehicle over these roads with ease. It was also striking that there was virtually no agriculture or any residence on the route. It was a barren stretch of low sand dunes topped occasionally with some sparse grass or scrub bushes. This would seriously affect any sabotage strategy.

As we approached the Ukrainian side of Kerch, there were some outcroppings of residences which lead into the more commercial and industrial areas. The town held in excess of 100,000 residents and had a few main boulevards. Some shipping and fishing activities were visible, but little else. The only target worthy of attention was the ferry line. It was the chokepoint between Russia and Crimea. Five ferries were in use and plied the narrow crossing of about five kilometers in no more than a half hour each way. Long lines of cars and trucks and individual passengers waited for as much as 40 hours to board the ferry. On each side of the Kerch Strait, heavy security inspected passports, visas and gave travelers as much harassment as they could. Complaints were loud and abusive, tempers flared. Russians, unlike much of the western world, are not respectful of others in lines and frequently attempt to butt ahead or join others further up in queue. This provoked much pushing and shoving. The ferries themselves were not large, only two levels and not in good repair. Over the years, maintenance had been neglected. Often, one or more of the ferries was sidelined for repairs. Because the strait was narrow and not deep, winds of 20 to 30 miles per hour could shut down the schedule for hours at a time. Many travelers slept in their cars or by the side of the road for days. Anything that would shut down the traffic between Russia and its new possession, Crimea, would be a major political irritant. Already, Crimeans were chafing because Ukraine, quite appropriately, had shut down anything that might aid the Russian occupation. Electricity and water, 80 percent of which came from the Ukraine, was cut off. Pensions and other government welfare services were discontinued. Private industry – banks, ATMs, insurance and virtually all international imports came to a standstill. Now, Russia had to supply this at great cost and was slow and inefficient in doing so, if at all. Already, Crimeans, although largely ethnic Russian and enamored of their roots were beginning to openly protest Russian occupation. A recent incident where electric stations were down and left people without power for weeks had caused much anger. Kerch traffic was a prime target. How to disable the ferries?

A land attack was out of the question. There was no cover for a mortar or hand held missile. There was no escape route. This would have to be a timed explosion set off by a water-based mine, or a bomb planted aboard the ferry. Would it be possible to smuggle on board an explosive device on each of several ferries to sink them in the harbor? Would it be possible to plant explosive devices on the side of the boat in the water? Either could be triggered by a remote cell phone devise at a preset time to coincide with the other attacks. We would need to calculate the amount and type of explosive for each boat. The boats were fairly small, not armored, nor double hulled. A relatively small blast would leave the ferries useless on their sides clogging up the harbor.

This would require two separate reconnaissance missions. First, they would have to see if a car or a passenger would be subjected to security searches before boarding one of the ferries. Second, they would have to research the naval mines necessary to take out the ferries in the harbor.

After sending a coded e-mail message, they were authorized to send the translator, Ilyosha, on board a ferry with a suitcase with a few suspicious items – water bottle, knives and modeling clay – inside the trunk of a vehicle. The entire round trip might take three to four days so the rest of the group were directed to stay at the home of some friendly people during that time. They would have to idle away their time wandering the streets as tourists. The host family was delighted to receive the stipend for housing them.

The site of their stay was an older apartment not far from the center of town. They shared the 14 year old daughter's bedroom while she slept temporarily on a cot in her parents' room. This inconvenience was not considered to be much in lieu of the generous stipend Alexei had made available. They were given breakfast of boiled eggs and toast with tea. The family was extremely grateful for the American coffee given to them as a house present. The father, Slovo, was trained as an engineer and worked in a fish processing factory operating the machinery on the line. The wife, Galena, was a bookkeeper for the government shipping lines. Both were considered middle class jobs. He was paid $50 per week in equivalent of American dollars, she $60. Galena took our money and the next day bought gold coins which she promptly stashed.

As they sat at night, Galena, a slightly plump but gregarious and funny woman with short blond hair and bad teeth in her late thirties, was eager to talk about the Russian occupation. Slovo was a tall, quiet man in his fifties who nodded somberly in agreement with his wife. She felt it must be like what she had been told wartime conditions were like. She and Slovo had enjoyed nice times growing up after Perestroika when Crimean economies were improving. Now was a disaster. Things were scarce, people were unemployed and drinking far too much. The Russian soldiers of the occupying forces were young, drunken louts who harassed women of all ages. They were now hated and avoided. Galena and Slovo were ethnic Ukrainians who were indistinguishable from the Russians. As first, the ethnic Russians had welcomed the occupying forces, now they were slowly beginning to long for the recent past. They had been recruited for minor espionage work at the Ukrainian church, by the friends. They were happy to see us as a harbinger of a better future.

For the next few days, they wandered the streets in this small town. Usually for lunch, they would stop at one of a number of small delis and buy some of the hard sausage they call kielbasa, but is more a dry, hard chewy pepperoni with a variety of flavors, garlic or pepper usually. Beer was incredibly cheap. A 16 ounce bottle was about $.20, but it was served warm. I have never understood why, but eastern Europeans and the British all drink their beer warm. Anyway, the beer was very good with a strong malty taste. Occasionally, we could get some kvass – a concoction made from bread, saturated in water and fermented. This was sold on numerous street corners and a full glass went for about $.05. Ice cream, a real local favorite, was also cheap and plentiful. The rest of the food for sale was a strange mixture of things we never see in the U.S. Parts of chicken or pigs that are rarely seen except ground up and sold as animal food. Parts of many kinds of fish we never see. But lots of sweets, especially chocolate all over.

In addition, there was a "black market" square, a kind of counter-culture commerce where individuals conducted business. Half empty bottles of shampoo or hair dye, used clothing in all stages of deterioration, massage tables, so-called antiques consisting of old Soviet military medals or uniforms, odd lots of shoes, galoshes or sneakers, all used, produce raised privately – radishes, kale, cherries, sunflower seeds – a mind blowing assortment of junk.

There were a few raunchy night clubs with women in various states of undress lounging in front. These were "B" girls for whom you would buy a drink and they would at least talk to you – other services to be negotiated.

Eventually, they broke out their books and just read to pass the time. Finally, Ilyosha returned with good news. His suitcase in the car was not opened, but men looked under, inspected his papers, looked in the back seat and trunk, but never opened or x-rayed the suitcase. When he tried to go lower into the hold of the ferry, there was a locked door, but there was an open cargo area which was filed with packages on pallets. These were resting on the bottom of the hold over the keel. In addition, there was a lower passenger area below deck where passengers went during inclement weather. It had a concession area that sold drinks and snacks. Some portholes at the upper area of the room showed the tips of waves outside. This placed the room itself below the water line.

The best option to blow a hole in the ferry would be a shape charge – a package of explosives designed to direct its entire blast into a targeted direction only and not sideways or to the rear. Without access to the hold itself, the use of a shape charge would be difficult. Any damage would require a much higher load of explosives which would then explode in a full radius of 360 degrees. It would have to be tweaked to condense the explosion down to 30 to 40 degrees. We would have to calculate the weight necessary to totally disable the hull. The explosive of choice would be C-4 or plastic, which came in bars resembling modeling clay and, like modeling clay, very malleable and could be detonated with a cell phone timing device. The maximum suitcase would have to carry less than 40 pounds. Would that be enough?

CHAPTER 39

The next possibility was to attack the ferries while they lay in port empty at night. Several possibilities presented themselves, but it would be necessary to see just how carefully guarded were the areas on water around the ports. To this end, we hired a small pleasure boat and rented fishing gear to see how close to the ports the boats could get without attracting attention. Boats and fishing gear were easy to rent, so we loaded up an inboard motorboat, put in a case of beer along with fishing gear. Ilyosha and two friends were fitted with small cameras to take pictures of as many places as they could. Ilyosha and his friends were to be in quite a few of the pictures. They set out on a route which took them ever closer to the ports until they were waved away by some of the shore patrol.

Of course, there were fairly wide shipping lanes that plied through the strait connecting the Sea of Azov and the Black Sea. As a result, the channel markers prevented Ilyosha from going through the strait in a northerly direction so he was limited to getting as close to the ports from the south. Sighting the shore, with what had been a golf range finder he was able to get within 200 meters of the port without interference on the Crimean side and 300 meters on the Russian side. There was no active shore patrol and no one had waved them off once they were on the outside of the channel markers. This presented the interesting possibility of having frogmen slip over the side at night with limpet mines to approach the ferries and attach the magnetic side of the mines to the sides of the ferries and return. The mines would then have a remote device attached to ignite the mine in the future. Five controlled explosions to the outside of the hulls would cause the ferries to roll over into the water and be disabled for weeks. This plan would have to be studied for feasibility, but offered high prospects for success.

CHAPTER 40

While driving back via the main highway westward on the Kerch peninsula, it occurred to them that one of the main stories from the Kerch residents had been about the destruction of the electric stations that had occurred. The perpetrators had never been identified, but rumored to have been Tatars – a group descended from the raiders of Genghis Khan in the 1300s. Stalin had peremptorily had them relocated from Crimea in the 1930's and 1940's. Today, they only comprised 15 percent of the population, but slowly over the last several years, they had been drifting back to the peninsula to join their brothers in the few enclaves remaining. In sufficient numbers, they could be a counterweight along with ethnic Ukrainians to the majority ethnic Russians. A massive well planned attack on the electric stations in some of the major cities could be attributed to them. So on the way back to the western side of Crimea, it was decided to examine the stations in Yalta, Simferopol and Sevastopol as possible targets. There was plenty of money left in the budget and they were way ahead of schedule. Even a week more would be no problem.

As expected, all three stations were unguarded and ancient. A satchel of C4 in each would put those cities in darkness for at least a month and cost Russia millions, not only to repair but to install security measures.

Hank and Joe were typing up their notes quietly in the back of Ilyosha's van as they again headed for the raft which had put them ashore just a few weeks earlier. They sent out a signal for a boat to meet them offshore and assembled their waterproof packs for the trip.

Soon, they would meet Alexei and our respective teams for a major planning session for our various targets.

CHAPTER 41

After a few days assembling notes, we had prepared a power point presentation for Alexei with photos, maps, and displays of various armaments. We went through the conclusions we had reached at the scene, but left all the options on the table for him to review and select.

He was 100% in favor of attacking the Belbek Airfield and disposing of as many of the TU-27 interceptor jets as possible. The plan was to be a joint attack by two mortar crews on one side of the airship and three snipers on the other. The mortar crews would be trained to develop, as nearly as possible, to use pin-point accuracy to destroy the jets and crater the runway. The snipers would use 50 caliber rifles to shoot at the fuel tanks on the wings. The attack would be limited to 15 minutes, at which time the men would be driven in vans north into the forests in the center of Crimea about one hour away. The vans would have been stolen with switched license plates. At an area about five miles away, the vans would be abandoned, and the men and their weapons would go into other vehicles for the route north. In the highway, at a certain strategic point, a farm vehicle heavily loaded would swing onto the highway behind the escape vehicles and do a blocking maneuver by driving slowly in an area where there were curves in the road. About 10 kilometers further down the road, strips of boards with protruding nails would be placed across the road to flatten the tires of any pursuing vehicles.

The three snipers each would have a spotter and range finders and the crew of six would have a driver. The two mortar crews would consist of three men each and a driver. One elderly man would drive the blocking truck, and one woman would pull out the strips on the highway. Everyone would have burn phones. The snipers and mortar crews would be trained in a remote farm in western Ukraine and develop a tight synchronized operation. Including large bonuses for the personnel, the cost of the escape vehicles and all weapons systems – approximately $300,000.

The next area of interest was the destruction of electric transmission stations in Simferopol and Sevastopol. In view of the relatively low risk of these operations, the towns of Kerch and Yalta were added. One operative in each city would arm a satchel of C4 with a timing device to be started by a telephone signal to a disposable cell phone.

Alexei enthusiastically approved all four. He had already selected a training base about 60 miles from Komenetsk-Podolsk in western Ukraine. Hank, an experienced infantryman, got the assignment to train and drill the nine men in the Belbek Airport mortar and sniper attack. It was not surprising that the mortars and 50 mm guns were readily available. Ilyosha returned to the Crimea to design the explosives placement in the four electrical stations. Sveta had her hair dyed from that striking blonde to a dull brown-gray mix. She acquired some old raincoat, a knit hat, and worn work boots and reconnoitered the fences at Kerch. She had five suitcases loaded with old radios and placed them in the lower deck. After a few days, she returned to see if they were still there. No sweat.

Now the hardest mission. We acquired two frogmen from the Ukrainian Army and dropped them 1000 yards from the ferry docks at about 8:00 p.m. They were to swim up to the ferries and return. We would await a report.

Joe trained the mortar teams along with Hank for the attack on the Simferopol Commercial Airport.

We wanted to be ready in a month.

CHAPTER 42

After weeks of training, it was now time for the attack. A large pleasure yacht cruised by the western coast, the crew began to slide rubber rafts over the side at 20 foot intervals. The rafts had several large waterproof boxes lashed to the floor and four people hopped into each raft and began to paddle eastward. It was now about 10:00 p.m. The rafts would reach shore around 11:00 p.m. The party from each boat dragged the craft up onto shore and lifted it until they were off the beach. A series of vans coasted down the shore road and picked up each party, deflated the boats and took off for the safe house thirty miles inland. The night was a bit cloudy, but the Black Sea was calm. The lapping of the waves on the shore was among the loudest noises. Soon the entire party stole into the darkness and was on their way eastward.

When the vans reached the safe house, the parties off loaded the rafts and boxes of equipment. They changed out of their wetsuits and walked smoothly up to the main house. Ilyosha and a middle aged couple were there to meet them. They sat around the kitchen table or in the living room and had a snack of pastries, yogurt and blinis in sour cream and raspberries.

Without much conversation, everyone either went upstairs to bed or staked out a mat and a sleeping bag on the floor and went to sleep.

At sun up the next morning, they began to stir. A large breakfast was laid out in the dining area and, as people trundled in, they filled their plates and sat with their training partners. Gradually, the cars and vans pulled up and began to load the gear necessary for the trip.

Ilyosha drove a car by himself and set off for Simferopol first. He would plant the explosives in four electrical transmission plants. He needed no help. Instead of military C4, he had been given Det Cord – a commercially available explosive – a bit weaker than C4, but equal in all other respects. It had the advantage of not being linked to any particular military force. This particular supply came from the oil fields of Azerbaijan.

Hank and Joe, along with the snipers and mortar crews, left for Belbek Airport. A Russian speaker was at the wheel of each of the two vans. Hank and Joe would be the spotters for the snipers and mortar crews.

Sveta drove alone with five suitcases to the city of Kerch. She was disguised as before as an older lady. For the time being, the idea of a frogman planting magnetic explosives on the side of the ferries was rejected as a bit too risky. The suitcases carried the lesser of the risks.

Another van had carried the mortar crews to Simferopol Commercial Airport with the mortars. A small house with a roof deck had been rented anonymously about 400 meters from the airport. From three sides, no one could see the mortars, and over the fourth side, a large panel was placed across the front as if some roofing was going on.

CHAPTER 43

Sveta was up early. She was unable to contain her excitement for the mission. She had previously taken trips on all five Kerch Strait ferries with rolling carry-on bags to see which items might be picked out on the x-ray machines that scanned passenger luggage. They had been able to disguise scissors, modeling clay, steak knives, large shampoo bottles, lighter fluid and a variety of other things from the people who were at the scanners. The scanners at Kerch were from a prior generation of devices which simply did not have the visual acuity to allow the scanner personnel to separate the harmful from the benign items of the passengers. She had gone back and forth from Russia to Crimea with the new Russian/Crimea passports in a fake name. With the recent takeover of Crimea by Russia, the Crimean citizens who had only held Ukrainian passports were now given a new document which identified them as residents of Crimea, but now under Russian control. It was easy to produce as many of the new fake passports as were needed, but the production of this new Crimean residence card was another small problem. It turned out that Russia had not had the time to produce a new passport type document with the same safeguards as the Russian passport. After a careful review by a few experts, only minor technological elements needed to be incorporated into these Crimean cards to have them pass inspection at the checkpoints at the border. There was essentially a magnetic strip containing some identification imbedded on the card somewhat similar to a credit card. It was relatively simple to decipher this electronic information and issue new magnetic strips for use of the fake IDs. Russia apparently was still lagging on the technology to create a more sophisticated ID system or simply was unwilling to spend the funds on such technology. It was also apparent that the computers examining the documents did not yet have a system to record how many trips in and out of the Crimea each traveler made. Since it was a short and cheap trip, many people made daily or weekly return trips for business purposes. The lines were long, the travelers angry and impatient, so the manpower at the security check were lax and careless.

Sveta had already had her lustrous blonde hair dyed into a frumpy brown with graying roots. She had on a well-worn men's small sweatshirt, a black skirt and scuffed black sneakers. She wore her hair wrapped in a kerchief and wore a pair of glasses with tortoise shell rims. Of course, under all those clothes was the lean, muscled, lithe body of a career gymnast with a blue and yellow trezub tattoo on her left shoulder – a remnant from her days on the Ukranian team. If she were ever stripped, her identify would be easily betrayed. So the disguise had to work. She limped painfully along in line. Fortunately, with the crush of tourists and vacationers back and forth through Kerch, the Russian authorities did not wish to appear to be too officious in their examination of what were supposed to be part of the "New Russia." So the whole vetting process of most travelers was minimal.

Each of Sveta's carry-on roller bags contained two five kilogram bricks of C4. Actually, it was not C4 – the military plastic explosive, but Det cord, a commercial explosive widely available for construction purposes. Above and below the bricks were a variety of items which could mask the wide expanse of the bricks -- scissors, shampoo bottles, and a variety of small metal containers. On the top layer was a collection of dirty clothes, mostly underwear, sufficiently redolent with body odor, to discourage any inspector from getting too familiar with the contents.

Sveta was to leave one brick on the lower level of the first ferry as close to the hull as possible in a small lunch bag from the snack stand. On the return trip, by another ferry, she would leave the second brick and so on.

Her friends' apartment was only three blocks from the ferry so she walked down early to get in line. After a few agonizing moments, she walked through the line for the scanner unscathed and retrieved her carry-on from the belt. As soon as she could, she went to the lower level and sat reading a trashy romance novel off to one side of the concession stand. As soon as the room started to fill up she started to look for a convenient place to drop her explosive lunch bag. Interestingly enough, the lower level consisted of girders with steel plates bolted on. At the bottom of each plate was a pocket between the steel plates and the edge of the horizontal girder, where a flange to provide extra support had been welded along the girder. Taking a seat near the hull, Sveta quietly opened her carry-on and took out a lunch bag and placed it in the pocket next to the hull. The ten pounds would easily take out the steel plate which would flood the concession area in a matter of seconds. The timing device made from a burn phone and electrodes into the brick was primed to explode from a single telephone call.

After a few unhurried minutes, Sveta rolled her carry-on bag back up to the upper deck and took a few gulps of salt sea air into her lungs to relieve the tension. She longed for a gym to do a few warmup routines, but that would have to wait.

She left the ferry on the Russian side and treated herself to a heaping plate of fried fish and waited for the afternoon ferry with her earphones on and an ABBA tape in iPod. Work well done usually had a lot of boring downtime until the return trip. She hobbled up to the end of the line of passengers going in the opposite direction with her second brick of Detcord in her battered roll-on luggage.

CHAPTER 44

Ilyosha drove a beat-up Lada with an official looking decal on the side indicating it was the property of the new russian electric company. He was dressed as an inspector and had a rolling suitcase replete with electric meter gauges and a clip board. He had visited each of the plants, gave a half-hearted flash of his laminated identification card which had been dipped lightly in coffee and given a few blows of a hammer. He also wore his own dark blue hard hat with his new name (appropriately chosen) stenciled on the back. In his carry-on, there was an Ipad on which he was taking a few shorthand notes. He also had downloaded a blueprint of each of the electric transmission sites. He was neatly dressed in a light blue polyester shirt and dark blue pants. His shoes were appropriately rubber soled work boots to prevent the transmission of electricity. He was able to explain that he was an inspector specially sent from the new russian utilities commission to evaluate and inspect the local power plants just recently absorbed into russian control. Of course, little money or maintenance had been spent to update or make necessary repairs to the plant since World War II at least. Like the rest of the Soviet infrastructure, it was in sorry shape from years of neglect.

His presence was welcome at the plants because the workers well knew the status of these jury-rigged systems. Ilyosha said that he had been tasked to prepare a budget and a list of priorities for bringing the plants into compliance. Of course, when the workers approached him with suggestions or questioned him on his findings, he was able to adopt the bureaucrat's stern face and say that his findings and opinions had to remain confidential until they had been reviewed by the higher-ups. The local workers knew what that meant and left him alone.

As a result, he was able to wander at leisure throughout the plant until he could locate the best area to leave a brick of the plastic explosive with the burn phone timing device.

He was able to complete the work at the four sites in two days each and return in the ancient white Lada to the farmhouse. He put the four burn phones on speed dial and then phoned in to Hank and Joe that all was in readiness. He then had a stiff shot of vodka and went to sleep for 12 hours.

Joe and three snipers found their locations on the north side of Belbek Airport. They laid three inflated air mattresses on the ground just behind a row of grape vines and cut through the lines to allow a six inch window to poke the long barrel of their Barrett M82 long range sniper rifles. These recoilless rifles shot 50 caliber ammunition and had a range of 2000 yards. Equipped with a Leopold 4.5 scope, they would aim at the wing fuel tanks of the TU-27 jets as they sat quietly on the ground. The snipers, recruited on temporary assignment from the Ukranian Army, were crack sharpshooters. Each had a spotter to sight through a telescope to indicate where the shots had landed and call out an adjustment to the sniper of his aim. Joe speed dialed a call to the command post in the farmhouse and the other units that they were ready and in place. Within seconds, Hank signaled that his mortar units on the south side were ready. Command at the farmhouse, gave the "go" signal. Sveta pressed her speed dial and ignited her bricks of plastic explosive at the lower decks of four ferries in Kerch. Ilyosha pressed his speed dial and ignited his bricks at four electric transmission stations.

The snipers, having previously divided up the planes, began firing their rifles. Each sniper got off five rounds, hitting four planes each. The mortar shells rained down on the remaining jets. Within 15 minutes, the mortar crews and sniper crews were packed up, in their vans and on the road north.

All four electric stations were reported in flames after a massive explosion by a local lookout. Six of the planes caught fire immediately and seven more exploded, spewing burning debris around the runway. The crews did not want to see if any other damage was done, as the fire alarms began to ring out, they all walked at a measured pace to their vans and took off back north. The man driving the heavy farm truck told them he could see no pursuit vehicles. When the vans passed, he and his heavy ancient truck lumbered onto the highway and stalled out blocking both lanes. He waited a full ten minutes until he could see any traffic before restarting the engine. After another ten minutes he called in on the burn phone and was told to go back home. About three kilometers down the road, the stolen vans were abandoned in a forest turnoff and the men and gear reloaded onto a large truck and headed for the farmhouse. The man in the old farm truck still had not seen any pursuit. Since he was now five kilometers back, the woman who was poised to put the nail studded strips on the highway was called off and waved as they went by.

At Simferopol Commercial Airport, explosions and large fires were reported, as the mortar crews calmly and deliberately disassembled their gear and walked to their van.

Within minutes of the Belbek explosion, all four electric stations exploded and three of the ferries had massive holes in their hulls and rolled over at the dock and submerged in ten feet of water. The other two were severely damaged, but still afloat. Simferopol Airport, dead quiet at this time of the evening, erupted in 15 minutes of explosions. Ten ancient passenger planes exploded and were on fire and craters five meters in diameter dotted the runway.

In less than two hours, all parties were on their way back to the farmhouse. They came in at intervals and all sat near the radio. They picked up the police frequencies and the public radio. The latter spoke simply of a series of terror attacks which failed because there were no serious casualties reported. At first, it was linked to a Muslim terror group, but then to Chechnyan rebels. The evening broadcasts were interrupted for updates saying that the search for the perpetrators had yielded a number of clues and they were expected to be in custody shortly.

The police radio band was ablast with commanders of all sorts swearing and ordering about their underlings. Fortunately, it was before dawn when the explosions took place and many were only beginning to awaken as they jumped in their cars and joined the search.

One commander had entered a Muslim community and had all males tested for gunpowder residue or explosives. Explosive sniffing dogs patrolled the streets of Simferopol and Kerch. The entire male Tatar population was brought into the high school gymnasium to be stripped, tested for explosives residue and interrogated. All cars were stopped and anyone with the slightest Ukrainian accent was also brought in for questioning.

Meanwhile, massive sections of Kerch, Simferopol, Yalta and Sevastopol were in total darkness – house lights, computers, televisions, street lights. Candle light began to appear at windows as the people began to wander into the street to ask what had happened.

Daylight yielded no further information. The Russian forces had no clue who did what and were taking major flak from Moscow. It was a total embarrassment and an undeniable sign of weakness of the Russian military establishment.

The internet, television and radio began to erupt with almost continuous coverage of the attack. It was labeled almost universally by the western news media as a "professionally executed, coordinated attack on seven diverse locations simultaneously carried out with devastating results." The Russian media reported it as an inept attack which yielded minimal damage. It was repeatedly noted that there were no deaths and, to date, no serious injuries reported. It was speculated that the attacks were attributed to various Muslim groups, various Chechnyan groups, NATO, the CIA, Ukraine, the Tatars, depending on the bias of the reporters. No evidence was available.

CHAPTER 45

The Russians immediately rounded up 10,000 troops and dispatched them to Kerch by plane and boat. The Kerch ferry only had two boats which were capable of immediate repair, but the Ukrainian side of the harbor was clogged with three shipwrecks. The Ukrainian-Russian border in the north was closed until further notice by both sides, the Ukrainians to slow any Russian police efforts, the Russians to prevent anyone from escaping.

All this was for naught. Three pleasure yachts had cruised up the west coast of Crimea days ago and had taken on several rubber rafts loaded with men and equipment in the dead of night.

Meanwhile, the raid of the different ports of Crimea had been at the top of the news for days. Photos filtered out of the wreckage sites over the internet. Reporters and film crews flocked to entrance routes to Crimea and tried to bribe their way in. The Russian pseudo-news channels tried to push various angles. At the top of the list was the CIA and NATO, both of whom vigorously denied the claims through their press representatives. The focus shifted to ISIS, Iran, Turkey, and Al Queda, who, although famous for claiming success in these matters, denied any involvement.

The Tatars, especially the men, were harshly interrogated and tracked for alibis. Most passed scrutiny. A few that did not were incarcerated and grilled further. Same for pro-Ukrainian Crimean politicians. Nothing of substance turned up.

After four days, a computer generated letter in Latin was delivered by a small boy to the Al Jazeera station in Cairo. It read in both Russian and Arabic:

"To Russia:

We have planned and prepared these attacks. You will note that we have taken special precautions to avoid human casualties. There have been no deaths. We believe that there have been a few minor injuries. For that, we apologize.

Our mission was solely to attack economic targets valuable to the thieving oligarchy that now controls the Russian motherland. Mr. Putin has embarked on a course of driving his country into bankruptcy and, for no apparent reason, has annexed Crimea. Crimea needs to import electricity and water from Ukraine. Ukraine has been subsidizing Crimea; which does not have a productive economy. The Russian economy is now in a shambles and cannot afford to police and patrol Crimea, much less subsidize it. Russia must let Crimea go.

We have hired a lawyer to negotiate our demands and communicate with appropriate representatives of Russia. Please contact Peter Stern at 215-555-7112 to set up a conference.

Here is a list of partial demands:

1. All Russian soldiers, material, vehicles and other equipment must be withdrawn from Crimea. This includes all pseudo-Russian soldiers from Crimea, Moldova and other puppet states that Russia has brought into its force to occupy Crimea. Anyone in uniform who was not a permanent resident of Crimea prior to March 2014 must return to Russia or whatever puppet state they came from.

2. All Tatars will be permitted to return to Crimea. Any Tatar applying to return will be given sufficient travel money and six months salary to tide them over until they can relocate.

3. All TU-27s and all naval vessels commissioned after 2000 shall return to Russia by safe passage through the Kerch Strait after it has been cleared.

4. You will permit an international team of qualified electricians

to repair all damaged electric power plants at our cost.

5. You will surrender the former President Yanukovich to Ukrainian custody and surrender all his accumulated wealth to a bank in Switzerland until a correct accounting of his assets can be completed. He will be directed to surrender all ill-gotten monies to the Ukrainian government.

6. To repair all damages to the Simferopol Airport, you will permit an independent tribunal to sell off landing rights to qualified commercial airlines. These funds will be used to make repairs to the Simferopol Airport.

7. You will make reparations to all Ukrainians who suffered a loss by virtue of your takeover. A fund of $90 billion rubles will be placed in escrow with a bank in Switzerland. An arbitration panel will hear all claims. One arbitrator shall be selected by Russia, one by Ukraine and they shall each select a third. The ruling of the arbitrators shall be final.

8. Grant independence to Chechnya, Osssetia and Ingushetia.

Kindly arrange to commence negotiations at your earliest convenience to avoid suffering further debilitating consequences.

The Committee for Crimean Freedom"

Of course, I had prepared the letter and had it delivered, all with the approval of the Blue Eagles.

I awaited a response as I sat by the computer at home in Philadelphia. I was sure by now my telephone was tapped. It did not take long before the press assembled outside and the telephone rang with requests for interviews. I knew this would clog up my line and frustrate the Russians. They would have to figure out a way to reach me. The Blue Eagles arranged for someone to deliver me groceries and for a team of four bodyguards.

Kindly arrange to commence negotiations at your earliest convenience to avoid suffering further debilitating consequences.

The Committee for Crimean Freedom"

Of course, I had prepared the letter and had it delivered, all with the approval of the Blue Eagles.

I awaited a response as I sat by the computer at home in Philadelphia. I was sure by now my telephone was tapped. It did not take long before the press assembled outside and the telephone rang with requests for interviews. I knew this would clog up my line and frustrate the Russians. They would have to figure out a way to reach me. The Blue Eagles arranged for someone to deliver me groceries and for a team of four bodyguards.

CHAPTER 46

This was not going to work. Unfortunately, posting my name and phone number on line had attracted a swarm of media coverage and curiosity seekers to my humble apartment. Even with police and private security, the people trampled the grass, tied up the phone lines, camped on my Internet and Facebook. There was no way for the Russians to answer the Al Jazeera posting. For several days I lay marooned in my apartment and only food deliveries could get through. Hank and Joe and the others could not help because it might tip off their connection to me and expose their part in the attacks; but I had to rely on their sound thinking for a way out of this massive clog of humanity. Even the United States could not help. They had credibly disavowed any knowledge or assistance in the attack.

I imagine Hank and Joe somehow were thinking this out clearly and found an honest broker to resolve the situation. Finland for years had been treading a fine line between Russia and NATO and had served as a back door diplomatic link which did not disclose the source of its contacts in the post. The Finnish ambassador to the U.S. had been able to commandeer a fleet of bullet proof SUV's to come to my humble abode with an equally impressive string of Philadelphia Police cars. They formed a gauntlet outside the entrance to my building and screened me off from the public crush so I could enter a random SUV. Traffic was stacked all the way to downtown Washington D.C. as I rode the three hours to the Finnish embassy on Massachusetts Avenue.

CHAPTER 47

Although the exterior of the Finnish embassy looks like an elegant Georgian colonial home, it is very Scandinavian inside. Outside it is a large brick building painted white with three large white columns over the front door. In front is a large empty circular driveway. The building is surrounded with neatly trimmed yew bushes. Inside, it felt like I had walked into another world. There was a profusion of wood – all teak and walnut and oak. The floors were bare except for small runners or area rugs of a simple wool design in grays and blues. On the walls were paintings of scenes of Finland, herds of caribou, snow-covered villages, open pastures filled with wild flowers and a few cattle.

I was greeted by a pretty, large pale blond woman with a neatly clipped hairdo, bangs and a simple undercut pageboy. My bags were swept up to a room in the rear and I was invited down for tea and biscuits. On the table were also some rough crackers and squares of goat cheese. I thanked my hosts for their intervention and tried to relax. I prepared some notes for my meeting with the Russians.

Before this trip to Washington, I had no notice when the phalange of SUV's and cop cars showed up at my flat. Although I knew I would have to go some place private, I didn't expect to leave Philadelphia. Since I had no idea when or where I would be going, I had hurriedly thrown my shirts and suits in a suitcase and packed a rolling duffel. I must say, the Finnish embassy folks couldn't have been nicer and their food was excellent. The D.C. cops were used to controlling crowds, especially on Embassy Row on Massachusetts Avenue. So, I sat and waited for some Russian dignitary to arrive. They did. For breakfast the next day. It was the Ambassador and a staff of five. The meal was all cordiality and pleasant remarks. They knew all about me, my full resume and even a few clips of me in Memphis, but no link to my organization. I have to say how great it felt to pick up the check at the end of the meal. I mean, when do you get to treat an entire country, especially a world power, even if a dwindling one, whom your client has just bombed?

The Ambassador, however, was ill-prepared or not authorized (probably the latter) to negotiate. He just wanted to know who I represented.

I had to make my little prepared speech. "Gentlemen and Ladies (there were two), as you know, I am a lawyer. I represent a client. In the U.S., we honor the principle of lawyer-client confidentiality, which means I will not betray my confidential communications between myself and my client. I can assure you that I do not represent NATO, the United States or any other recognized government. I also did not participate in the planning or execution of the events which have taken place in the Crimea. However, I have full authority to enter into an agreement, if one can be reached, with Russia."

The questions ensued, but not related to the actual incident or demand on Al Jazeera.

"You are an American?"

"Yes."

"Do you represent a group of Americans?"

"Sorry, I will not reveal who my clients are."

"Do you know the extent of the damage your client has caused?"

"Yes. I have seen the news and other reports."

"Did your client report the damage to you?"

"Sorry, I cannot disclose client communications, if any."

"Are you the only lawyer involved on your side?"

"Yes."

"What ethnicity are you?"

"I believe that question is irrelevant."

"We believe you are Jewish and your great-grandparents were émigrés from Ukraine. Is that true?"

"I am an American, my religious beliefs are irrelevant."

"Why did your client hire a Jewish lawyer?"

"He, she, it or they must have thought me competent."

"Are you associated with the State of Israel?"

"No. I have no association with any formally recognized government, as I said before."

"When was the last time you spoke with your client?

"That is confidential information. Okay. Now, I have been patient about these incessant questions. Now it is my turn.

"Isn't it true that Russian soldiers used military force to take over the territory of Crimea?"

"No. Volunteers came in to support the ethnic Russians in Crimea who were unhappy with Ukrainian control of the region."

"Then, I am bargaining with the wrong people. You, I believe, represent Russia, not the 'ethnic Russians of Crimea.' Whom should I be meeting with then?"

"We are empowered to speak for them in view of the election which recognized a new government."

"I see. Are you prepared to recognize my demands to this quasi-Crimean organization?"

"Yes. We have seen your damage and heard your demands"

"What do you propose to resolve this matter?"

"What will your client do if we do nothing?"

"I don't know. I think you have seen evidence of his ability to conduct well-planned surgical strikes on targets of value to Russia without loss of human life. Russia, if anyone, has lost considerable financial value. Even if I do not accept that Russia can represent legally the Crimean people, I believe it is in the interest of Russia to stop my client from targeting Russian assets. Will you heed our demands?"

"What do you envision will be the government of Crimea if we can reach an agreement?"

"Some substantial degree of autonomy, with some degree of Ukrainian authority and very substantial Russian licenses for commerce, access to the Black Sea, docking rights at Sevastopol and extensive negotiation on trade tariffs."

"You want us to return Crimea to Ukrainian control?"

"I didn't say that. I said there would be a substantial degree of autonomy – to be negotiated. Perhaps I should be talking to some Crimean representatives on this issue."

"Why would we release Crimea from our . . . let us say sphere of influence?"

"Okay, you want me to be frank. Let's try this. Russia, under its present leadership is suffering from severe financial difficulties. It has blown 52 billion dollars on the Socchi Winter Olympics. It then invaded and took over Crimea and further supported Russian forces in invading eastern Ukraine, for which it drew down heavy international sanctions. That, in turn has crippled its trade, ruined its currency and its reserves of currency. It has taken over a territory in Crimea which required heavy subsidization from Ukraine. Ukraine is an overwhelming source of water and electricity to Crimea, which Russia cannot replace except at great cost. Russia's only land access to Crimea is through the port of Kerch, which is currently only serviced by inefficient ferry traffic, which is not in operation."

The Ambassador and his aides were getting more and more agitated. They needed to listen to me and could not leave, on the other hand I was essentially one lonely person insulting them and belittling them and their political leader. Finally, the Ambassador erupted,

"You blew it up. That's why it is not in operation."

"Not me, but probably my client. But let's assume that it's true. You have lost many valuable TU-27 jets – what we believe at a cost of at least $20 billion each. These are Russian, not Ukrainian losses. You, Russia, have lost many commercial air lines, all these losses except the electric installations were Russian. At what cost will Russia continue to protect and defend Crimea and Russian assets in Crimea?

"How many guns, planes, men and pieces of equipment will Russia withdraw from its confrontations with NATO to protect and defend Crimea, the Strait of Kerch, its naval base in Sevastopol? At what cost? And for a country approaching bankruptcy?"

"We are not bankrupt; that is a lie."

"I see. What were your currency reserves in 2013 and what are they now? When or where is the ruble accepted for international trade now? What were your petroleum profits in 2013 and what are they now? What has American shale oil done to the price of oil? Can you even afford this dialogue today?"

The Ambassador was furious. "You, you little Jewish shyster. I'll . . ."

"Ah, now the anti-Semitism. If you'd kept a few Jews, you would not be in the trouble you're in . . ."

"I'm sorry I didn't mean that. We must approach a resolution." I had remembered my early training as a lawyer in negotiation. "He whom the gods would destroy, first they make mad." He was mad all right, and no longer smug. He was blowing his cool and he was an underling. He couldn't just walk out with nothing to report. He continued after a few deep breaths, "Alright, alright, if we do not reach an agreement, what will your client do?" "Well, first and most obvious he will repair at his own expense the electric facilities that were blown up. Our report showed that they were in a terrible state of repair and still used technology from the 1920s and '30s. Our offer includes the obligation to give Crimea brand new state-of-the-art facilities. The longer you wait, the longer the Crimeans will be in the dark. Our offer includes free WiFi, optic fibre cables, the whole nine yards."

"What will they actually do next? I have no idea, it was not discussed, but let me think of some expensive vulnerabilities. Mining Kerch harbor and strait, mining the Sevastopol naval base, mortaring discretely Russian military installations, bombing all Russian military facilities, assassinating high- ranking Russian officers.

"Have you seen the road from Kerch to the eastern coast of Crimea? One main highway and almost no passable side roads. What of Russian trucks? What could we do to them? Crater the highway, fire at the trucks, many many evil things I can think of. How many men will Russia commit to defend all the things it can think up that my client might do?

"We do not wish to harm human beings, even Russian enlisted men, and we do not wish to harm Crimean people. But at least you must impose security restrictions, and expend funds to protect them. I can't promise anything without a comprehensive deal."

"Very well, Mr. Stern, I have your point. I will discuss this with our government."

"Come now, Mr. Ledvedov, do not leave on that note. We are just servants serving masters. Call home. Tell them what I said. Then let us enjoy Washington D.C. What kind of food do you like?"

"I couldn't do that."

"Sure you can. I give you a choice, French, Italian or seafood?"

"I will let you know." It still would have been cool if I could pick up the tab for my Russian guests.

CHAPTER 48

Of course, the Russians declined my invitation for dinner. I managed discretly to get a hotel room in a luxury hotel on the beltway. Joe hired two bodyguards from a local security agency. All very confidential. I still knew Joe and Hank were out there somewhere. One of my new rent-a-cops handed me a note. It read: "Go get 'em, tiger."

Meanwhile, my telephone started to clear up. I ticked off thousands of calls and found several from the Ukrainian embassy in Washington. I was asked to meet discretely with them. An old friend of mine from college had a very nice law practice in Silver Spring, Maryland, just outside of D.C. Jim Henderson now had a decent sized firm in its own building just off the Beltway. When I called him, he could not stop laughing and saying, "Wow. What the fuck have you gotten into?" Jim was a big stocky guy who had played tackle at Yale. He was solid and reliable. I, of course, did not reveal my client or any of the proceedings, but asked if I could borrow his conference room for a meeting. He howled with laughter – "You want to discuss the future of Crimea with the Ukrainians in my office?"

"That's about it, yes Jim."

"Well, okay."

"Now, Jim, this is hush-hush. No one can know we were there or that we met. We'll have to sweep the room for bugs and all that."

"No problem. We even do that in ordinary lawsuits now."

"Ok, I'll get back to you. It may be at night, maybe early evening."

"That's good. We have a janitor that can let you in and lock up afterwards."

"Great. Thanks."

That evening I was driven to Jim's office by my two bodyguards. I was sure Hank and Joe had caught up with me somehow and were hiding discretely in the weeds somewhere with substantial fire power. I got to the office a half hour before the Ukrainians and had the office swept for bugs. Jim had cleared out the office for me. Soon, three ominous black SUVs rolled into the parking lot and discharged two women and three men at the building. The janitor looked at their ID's and sent them up.

I sat by myself at one end of the table and the five others squatted at the other end looking grim. Uh-oh. That was not a good sign. So I started with a smile.

"Good evening. Dobre vechia (Ukrainian for Good Evening). I am the lawyer for the people who are responsible for the recent activities in Crimea. As a lawyer, I cannot reveal confidential information I have received from my client, but I am prepared to discuss anything else. Can I have you put your names on this sheet of paper?" Meanwhile I slid several of my business cards across the table.

Some of the people slid business cards back; others filled out the page of yellow legal paper.

I continued, "I must ask that all bodyguards or security personnel leave. I would only like to speak to diplomatic or military representatives." Two men left, after some whispered dispute. There was one man, Antonin Popov, the Ambassador himself, and two female aides, Olga Pomrenko, and Elma Katieva. Each had given me a business card and sat there looking serious.

The Ambassador was a squat, solid man in a very nice dark suit, with a sparkling white shirt and a silk tie with the Ukrainian flag stitched on a field of light blue. Someone had told him how to dress like an American businessman. He had black hair heavily oiled and combed straight back. It was easy to see he had dyed his hair – it had that shoe polish look. He had heavy black jowls and a stern forbidding expression. The two women were old-style Soviet in fashion. One, a square middle-aged woman in a square grey suit had her hair cut in severe bangs and short on the sides. The other one was tall and had long black hair, also with the shoe polish effect in a navy suit with a long skirt.

To undercut this appearance I wore khakis, sneakers and a golf shirt The Ambassador started. "What your client has done is very grave. We are currently involved in very delicate negotiations with Russia over the matters in eastern Ukraine. If there is even a hint that we are involved in your acts in Crimea, we will see more fighting and bloodshed."

"Quite so. I am very much aware of your point. You may be sure that we will disavow any connection to your country. It happens to be the truth. In fact, we honestly can disavow any connection to any recognized government."

"But you may have disrupted our negotiations for military aid and financial assistance from NATO and the West. You have caused a major catastrophe in our plans for rehabilitating our country."

"OK. Now its time for some truth. First, your country has a long tradition of corruption which imitates the Soviet system. The West will never provide you much more than humanitarian assistance until you can correct your own ineffective, inefficient and corrupt system.

The Ambassador tried to speak; I continued.

"NATO and the U.S. will not intervene on your behalf on a military basis in a confrontation with Russians no matter how much Russia denies its involvement in eastern Ukraine.

The sanctions the West has imposed on Russia are doing their job and Russia, if it persists on its present course, will be bankrupt and, without its oil revenue, will be relegated to a second-rate regional power at best. As a result, it will be unable to support or defend Crimea in any case.

"Our actions will either force Russia to accept some or all of our demands, or to spend billions it does not have defending its position of control in Crimea. It doesn't matter to us.

"Russia will never agree to lose face in a confrontation with an unknown terrorist group." The Ambassador tried to break in once again.

"True. But also Russia at some point must balance its financial position and its resulting deficiencies in domestic spending with its prospect of total financial collapse. The Star Wars SDI system threat of President Reagan eventually caused the entire Soviet Union to fall apart. Wars are fought first on the economic front and Russia is losing in a rout. It can only survive by directing its people's anger against NATO or the U.S. Eventually, their eyes will be opened and they will demand a new government. Simply put, Russia cannot afford to keep Crimea and we will get whatever we can from them as they slowly and quietly surrender without losing face."

"But we will not allow you to dictate terms without consulting Ukraine." The Ambassador said grumpily.

"You will be consulted."

"But the Crimea is mostly ethnic Russians. They will never vote for Ukrainian control."

"True. They will have some autonomy. How much, you and we will determine in an agreement with Russia."

"Will they agree to this?"

"We think so. I expect their reply shortly."

"We can't appear to be too close. They may suspect our involvement."

"You could denounce us publicly and insist on the rule of law."

"Yes, we could do that."

"You could appeal to ethnic Ukrainians and ask them for calm and not to engage in similar acts."

"Maybe not. I think we should keep quiet on that score. Just what do you want anyway?"

"A reform government that is free of corruption that will attract international investment."

"So, no Russian or Ukrainian oligarchs running things."

"We'll see who can step up."

The Ambassador gave an exasperated gesture with his hands. "This is impossible. Crimea is 75% ethnic Russians, they will never now vote for a return to Ukrainian control. They may hate the conditions they find themselves in, but Russians are used to suffering - lack of food, heat, electricity, standing in lines, corruption, black markets. They will never vote for anything Ukrainian no matter how many Tatars you bring home. The Soviet Union taught us to be suspicious and trust no one. The czars were the same."

"True. But if Crimea can be given enough freedom, enough free market, enough aid, enough foreign investment, it will shame Russia by comparison."

"That will take forever. You can't re-educate the Crimean peasants in a few years. They are used to the old ways and will resist change."

"But the Czechs, the Germans, the Polish . . ."

"We are not like them. We have suffered under the yoke of the czars and the Soviets. Stalin killed off 50 million of our brightest and best – engineers, intellectuals, doctors, professors, lawyers. He depleted the gene pool. You can't change that."

"I have to agree. But I want to accomplish a few things.

1. Autonomy for Crimea – freedom from Russian control.
2. Free markets and expanded capitalism.
3. No corruption.
4. No military base for Russia."

"Well and good."

"And what do you think they will agree to?"

"They will nibble around at our terms, stall things out and hope the whole thing blows over."

"Probably. What will you do then."

"We will push, harass and irritate."

"Why?"

"To distract Russia, to open a new front even if a bit small and to get them to back down from their grandiose schemes until the new government wishes to join the West in maintaining peace and fostering prosperity."

"Okay, I see."

"Look, let's see how the negotiations play out. My people will be in touch with you."

"Who are your people?"

"Nice try, comrade. We'll be in touch." I got up to leave and shook hands with everyone. I heard them muttering as they left.

CHAPTER 49

My 15 minutes of fame had thankfully passed and I was able to walk around D.C. in peace. Of course, I could not have direct contact with Hank or Joe, but they did manage to exchange messages with me through our hired rent-a-cops who were my bodyguards. It was also comforting to see occasional glimpses of some of my people passing by discretely on the street.

I went out for a very nice breakfast and a trip to the local version of my gym franchise for a workout, took a sauna and got ready for my next session with the Russians at the Finnish Embassy. I sat in the conference room as they trundled in grimly. They obviously had gotten no new authority and weren't going to offer anything.

"Mr. Ambassador, good morning. What can we do today?" "Not much, Mr. Stern. You leave us little to work with. Your people attack us and then make demands we cannot meet."

"Alright. Let us look at the practical solutions. Crimea was a losing proposition for Ukraine. It had to subsidize its electricity, its water, and many other parts of its economy. Certainly Russia does not need any additional expenses. With the occupation, Russia has to spend funds it can ill afford to lay out to support its army and occupation forces. It also has to pay Ukraine for the water and electricity which Crimea cannot produce. The tourism business in Crimea – its overwhelmingly only source of outside revenue - has dried up almost completely. Certainly, the Europeans and the Ukrainians are not coming. Your airplane traffic is one tenth what it was, as is the rail traffic from Ukraine. You have now lost the Kerch ferry traffic as well.

"The Russian economy is a disaster. Your oil revenues are way down, you're losing your currency reserves at an alarming rate, no one will accept your ruble for any transactions. Need I say more?"

"No, Mr. Stern you need not. The U.S. and NATO are fighting an economic war and are winning. Off the record, we agree."

"There is no valid strategic reason why Russia should want to keep Crimea under its control either. Your Sevastopol fleet is a collection of old World War II vessels and submarines – easily defensed. They would never be able to leave the Black Sea via Constantinople.

Your Belbek military airport is extremely vulnerable to attack, even with the TU-27 interceptor jets. The U.S. and NATO would not allow the provocation of offensive bombers at the site.

"As far as commercial port access, I believe I could guarantee the free port of Yalta or Sevastopol for a shipping capacity Russia might need as well as access to the port over land through Crimea.

"So you've got your warm water port. We would only reserve the right to inspect all cargo and exclude any military equipment."

"What would you expect from Russia in return?"

"Removal of all military personnel and all Russian citizens who have arrived since 2014. Autonomy for Crimea on certain issues to be determined with recognition of Ukrainian sovereignty on all other issues. Reparations and compensation for the recent Russian occupation."

"What would you do in return?"

"First we would, at our own expense, repair, refurbish and modernize all the electric plants we blew up. The work to be done by either Swedish or Israeli firms.

"Second, we would provide a bank for micro-loans to businesses to be commenced in Crimea.

"Third, we would repair or replace the Kerch ferries, provided all Russians wishing to enter Crimea would be limited to a 30-day tourist visa and have no military affiliation.

"That's peanuts. We could do that. But Russia would be forced to acknowledge a defeat and a loss of prestige."

"So now that's it. It's all about Russia's empty claim to remain as a world power. Certainly, this would embarrass Putin personally."

"True."

"Alright, I would agree then on a temporary solution without an overall political one.

1. We repair the electric facilities with Swedish or Israeli companies.

2. We replace the Kerch ferries, provided that travel by Russians is restricted to 30-day visas for vacation purposes only.

3. Russia would foot the bill for the return to Crimea of all Tatars expelled, and include a six-month compensation package.

Let's try this for now."

"Would you agree to halt all terrorist acts within Crimea?"

"Of course, that's not an enforceable agreement. I mean, we are, after all, terrorists. But, as a matter of honor, we would agree to no further hostilities for a period of one year. Provided there are no human rights violations by the Russian occupation forces against non-ethnic Russians."

"What would you do if we don't agree?"

"As I have said, I'm only a lawyer, not a military man. I am not involved in the planning of these ventures. I do not participate in any way."

"But you have a military background."

"Yes, but mainly as a desk man or a staff adjutant, not as a field operative." "True. So we see. But, let's imagine what you might envision as a next move if we can't agree."

"You know as well as I. But for academic discussion, let's assume they keep to the rule that civilian or even military casualties would be limited. I would ask you first, how well are your imports protected, your electric facilities, your naval vessels. At a minimum, I would expect

Russia to expend substantial effort to protect these assets. I can see massive purchases of metal detecting machines, explosive sniffing dogs, large numbers of security personnel. I could foresee annual security expenditures out of a very thin Russian budget of many millions. Then suppose the military personnel were targeted. How would you protect against snipers going after senior officers, or roadside IEDs exploding on combat troop transports. The U.S. spends billions protecting against this. I would expect Russia would have to as well.

"Alright, comrade, we get the picture. We will get back to you."

"Very well, you have my cell phone and email. Don't be a stranger."

The Russian trio rose and grimly filed out.

CHAPTER 50

After the Russian contingent left for the second time, I noticed that the press, which had assembled in front of the embassy, had disappeared. I was, alas, yesterday's news. I received a note from one of my rent-a-cop body guards that I was to meet Alexei, Hank and Joe at a secure location, outside D.C. I was to take evasive measures getting there and I would have a blocking crew set up behind me at 10:00 a.m. the next morning. I went to the rear of the Finnish Embassy and looked for my car along with the two bodyguards. I saw an Enterprise Yaris in black sitting in a corner of the parking lot. Yo! Another Yaris. What was this? The bodyguard got in and motioned me to the front seat. We were off to Reston, Virginia, about 30 miles outside D.C. on Route 50 into Virginia. With all this traffic, this would be an hour ride. I put on my headphones, dialed in an audio book, closed my eyes and listened to narrative. As we went through Arlington, we circled around the Marriott parking lot just off the Key Bridge to see if there was anyone following us. After a brief stop, we got back on the road. When we got to the residential areas, we again circled through a few streets. Still no tail.

I was never able to spot the blocking car, but we did a few more circles through points along the route. Finally, we pulled into the parking area of a Reston townhouse development and hustled into the rear door out of sight. Around the kitchen table were Alexei, Hank and Joe.

"Hello guys. How come all I get is a Yaris?"

"We're on a budget and no one is gonna believe a fancy lawyer is renting a Yaris. Anyway, you weren't followed, were you? Now, what can you tell us."

I went through my notes of the first two meetings in detail, going through my offers and their responses, which were unfortunately minimal.

Alexei had taken notes as I went through everything. He looked up. "I'm not surprised. This is standard Russian negotiating technique. Delay. Delay. Delay. Offer up piecemeal. More delay. I am not at all disappointed. Unfortunately, Peter, your job is more of a necessary pawn. I frankly don't expect a deal. Russia, and especially Putin, will never agree to anything that smacks of surrender or a loss of face. Don't worry about it. Basically, what I wanted to accomplish has been done. Russia has already lost face and a hell of a lot of money. I want you to continue to make these demands and I want Russia to stonewall you."

"What I would like to do next is step in myself and offer over national media to pay for the repair of the electric stations and restore the ferry and the commercial airport is Simferopol. I will then ask to charge fees for the ferry, and purchase landing rights at the airport for a new charter airline I will set up to take passengers from Kiev, some European cities, and possibly some Russian ones for vacation packages to Yalta and other spots on the Black Sea. I want to control as many of the vacation packages as I can when tourism returns to the area.

"I will make my proposals very public and try to embarrass Russia into accepting. I expect to open a series of branch banks with ATM's and credit cards throughout the Crimea, and set up some telephone towers for service. I would also like to get rights to a casino. Of course, this will take a substantial amount of bribery and personal influence on my part, but frankly, it is easier to deal with Russian corruption than to wade through Ukrainian politics. A corrupt regime controlled by Putin can deliver what I want. In Ukraine, I don't know who I'd have to bribe. Unfortunately, that is the state of the world. I had budgeted a lot more for your activities to date, so I am tripling the payment of your bill which I have wired into your Swiss bank account.

"I am also giving Hank a week in a suite in Paris for two. He may invite whom he wishes." Of course, Joe and I looked at Hank who was reddening at the exposure of his interest in Sveta of which now even Alexei knew.

"Peter, I wish to have you show some nonchalance in your negotiating process and go on a vacation of your own. I have put up $10,000 in a travel account on your Visa card. Tell the Russians you have other things to do and then go on a carefree vacation for a while."

"Joe, I want you to work with Ilyosha on plans for the ferry and the electric stations with some friends of mine in Sweden."

"Peter, return to the Russians and tell them nothing. Let me negotiate with Putin's circle myself."

I had to speak up. "What do I tell the Ukrainians?"

"Tell them you are negotiating for a ceasefire in eastern Ukraine and a return of Crimea to Ukrainian sovereignty subject to major concessions for local autonomy. Look, Ukraine can't afford to take back Crimea, Russia can't afford to keep it, and both know that my investing in Crimea is a godsend. With very little money, I can restore the tourism industry, the airplane business, the ferry and the electric utility. This could be a multibillion dollar deal. But it will be a win-win for everyone without a significant casualty."

Not having the business acumen or perspective Alexei did, we had to marvel at his plan. He would take a fallow asset and develop it into a huge money maker.

"I also want to develop the west coast into an international vacation destination. With enough investment, I believe I could create lots of ethnic Ukrainian jobs."

"Alexei, it really sounds great. But, basically, you want us to do nothing for at least a week, and then you'll tell us what to do?"

"That's right. Take a rest and let me handle this with Russia for a while."

CHAPTER 51

lexei was so pleased, he brought in Sveta for a short visit and picked up the tab at a great restaurant in Philadelphia. It was one of those fancy chain restaurants, but the food and the service were exquisite. Since it was Alexei, we ordered a little caviar on toast for a light appetizer. Joe and I went for big prime ribs; Hank, who was in thrall with Sveta, ordered something French. It looked like veal with crabmeat and some cream sauce and a "light white Chardonnay." Hank obviously had lost it. Sveta did not disappoint and ordered a giant porterhouse steak with a huge alembic of Heinekin

We heard Sveta mutter a few words to Hank, including the word "medved." He responded calling her "cucumber."

Joe and I could not let the moment pass. We had to ask what this cutesy stuff was. It turns out "medved" means bear in Russian. OK, fair enough. But "cucumber" translated into Russian is "agorits," which was Sveta's last name, "Agoritsova". Sveta refused to be cowed by our teasing. She explained that many Russian names are odd like that. The famous conductor-composer Smetana is named "sour cream" Kapusta is cabbage and so on.

During dinner, I made a call to Fontina Fitzhugh. She now was a prosecutor in Tennessee. She was not attached and was open to a long weekend somewhere. New Orleans was a good choice, so I arranged some plane tickets for both of us and booked one of the fancy hotels on Bourbon Street.

Joe lay low for the time being. I suspected he had a new girl friend, but he was not ready for a prime-time introduction.

Finally, for desert we ordered a giant chocolate mousse and four spoons. The mousse died a noble death and suffered no pain.

CHAPTER 52

I had ordered airline tickets for Fontina and myself and reserved a hotel near the French Quarter. Fontina arrived and checked in and went up to the room. Fontina was seated in an arm chair reading a novel. I had a small overnight bag and dropped it on the floor as Fontina got up. She was dressed in khaki Bermuda shorts, a white tee shirt and sneakers. Her hair was up in pig tails. What happened to the glamorous Fontina I knew?

"How ya doing, Pete?" she said.

"Whoa, is this Fontina? Where's the high fashion?"

"I decided I wanted you to see the real me. Is it so bad?"

"No . . . no . . . but . . . but" I knew instinctively anything I said would be wrong.

"Which Fontina do you like better?" Wisely, I didn't answer.

"I don't know. Let's go for a walk around town."

"Great idea. Then I want to eat some real New Orleans food."

We took the elevator down and started to walk down Bourbon Street. As we got to the end of the street, two beefy guys in football jerseys and shorts stepped out of an alley and shoved guns at us.

"Pliz, Meester Stern, into the wan." Strong Russian accents. I turned to look at Fontina. The men motioned her away with the points of their pistols. She complied, with a puzzled worried look on her face.

I shrugged my shoulders and mimed an apology, but followed the men as they directed. I got into a black Cadillac with heavily tinted windows. The two gunmen followed with their guns continuously pointed at me.

"Where are we going?" I asked.

"Shut up. Dunt ask." I shut up as we drove out of town. A black hood was put on my head and I could feel plastic restrains put on my wrists. We drove for over a half hour and came to a stop on what felt like bare ground, not asphalt. Definitely a soft surface. I got out and was walking on what felt like grass for about 50 steps and then was ordered up three steps and through some kind of entrance. The floor was wood and creaked. It might have been a residence. I was ushered into a room on the first floor and pushed into what felt like a kitchen chair with a padded seat.

"Mister Stern, we need some answers."

"What have you done with my date?"

"No worry Mr. Stern. Ms. Fitzhugh is already back at the hotel. She is not of interest to us."

"First, who is 'us'?"

"Mr. Stern, we ask questions now." The voice was male, with a slight accent, not Russian, not German, something else.

"I have told everyone, the Russians and the Ukrainians, that I am a lawyer. I preserve attorney-client privilege. I do not reveal confidential client information. I am sure you know that."

"Are you working for the same people as in Memphis?" OK, so they had done some research, big deal.

"I have several clients." No sense denying Memphis. "I don't wish to make this unpleasant. It would be less painful if you could answer our questions."

"Ah, threats of torture. You must be Russian. Now, let me be reasonable with you, as I have in the past. My client is capable of inflicting heavy damages on you and your country. Much more than harm to one simple lawyer. We have harmed no people so far. Let us keep it at that.

"Second, I know nothing. I am not told in advance of any

operations. I am not involved in the planning or implementation of any operations. I am simply their public face. I can give you no useful information."

"Ah, Mister Stern, we know you were former CIA and military."

"If your information is so good, then you know I was a desk man; not a field operative. That is why I quit."

"Maybe you seek action now."

"I seek to represent my client, who has paid me well."

"You don't need money. You are in this for the excitement."

"Perhaps. But I also like the idea of eradicating evil."

"Are we evil?"

"Who are you?, first. Then I'll answer."

"Why do you think we are evil?"

"You kidnapped me for one, and you threatened me with torture. If that ain't evil . . ."

"Why are you doing this?" I had been stalling. I knew my bodyguard had been following me at a discrete distance and would alert Hank and Joe. I figured Fontina might call the police. I had not been relieved of my cell phone until we had been in the Cadillac, so at least they would know the general direction I had been taken. If I could stall out long enough, help would be on the way, Maybe.

"Why am I doing this? I like to get paid. I like adventure. I am not in favor of Russia illegally occupying Crimea. . . . I can't think of anything more right now."

"What do you think we will do to you?"

"Nothing. As you might have guessed, my client's retaliation would be very strong. You now know what they can do."

"What can they do?"

"More of the same. Maybe in Russia proper. You have little or no security presence in your towns. We can disable electric facilities, damage roads and bridges, blow up commercial aircraft and military jets, disrupt rail traffic, and that's if we're nice. We can kidnap or assassinate Russian officers. Count up the expense of defending these people. They will not be intimidated just because you kidnap me. You must see that."

"What do you really want?"

"I told your people already." Around and around this went for a few hours. My tone grew more monotonous and sarcastic, theirs more exasperated. But they had not harmed me in any way. It must be at least 6:00 p.m. now. Dark would come soon. Where were Hank and Joe? "Look, you're creating problems here. First, if anything happens to me, they will blame you. I've been in the news. People know I am acting only in a diplomatic capacity as a negotiator. By killing or harming an ambassador, you will receive major bad press and have little credibility in the future. People don't kill ambassadors anymore."

"Plus, even if you knew who my clients were, it wouldn't help. You have already suffered major economic losses and have had your lack of security exposed. You now must spend billions to prevent such attacks in the future. We have already won. You have been undressed in public. Putin is a paper tiger. If you were to kill me and the few of my clients I actually know, it will not prevent the rest of them from retaliating. Can you afford to prevent similar attacks on your other cities in Russia, by the rest of my clients? No.

"Plus, we have incurred no deaths or major casualties in our operations so far.

If you begin to harm me or my clients physically, you have opened a new front."

"What we ask is not so much? We repair your ferries, we repair and vastly improve Crimea's main electric stations at no cost to you. The return of the Tatars is a minimal expense and a minimal threat to you or your political majority in Crimea. The only thing you lose is a loss of face, a damage to your image for the other items." I was about to launch into an analysis of the economic decline of Russia, the reduction of its military power, an analysis of the oil market vis-à-vis shale oil, solar and wind energy; but I could tell I was losing my audience. These men were not educated, nor did they have the power to negotiate. They were thugs whose mission was to kidnap me. Their sole purpose was to get me to reveal my clients. But, they were permitting me to blab on. Were they waiting for someone else to arrive? Why were they letting me talk? Why not go straight to torture or truth serum? So I told them I was hungry, had come to New Orleans for the food and wanted some good Creole cooking. There was no response – only silence. Here I was sitting in a room somewhere, with a hood on my head and plastic handcuffs on my wrists. My inquisitors had just left me. What was next? I called out several times. No voices, no noise. I stood up. Nothing. I had been reluctant to bring my hands up to my hood. If I saw any of my captors, it might mean danger for me. If I could recognize them, I might be a dead man. But I could raise my hands up to my hood. I could feel the duct tape around my neck. I could reach the end of the duct tape. I could pull it. I could tear it away. I could unravel it from around my neck. Rolls of duct tape fell to the floor. I could feel the hood around my neck loosen. I came to the end of the duct tape and tore it off the hood. I lifted the hood. I could see a small room – a bedroom, barely furnished, but with twin beds. I stood up. No creaks, no sounds.

The windows of the room had shades which were duct taped to the walls. The room was mostly dark, but slivers of light came from the sides of the shades. I turned around and looked for the door. I tried the knob. The knob moved, but the door would not open. Something was blocking it from the other side. I went over to the shade and pulled it free of the tape. It was light out - about early evening. The window would not open. It had been nailed shut. With some fear, I wrapped the hood around my finger and punched at the glass. It broke. I used the hood to remove the glass around the edges of the window. I could look out. I was on the side of a small house with a side yard about four feet wide. Beyond the yard was a wooden fence and the house next door with a similar four-foot yard. I was about 12 feet from the ground. I used the broken glass to cut the plastic restraints. I could hang from the window out into the yard and shorten my drop to about eight feet. I dropped and fell face first into the shingles on the side of the house. So far, so good. I was fine. My feet did not hurt from the drop nor my forehead from the fall. I was okay. I walked to the front of the house into a small yard. The driveway on the other side of the house was empty. I walked out into the street and started to walk. The street was a narrow two-lane macadam one with no sidewalks. Similar small houses lined the street. There were people, children, a few dogs busy in the street. I thought I should put as much distance as possible from the house I had been kept in before asking for help. I walked a few blocks until I could hear some road traffic to my left. I walked toward the noise and could see a concrete four lane highway – a street sign – Jackson Boulevard. I turned onto Jackson and could see a Gulf gas station with a mini-mart. I had no wallet, no funds, no phone, but they might let me use a phone.

As I got nearer, I had to ask myself what had just happened. What happened to the interrogation? Why had they seemingly just abandoned me? What was going on?

Then who would I call? The hotel? Fontina? The emergency number of the Blue Eagles? Maybe, my interrogators had decided to let me loose so they could trail me to my clients. The emergency number was well protected. I could call in, ask for help and a cut out would then call the Blue Eagles. And where was my bodyguard? I was pretty sure the Blue Eagles had already been alerted, but did not know where I was. They could send some independent security company to come and pick me up. No, the interrogators would not track me then. I think it would be best if I just went back to the hotel and waited. If I could get to my room I could get to some cash I had buried in a secret compartment in my overnight bag. Then I could pay the cab.

I walked into the Gulf mini-mart and the nice old black man behind the plexiglass window handed me his phone to call the local cab company. I took his name and number for a reward. The cab ride turned out to be only about ten minutes, apparently my kidnappers were driving around to avoid my tracking their route to the house. I went up to my room, got the cash and paid the cabby. Fontina had left a message at the desk. I called the emergency Blue Eagles number and got a call back almost immediately. Joe said that the bodyguard had called in. My credit card had been cancelled and my phone cut off. I told them about my brief interrogation and my puzzling abandonment and escape. While I was on the phone, my bodyguard came up to the room with $200 in cash and a burner phone for me. I called Fontina. She had already exchanged her ticket for one back to Memphis and was at the airport now. I told her I'd catch up with her soon. So, here I was sitting in my hotel room alone. I needed some ID to get on the plane back to Philadelphia, the best I could do was enjoy New Orleans and relax.

CHAPTER 53

Without Fontina, New Orleans was not as much fun as I hoped. As a single guy eating at nice restaurants, going to tourist sites, even riding the Street Car Named Desire, I was unhappy. I began to receive a few messages from Hank and Joe on the burn phone I got for untraceable communications. They were getting very positive feedback from Alexei that his offer to Russia to take over the electric stations in Crimea, restart the ferry service, and purchase land in west Crimea for development as a resort was going well. Alexei basically told us to stand down on our negotiation efforts while he pursued his offers. Frankly, I was a little miffed about this. I felt he had hired us into an international incident on the pretext that we were righting some vast wrong by ridding Crimea of the Russian military. In reality, I felt he simply wanted to hop in with huge economic opportunities for himself that we helped him create. I mean Russia is broke, its economy and ruble are in the dumper and they can't afford to spend a nickel on the Crimean peninsula and are risking a backlash of public opinion that might spread to Russia itself. Alexei was brilliant in realizing Russia's vulnerable position and seizing on it for huge economic returns. I can't say that I blamed him. Besides, we were very well paid. I mean very. Our fee was trebled and in an offshore account. Our people were happy. I might mention that Hank and Sveta were an item – a very interesting item. A big 6'3" 250 pound hulk and a 5' 110 pound gymnast. Hank was learning Russian and ballet terms. Sveta had applied to a few schools to be a gymnastics teacher in the eastern U.S.

I had money added to my considerable stash which I didn't know how to spend. But I had been invigorated by the work we were doing. All these thoughts were going through my head as I flew back to Philadelphia. I rolled my carry-on bag off the plane and out the elevated tunnel to the baggage claim area when three guys in casual clothes sidled up to me. I had expected one of Joe's guys to come pick me up outside baggage claim, but I was being blocked from going there. Having already been kidnapped and waylaid in New Orleans, I thought this was all over. I mean, Alexei told us to stand down. That meant the Russians weren't going to take any further action until they did or did not make the deal with Alexei. Who the hell were these guys?

"Mr. Stern, could you please come with us?"

"Oh shit, what is this now? Who the hell are you?" One of the guys opened a warmup jacket to reveal his hand on a taser. I had no desire to be tased in a public place. Besides, these guys spoke unaccented English.

"We are government."

"Whose? Mine?"

"Yes. We need to speak with you."

"Make an appointment. I'm tired and hungry and I want to go home."

"Sure. Sure. Please don't make this difficult."

"If you're U.S., I don't need to do a thing unless I'm under arrest."

"This won't take long. Can you walk with us to an office here at the airport?"

"Why should I?"

"It's a matter of national concern." I could see I wasn't going to get home soon. I had been thinking of thawing some frozen lasagna and watching sports on TV. Well, Philly sports on TV was not a welcome thought. The Sixers stink, the Phillies stink, the Flyers are interesting but still play like goons and stink, and the Eagles were in a "rebuilding phase" because the last coach had an ego the size of Mars. The lasagna could keep.

"Okay, I'll come, but I want dinner, a beer and a ride home." I'm tough when I want to be. By this time, I could see Joe coming towards me in the walkway. I motioned him to stay away. He straightened up and leaned against a post, keeping an eye on me.

I could see the three guys looking at each other. The guy who looked like the leader shrugged. OK. I was in for dinner, a beer and a ride. We went to an office in the security area with a wooden conference table and chairs. The leader pulled out his cell phone.

"What do you want?"

"I want a crab cake, cheese fries with Old Bay, and a Coors Light from Chickie and Pete's."

I knew this existed because I had had it before. It was good and the United States could afford it. I saw the leader turn and place the take-out order. The other two sat opposite me at the table and pulled out notebooks. When the leader sat down, he opened.

"Mr. Stern, I am Joe Fusco. This is Kenny Johnson and Matt Turner, we are all agency."

I knew darn well what they meant, but I was going to play hard to get. "What agency?" They pulled out their CIA badges.

"Oh, that agency. What do you want?"

Fusco started. I knew his name wasn't Fusco. He was 6'1" tall with strawberry blond hair and a Midwestern twang. "Who do you work for?"

"I'm sorry, that is confidential client information. As a lawyer, I must protect my clients' privilege." I was getting good at this line.

"They are meddling in international affairs and might be arrested under the Terrorist Act."

"You mean the Patriot Act, which is up for renewal as we speak. We have undertaken no acts on American soil that I am aware of. You have no jurisdiction."

"Your clients undertook terrorist activities in Crimea and caused considerable damages. The Russians have protested to us and we have denied it. They believe because you are involved that we are lying and that your people are either CIA or hired by us. Is that true?"

"As I told the Russians, the Ukrainians and now you, we are not CIA or hired by any arm of the federal government. I am authorized to say that and it is true."

"Will you cooperate with us?"

"No. That might create a conflict of interest. If you have specific proposals, I will convey that to my client."

"You have said 'client' and 'clients', which is it?"

"Both."

"You have embarrassed Russia and destabilized our relations with them. Putin may engage in more provocative offensive acts against us or NATO because you made him look bad."

"So. I don't see the U.S. doing anything to cause Putin to back off. Maybe, you should claim our acts. We did a very clean job with no real casualties and made Putin look like a paper tiger."

"But he is angry and dangerous."

"True. But he has no money, is going broke and soon his people will begin to complain."

"Is that why you did what you did?"

"I can't say."

"Look. We have orders to tell you to back off." By now, my dinner arrived. I started to eat. It was only 5:30, but I had skipped lunch.

"Suppose we do as you say, what's in it for us?"

"The best wishes of a grateful nation."

"Look, give me your card. I don't care about your name, but at least give me a real telephone number or email and after I talk to my client/clients, I'll be in touch. I just convey messages, I don't do policy. Maybe, we can work together." The crab cake was really good – chunks of crab. The fries were good. I offered them to my interrogators. They weren't shy and took almost half. The beer was just right at the end of the day.

"Sounds good." They got up and left. I finished my meal and walked back to the tunnel. Joe was still there. He was sitting on a cigarette trash can, playing a game boy. I waved and we went down the stairs together. He had parked in the short-term lot. His car, a beat up 2004 Jeep SUV.

"Yo, Joe. This heap. Usually, I get at least a Yaris. This heap does not befit my talents."

"Sorry. I go Point A to Point B. No fuss." He swept the car for bugs and bombs with a hand-held device. We got in. It wasn't until we got on the Expressway that he spoke.

"OK. What happened?" I tried to give him every detail. Fontina. The first kidnapping. The walks around New Orleans. The flight home. The CIA chat. I am a lawyer and I know detail is important. I gave him all the details. It took the whole ride home. He dropped me off at my apartment house.

"Jake, I need to see you tomorrow about 10:00. We want a full discussion with Alexei."

"Oh, and by the way, Sveta wishes to fix you up with one of her girl friends, a Nina Vishnili. She's a ballet dancer from Georgia, the former Russian republic near Ukraine."

"Uh oh, Joe, what are you getting me into?"

"Have I steered you wrong before? Besides it's just dinner with them and a show."

"A show, huh?"

"Just a ballet. Sveta really likes it and both of the girls want to see this new dancer. He's supposed to be fantastic."

"Ok, we'll see. Where's dinner?"

"My treat at the Oyster House, really great seafood and just a walk to the theater. At 6:30 let's say."

"Good, see you there."

CHAPTER 54

The next day I took appropriate countermeasures to be sure I was not followed. I left my apartment complex, drove around the block and re-entered through the gate which was manned by a guard checking IDs. My car ID buzzed the gate and I drove through. No one followed. I drove around the complex and left by the other gate. I drove in the Penn Charter School driveway just across the street and stopped behind the school and waited to see if anyone had followed. So far, I was home free. I went out the other entrance to the school and took Henry Avenue into north Philadelphia, parked on one street and walked into our headquarters in the rear of Venango Street. Joe was there already and Hank was delivering Alexei and his translator circuitously from the Russian neighborhood in the far northeast on Bustleton.

They all came in and sat around our boardroom table. Joe started. "Alexei, I wanted to thank you for your generous compensation, way above our contract. But, we are a bit concerned about some things. We undertook this job because we wanted to do some good in the world. We felt that knocking Putin down a peg would put a stop to his adventurism and make the world a little safer. Now, it seems as if our efforts were mainly to enrich you and create an opportunity to acquire assets in Crimea for your own benefit. We don't engage in terror for profit. We want to know what your motives are and what is your end game. How do you expect this to play out?"

"Ah, I see. You are altruists and want to be fairly paid for doing good. You mistrust me now. First, let me say that what you have done has already accomplished my goal. Russia must back off to avoid any confrontations from an unknown enemy – you. It was not NATO, the U.S., Ukraine or some country with a political agenda. We will hear little more from Putin. He cannot provide security throughout Crimea to prevent further terrorism. He knows now that a small organized force can create havoc not only in Crimea, but in his own country. He is tasting the effects terrorism had on Israel and the U.S. and does not like it, although he and the Soviets financed terrorism in the past. They were nowhere near as professional or effective. You took no lives, you were surgical and you made an undeniable statement by a group simply seeking world peace. I applaud you.

"Now, as to me and my financial profit. I have access to the inner circle and am known by Putin's cronies as a fellow oligarch. I can make a credible offer. If I don't someone else will. I intend to develop industry in Crimea and hire the Ukrainian ethnic group who have suffered Russian ethnic domination since Stalin sent them there. I will renovate the electric utilities and staff it with Ukrainians. I will repair the ferries and staff them with Ukrainians. I will develop a huge vacation complex in western Crimea on the Black Sea to attract vacationers for eight months of the year. It will have modern all-inclusive hotels, golf courses and marinas. All this will employ tens of thousands of Ukrainian ethnics. I will provide schools and health care for the Ukrainian minority. But slowly, and imperceptibly. Then the Ukrainians will vote the Russians out."

"Ok. I can see your plan. So what do you want us to do?"

"Three things. Make the Russians pledge to bring their military forces home. Make the Russians pledge to give total autonomy to Crimea – have votes and their own elected leaders. And lastly, demilitarize the entire peninsula – only defensive weapons – no bombers, no nuclear subs, no nuclear weapons, only defensive troops of integrated forces – both Russian and Ukrainian ethnics.

"If we design the elections to be indirect, somewhat like Great Britain's, we will have a minority of Ukrainians and Tartars elected and then they will be appointed ministers in various cabinet posts. This will tone down the Russian majority and possibly lead to coalition governments.

"As you can see, I have thought about the end game – an autonomous, demilitarized Crimea."

After some thought, I had to speak up. "I can see you will be a behind-the-scenes manager of the new government state."

"Quite so."

"But I see a number of problems. First, if the current Russian occupying force allows you to repair the electric utilities and the ferries, and sells you the land in the western Crimea, how will you get good title? I mean, they don't own it. Maybe Ukraine owns it. But who will be the seller."

"I am negotiating with both Russia and Ukraine to sign a treaty giving me good title and guaranteeing my ownership."

"What if they back out after you've spent your money?"

"The U.S. will guarantee it, by posting a bond which I will pay for."

"Very interesting. You've been busy. So all three – the U.S., Russia and Ukraine have all been meeting about this?"

"Yes. A resolution was reached while you were being held captive in New Orleans. That's why they let you go."

"But what about my vacation with a beautiful woman?"

"Sorry about that. Maybe the Ruskies will make it up to you."

"What if the Russian ethnics try to sabotage your new investments? Won't you have to spend heavy on security? I mean if you hire only Ukrainian ethnics, Russia will be mad and could instigate some covert action against you."

"True. Always a possibility. I want to hire you for further long-term work. I want you to hire and train some informants to sniff out any of these plots."

"Ah. Very interesting. How will we pay them?"

"I won't pay you directly. I will be giving you a piece of the action and a seat on the board of directors. That way you will have a stake in the survival of the enterprise.

"Who will own this?"

"You alone will. You will hold it in trust for your organization, but it will be a secret trust."

"I can see that, but I'll have to talk to my people." Hank and Joe nodded in agreement.

"How soon do you need to hear from us?"

"Today, if possible. Holding everyone together on this will be a problem if it drags on."

"I think we can move quickly."

I ran down the list of other things I had included in my demand letter. Alexei seemed to feel that as long as he got the three things he wanted, he could sacrifice the rest. I thought I should appear to be ignorant of our talk today and, as a pretext, insist on some of the items and then yield slowly and reluctantly on them later. It was crucial that we keep the appearance of having no connection to Alexei. On this we agreed. I told Alexei we would contact him by a burn cell phone later in the day.

CHAPTER 55

I drove into Center City and parked near the Academy of Music and walked over to the Oyster House. Hank and the two women were already seated and had drinks. Nina was petite and had the look of a Georgian – dark hair, dark eyes and pale white clear complexion. A definite beauty. Sveta explained that Nina was a prima ballerina with an American company in North Carolina, but had been to the highly rated ballet school in Kiev. Sveta and Nina were sharing a pitcher of draft Heineken. I sat and just asked for a glass from the pitcher. Sveta and Nina had been giving Hank a preview of the ballet that night – Le Corsair. They caught me up and then launched into the solo performances we would see that night which were to be spectacular. Hank explained, much to the delight of the two women, what some of the moves were – in French – and described how much strength and flexibility was required. Of course, Nina had not been given any hint of what Hank and I were doing for a living, but her English was exceptionally good and she explained that in addition to her performing as a soloist in North Carolina, she also taught Russian there.

Somehow, and I truly don't know how, we got into a discussion of the ridiculous situation in the Ukraine with the Russians taking over the Crimea and the out-of-control battle in eastern Ukraine. Nina laughed heartily though at the recent sabotage in Crimea and how Putin had egg on his face. She hated Putin and was very much pro-Ukrainian although she was from Georgia. Her parents had not done well under Stalin and she could feel a return to the mean old days of Soviet Russia coming back. Sveta gave us an apologetic grimace as Hank and I exchanged glances. Were we being set up? Or was this a frank opinion? Most people from the former Soviet Union were very private about their politics – you never knew who might be listening, but Nina was now an American citizen and firmly ensconced in her new country.

Something mischievous arose in me. "So, Nina, which act of sabotage did you like best?"

"Although the blowing up of those ego baubles, those TU-27s right in the military airport was the most costly, I think the bombing of the ferries was great. It blocked up the entire peninsula like a bad toilet. It was really cool." I was careful not to look at Sveta. She might be blushing or something.

Hank said, "You know, Peter here is the attorney negotiating the demand terms with the Russians. He's the lawyer for the group that did all this."

"Wow! The lawyer. You don't represent a country or anything?"

"No. No country. Just an independent group."

"An independent group? That's something. Who can guess what they are up to?"

"Nina, you know I can't say anything about this."

"Oh . . . yes . . .yes. I get it. Sorry. Let's talk ballet. I forget not to talk politics."

"Well, let me ask you something. How do you feel about the U.S.?"

"Ok. Now I'm going to be frank. I'm a little disappointed. This country is very materialistic – too much time and money is spent on clothes, fashion, cosmetics and fancy cars. In some ways, I agree with socialism. I would like to see more money spent on education, science and poverty."

"We would call you a liberal here."

"I think that would be fair. I don't believe in fancy clothes or jewelry."

"Many American women do."

"Yes. I like to dance, I like to cook and I walk around in my jeans and a turtle neck. That's it." I was wondering if Hank had told her about my ex – she was a big-firm lawyer's wife with a big clothes budget, country club, nice car. She was a nice person I have to admit, but she just never liked the long hours I spent at work. Nina was an independent. She could take care of herself.

"Were you in the Kiev school during the Soviet era?"

She smiled giving me a sideways glance. "How old do you think I am? That was 1991. I was only five years old then. They don't take you till you're 12." Doing quick math in my head, let's see – she's about 30.

Hank and Sveta were now heartily amused by the interplay between me and Nina. She was sharp, a bit tart-tongued and a bit saucy. She was putting me through my paces. Dinner was great. This was a place for seafood. Somehow the girls and I put away a second pitcher of Heineken, but what the hell. We made it to the theatre on time. Would I be too much of a pig if I said I couldn't help noticing Nina's calf muscles and firm little butt. Yes, I confess I noticed. Noticed and appreciated.

Well, the performance was great. The female soloist was exquisite, precise, feminine and delicate. The male did an amazing combination of leaps and turns. I have to say, these people were athletes. But for the women, I can see that women view this as an ideal. Men want to grow up and be linebackers – women must aspire to look like this delicate beauty. I imagined Nina doing these steps, which I was told are variations.

Nina was staying with Sveta, who was staying at Hank's house, so she rode home with them. But, no fool I, I arranged to meet Nina the next day. I would take her to the Russian supermarket on Bustleton Avenue and she would shop for dinner – a dinner she would prepare at my apartment. Just a date without Hank and Sveta.

I took a look at my kitchen and was appalled. What would a woman think? Especially a cook. Especially a ballet dancer – I'll bet they are a little compulsive.

I spent all morning the next day cleaning and vacuuming. What a pain! Do people do this all the time?

CHAPTER 56

I picked Nina up at Hank's home. Although we had made substantial bucks in the last few escapades, Hank still lived in a nice row house in Roxborough, which had a spectacular view of the whole Schuylkill River valley – a truly prized vista of many famous and not so famous Philadelphia painters. It was a little after 1:00 and I took the Expressway out the Roosevelt Boulevard all the way to the new Russian enclave in the far northeast. We drove up to the parking lot for the shopping center where the Russian stores and delis served their customer base. As we walked through the lot, three black SUVs circled around quickly and cut us off. Three men in suits, dark sunglasses and hearing aids jumped out and confronted us.

"Sorry ma'am. Mr. Stern, come with us."

"Ah, yo fellas, not now, I'm on a date."

"Sir, we can force you."

"What about her?"

"She can take a cab home"

"Great, just great. This is killing my social life."

"Yes sir. In the truck please." I turned and handed $40 to Nina and said, "Sorry, Nina. Duty calls. Take a cab back. I'll make it up to you." I mean, this is a great way to impress women, but I couldn't help but think Nina was having a déjà vu moment from the Soviets.

She waved and said, "I understand. See you soon." Ok, not so bad.

I got in the SUV and lo and behold, was not cuffed or blindfolded, just a passenger.

"Ok, men. Who are you? Russkies, Ukies or the home team."

"You'll see when we get there."

"How did you find me?"

"We put a tracer on your car."

"It wasn't my date?"

"No, sir. You are easy to trace. We had your cell phone too." "I'll remember next time."

We drove in silence to a motel outside of Langhorne on U.S. 1 and went into a room. There were five men in the room. The men who picked me up escorted me in, left and shut the door.

I was pissed. "This is the second date you have messed up. You have my phone number, just call. Why this strong-arm shit on the streets?"

The first man spoke. "Mr. Stern, I am a representative of the U.S. government. We apologize for the suddenness of your taking, but as you will soon see, time is very important."

"This is Mr. Antropov of the Russian Foreign Service and Mr. Federenko of the Ukrainian. They both speak English well, but have brought along translators in case there are problems."

"OK, what do you want?"

"We are prepared to bargain in good faith to end your campaign in the Crimea." The Russian spoke. He was a different man this time – a dark complexion, thin face, and in a tight double-breasted suit. The Ukrainian was a middle-aged blond with a round face and apple cheeks.

"OK, let's hear it."

"First, we have selected a contractor to repair the ferries and the electric stations. There is no need for you to do so. We are willing to agree to making the Crimea autonomous, and will withdraw any Russian troops not on site before 2014. We will agree to have no offensive weapons at Belbek Airport or the Sevastopol Naval Base."

"Well, first, that is not good enough. We had more issues you have not addressed and the exact details of the aims of your offer are not spelled out. It could take months to iron them out."

"What do you intend to do if we don't agree?"

"As you know, I am only the lawyer, the ambassador in effect. I don't know of their future plans or their contingencies."

"What do you think they could do?"

"I have very limited knowledge of covert work, so I am just using a layman's knowledge. But, I certainly could see blowing up more planes, blowing up air control towers, blowing up more electric stations, mining the Kerch Strait or the Sevastopol Naval Base harbor. I mean I could go on. We could do the same thing in Russian cities of our choosing. I'm sure you could think of these things as well. The idea is not to cause damage, but to cause Russia to spend money it doesn't have to provide security. Now you see how the U.S. and Israel feel. We spend billions to provide defense against terrorists you have financed."

"I see. Well, what else do you want?"

"Let me go down my demand letter. OK. Number 1 – remove all Russian soldiers and material as of March 2014. OK you agree. Number 2 – ah, here's one. Repatriate all Tatars with travel funds and six months salary to relocate."

"W could agree to that."

"All TU-27's and newer naval vessels out."

"I'll ask about that. These are defensive weapons."

"Repair electric stations. That will be done. Attach and return to Ukraine all assets former President Yarnukovich looted from Ukraine."

"I don't know if we would consider that. Perhaps you could negotiate with him and we might help in the persuasion."

"Miss Vishnili awaits you at your apartment. She was driven home by our people and did not need the cab fare. She has been given a gift certificate to LeBec Fin, the finest restaurant in Philadelphia. We have also invited her to perform at a gala ballet performance in Odessa and given round-trip air tickets from Philadelphia to Odessa as well as a deluxe suite at the Iberostar Hotel there. Her anger appears to have subsided. We can only suggest that the wrath of the two women may be less damaging than the possibility of keeping them both happy."

"I see. I see. You didn't tell one about the other?"

"Sir, we are diplomats. Give us some credit for discretion."

CHAPTER 57

I was asked to come to the warehouse which served as our headquarters for a surprise one morning. I used the usual counter-measure to avoid being tailed and pulled into the parking lot of the warehouse on Venango Street. As I came into the large loft space, Hank and Joe greeted me and lead me past the coffee pot to the conference room. They switched on the computer and as soon as the large screen TV lit up, I could see a still of the site of my kidnapping in New Orleans. I heard my bodyguard being interviewed off screen.

"I followed Mr. Stern and his date to this spot on the way to the tourist station for the Streetcar Named Desire which winds through the streets of New Orleans. At this point, two black SUVs with heavily tinted windows pulled up and abducted Mr. Stern. They then disappeared in the opposite direction heading west. Ms. Fitzhugh was left on the sidewalk. Before she could alarm the police, I came up to her and advised her who I was and gave her money for a cab back to her hotel. I assured her Mr. Stern would not be harmed. She as first was speechless and unable to react. Then she began to curse mildly and say something about needing a normal man. In the midst of her recovery from shock, she explained that she had tried to be a "simple girl" and had worn a white tee shirt and put her hair in braids. She just wanted a normal man and a normal life. She eventually calmed down and left.

"I had managed to get the license plate of the SUVs and traced them to a limousine company which had rented the SUVs to a corporate lessee using a credit card. I had Ms. Johnson trace the credit card. She also logged into the security cameras in the eastern section of New Orleans and was able to pick up the SUVs in the Maurigny neighborhood on St. Claude Avenue in the Chalmette parish. We were finally able to track in on Mr. Stern's homing device, but by the time we located the house where he was detained, he was already back in his hotel. We went in to the house and took fingerprints and DNA from some of their plastic coffee cups. Two of the men were ex-U.S. military and one was a member of the Ukrainian diplomatic corps."

"Ukrainian" Joe blurted out, hammering his fist on the table.

The transmission from the bodyguard came to an abrupt halt and the scene shifted to what looked like the inside of a trailer. Three men in dark clothing lay blindfolded face down on the floor with their hands secured behind them in plastic restraining devices know an "pop ties". Two men lifted up the man on the right side and lead him into the outer area, placed in a lawn chair. He was a plump middle-aged man with thinning grey hair.

"Who are you?" A voice off camera asked. Silence.

"Do you know you are guilty of kidnapping?" Again silence.

"We know who you are and we know you are a Ukrainian diplomat. So you may claim immunity, but not from us. We are not government." Still silence.

"Very well, then. Have him stripped and beaten."

"Sergei"

"Ah, Sergei. Sergei who?"

"Sergei Silenko."

"Not your cover name. We know better than that. Your real name!"

"Dimitri Stashevich."

"Very good. Now we are getting somewhere."

"So it seems"

"Tell your people to lay off. We can strike them at any time as well as we struck in Crimea. Do you get it?"

"Yes. Well, we never harmed him. In fact, we abandoned the whole project."

"Why?"

"Because we reached a satisfactory arrangement with Russia and an international investor."

"Who was this investor?"

"I don't know, but you soon will. He is repairing the damaged electric stations at his own expense and restoring the ferry line."

"He is doing this out of the goodness of his heart?"

"No. No. He bought the electric companies and the ferry line from Russia and agreed to restore all services at his expense."

"And you agreed?"

"We joined Russia in the transaction. We had no choice. We cannot recover Crimea at this point and the Russian ethnic majority supports the Russian occupation. Besides, he has made some concessions to hire ethnic Ukrainians. Or so I understood. When my government agreed, we had no further business with Mr. Stern."

"So you abandoned him, blindfolded and restrained."

"We are sorry about that. We will try to make amends."

At that point, we signaled the computer operator to pause. Hank, Joe and I retired to the other room. Hank turned to me. "What do you think?"

"He has diplomatic immunity. I was not harmed and we cannot have him arrested without blowing our identity. So we have to let him go."

"What about the other two? The hired muscle?"

"Let's get their names and report them to the CIA as Ukrainian agents and leave it at that."

"I still want to leave them blindfolded and restrained in some strange neighborhood like they left me."

"Fair enough. We'll leave them a note that says, "Don't mess with Pete.""

"Good. Let's do it!"

I left the meeting after reviewing my kidnapping in New Orleans with an unfulfilled feeling. Yes, we had completed a series of dangerous and difficult missions in a professional manner, and accomplished the goals our patron set out. We were handsomely rewarded. Yet, the fact that we had been manipulated into doing acts of international mischief to achieve financial gain for a single wealthy individual did not sit well. We were not mere soldiers of fortune to be hired for private wars. Our mission was to use our skills to right wrongs in the world, outside the bounds of politics.

Of course, our patrons were men of wealth and stood to benefit financially by our success; but we hoped to set the world on a path to peace and equality. Without that, we were no more than terrorist thugs.

To lighten my mood, I placed a call to Nina on my cell, but she had already texted me: she was returning to North Carolina. I thought about texting Fontina, but knew she would still be angry about the incident in New Orleans.

These two romantic failures depressed me further. I should feel elated. In a short time I had accomplished great things. By now, I was on the way up to my apartment on the elevator. But there, sitting on the bench outside by door, was Adedayo, an old friend from Nigeria. He liked to use the English name Alphonse in the United States. He had been one of the young foreign military I had been assigned to in my days at the CIA. We brought in junior officers for training in the U.S., and it was my job to keep them out of trouble, and see to their needs. Adedayo was a bright, quick student with a great future in his country. His family was well-connected. If he could avoid being drawn into military coups, he could become a leader. I wrote all this up in my report to be included in his folder for later use.

"Addie" (I liked that name better) "What brings you here?"

"Peter, wonderful to see you again. I have just now heard of your work in that Crimean affair. My country has sent me to talk to you."

"Come in, come in, have some coffee. By all means, let's talk." At this point,

I knew little about Nigeria, but another adventure beckoned. What could he want?